PENGUIN METRO READS

WHISPER TO ME YOUR LIES

Novoneel Chakraborty is the prolific author of fifteen bestselling thriller novels, two e-novellas and one bestselling short-story collection, with his works being translated into multiple Indian languages. Almost all his novels have debuted in the top three Nielsen listings across India and have continued to be in the top positions on various bestseller lists for several months after release.

His Forever series made it to the *Times of India*'s Most Stunning Books of 2017 list, while the Stranger trilogy became a phenomenal hit among young adults, with Amazon tagging it, along with his erotic thriller *Black Suits You*, as their memorable reads of the year. He has sold over 1 million copies and is India's most popular thriller novelist.

His latest releases, *Cross Your Heart, Take My Name* and *Roses Are Blood Red*, are still on the top ten lists across India. His twists, dark plots and strong female protagonists have earned him the moniker 'Sidney Sheldon of India'.

The Stranger trilogy, his immensely popular thriller series, has been translated into six Indian languages. The trilogy has also been adapted into a successful web series by Applause Entertainment on MX Player, amassing a whopping 450 million-plus views. His erotic thriller novel *Black Suits You* has been adapted into a hit web series by ALTBalaji, along with the digital exclusive novella *Red Suits You*, which is all set to be adapted soon.

Apart from novels, Novoneel has written and developed several hit TV and original web shows for premier channels like MX Player, Sony, Star Plus, Zee and Zee5. He lives and works in Mumbai.

WHISPER TO ME YOUR LIES

NOVONEEL CHAKRABORTY

An imprint of Penguin Random House

PENGUIN METRO READS

USA | Canada | UK | Ireland | Australia
New Zealand | India | South Africa | China

Penguin Metro Reads is part of the Penguin Random House group of companies whose addresses can be found at global.penguinrandomhouse.com

Published by Penguin Random House India Pvt. Ltd
4th Floor, Capital Tower 1, MG Road,
Gurugram 122 002, Haryana, India

First published in Penguin Metro Reads by Penguin Random House India 2021

10 9 8 7 6 5 4 3 2

ISBN 9780143449522

Typeset in Requiem Text and Bembo Std by Manipal Technologies Limited, Manipal
Printed at Thomson Press India Ltd, New Delhi

www.penguin.co.in

To man's greatest blessing and curse—family

Prologue

Victim Number 27
Gurugram Police Station
Present, 8.45 a.m.

'I don't think I'll ever forget what happened.'

Ekantika said, still unable to control her shuddering. She had drunk two 750 ml bottles of Bisleri water in the last half an hour and yet her throat felt dry. She'd thrown up twice. Her mind was processing everything slowly, zoning in and out of her emotional trance. In fact, the police officer sitting in front of her had to repeat his questions a few times for her to answer.

Ekantika noticed the interrogating officer, Inspector Gagan Babbar, sip his coffee for the first time and then keep it on the table separating them. He folded his arms and looked arrow-straight at her. It was her cue to continue. She glanced at him, then at the lady officer, assistant sub-inspector Preeti Jangra, standing beside him with a register, and continued.

'We came out of the movie hall around 11.15 at night.'

'You mean your live-in partner, Faizaan Ahmad, and you came out of Ambience Mall, Gurugram?' Inspector

Gagan asked. A crime had happened. Thus, everything had to be specific. The movie tickets were already taken from the deceased's wallet. The information on them and what Ekantika had told them were correct, Preeti noted.

Ekantika only nodded as a response to Gagan. It wasn't difficult to gauge her emotions. For both Gagan and Preeti, everything they noticed in her at that point in time was normal, obvious.

'No nods. You have to speak up,' Gagan said.

'Yes. We came out of Ambience Mall around 11.15. He was feeling a little emotional because of how the film ended. He is . . .' She checked herself and then, swallowing a lump, said, 'He was an emotional person. That's one of the things I liked about him. Something which is so rare in men.'

Ekantika went into a thoughtful trance. Gagan lifted his cup and took another sip. He put it on the table with a thud so her trance broke.

'I'm sorry,' She said and continued, 'He wanted to let off some steam so first we walked till the car park, then drove out of the mall premises only to park right outside. We smoked there. He felt better. We got a little intimate as well.'

'How little?'

'We kissed. Smooched actually. Not a horny smooch. Simple, emotional. Then we were on our way. I put on some music and we enjoyed the drive till we reached our society complex.'

Preeti made a note to ask the forensics team if they had found Ekantika's saliva match in Faizaan's mouth.

'Did you see any car or bike following you?' Gagan asked.

'None that I'm aware of. There were hardly any vehicles on the road at that time.'

Even the CCTVs on the road have captured the same. Hardly any vehicles, Gagan thought.

'We reached our society within twenty minutes or so. In between my mother had called to check if I was home.'

'Your mother's name, please?' Preeti asked.

'Charulata Pakrashi.'

'She calls you every night at the same time or was it only tonight . . .'

'Generally, she calls me around ten at night, but I had told her I would be at the movies till 11.15.'

'She knows you lived-in?' Gagan interjected.

'No.'

'Why not?'

'My mother does not understand the concept. You can say she is old-fashioned, and a little too concerned about me all the time. Especially because this is an alien city.' Ekantika gulped some water.

'Please continue,' Gagan said.

'It was a short call. As we drove in, the guards opened the main gate of the society. The usual drill, whenever we came from outside, was that Faizaan dropped me by our wing while he went to park the car. The same happened last night. He dropped me right outside our wing. I told him to be quick as I wanted to answer nature's call. He gave me the flat keys and asked me to go right ahead. That he would park and come. I took the keys from him and rushed into the wing. I went up in the elevator to our fourteenth-floor flat.'

The elevator CCTV capture had her getting inside the elevator. She was in it till the fourteenth floor and then got out, Gagan thought.

'Once I was in the flat, I rushed to the washroom. I relieved myself in two–three minutes and came out, changed and was waiting for Faizaan. He didn't come. I called him twice on his phone but he didn't answer.'

Her phone log showed the two calls as well as the one with her mother, Preeti made a mental note.

There was a momentary eye lock between Gagan and Preeti after which Ekantika continued, 'Then I immediately WhatsApped him. The message was delivered but wasn't read. Obviously I sensed something wasn't right. On a hunch, I picked up the flat keys and went down. I was heading to the parking when I saw a person moving out from the other side. I didn't care much and continued to head towards our car which, I found, was neatly parked where it's always parked. But Faizaan was nowhere to be seen. I called him on his phone again. Though the call was ringing at his end, I heard nothing. As I went closer, I noticed a flash of light from within the car. I inched closer, and realized his phone was ringing inside. In its dim light, I saw Faizaan sitting on the driver's seat like a dead duck.'

There was silence. Inspector Gagan Babbar could see she had choked on the last words. Ekantika gulped a little more water from the Bisleri bottle beside her. A quiet minute later, she said, 'I tried to open the car's door in panic but it was locked from the inside. That's exactly when I dialed 100.'

Gagan finished his coffee by the time she was done talking.

'We are awaiting the viscera report but the initial post-mortem report says . . .' Gagan paused and said, '. . . that it is death by asphyxiation. The deceased, Faizaan Ahmad, had been made to inhale chloroform first. And then a 3.3-inch-long piece of cello-tape was neatly stuck to block his nostrils and 6 inches of cello-tape was used to block his mouth in a way that he couldn't breathe.'

He stood up, adjusted his trousers a bit so they went atop his bulging belly line and said, 'With what we have got right now, we can say it resembles the work of the cello-tape serial killer of the nineties to a T.'

Ekantika looked up at him in anticipation.

'The cello-tape serial killer?' She sounded as if she couldn't connect the two.

'The most baffling and neat serial killings that India has ever seen but could never solve. Our own Zodiac killer kind.'

Ekantika swallowed a lump, trying to understand the gravity of the situation. *Her boyfriend was murdered by a serial killer?* They could see the fear scribbled on her face.

'Not that I want to scare you,' Gagan continued, 'but we found out something which tells me that the target of the cello-tape killer wasn't your boyfriend.' A pause later, he added, 'It was probably you.'

For a moment, everything went black for Ekantika.

BOOK 1: LOVE AND SOME CRIME

1

Ekantika's audio statement to the Haryana Police

It started with his need for *sexorcism*. Honestly, I didn't know what that word meant when I heard it for the first time from Faizaan. He told me later that sexorcism means having sex with random people to exorcise their ex from their system. I never understood how an emotionally embossed ex could be removed with sexual promiscuity. It's like changing the interiors of a place in an attempt to forget the memories you had of that place. And why remove anyone? I would rather keep everyone—good, bad and ugly—within me. As much as their leaving me made me, my keeping them within me will also shape my personality in perhaps a stronger way. Anyway, I never had any ex, so forget that. I don't know why I said it. When I close my eyes to think where I should begin, this moment came to me first so I just blurted it out. Let me now begin from the beginning.

2019. It had been a year since I had come to New Delhi after my graduation in Economics (Hons) from Baruipur College in West Bengal. Shifting here was more scary for my mother than me. This was the first time I had to move out of

Baruipur because of my UPSC aspirations. A little personal research told me that enrolling at a coaching institute in New Delhi would help me immensely. Topsie Coaching Centre it was. They had the most immaculate record as far as producing IAS officers was concerned. In fact, the girl who topped the year I graduated also happened to praise the centre in her interview I'd read on one of the news portals. It helped me lock my decision. And also convince my mother to allow me to move out, as the topper girl from Andhra Pradesh was also from a small town like me.

I come from a world where people don't usually question verbal validation and take it rather seriously. That too if it's coming from a topper. That was it. I enrolled myself in Topsie, appeared for their online internal entrance exam, passed, paid my fees in advance and then arrived in New Delhi.

For the initial two months, ma was there with me. She helped me set up the one-room rented flat in Karol Bagh. Ma wanted me to share it with a roomie. But I was against it. I have this phobia of strangers. I just can't one day start sharing my place with someone else. Or things. Or people. Anyway, I'm smarter than my mother thinks I am. That's, by the way, every Indian youngster's story. But who is going to explain that to an Indian mother? She used to constantly watch *Vardaat*, *Crime Patrol* and *Savdhaan India* and assumed her daughter would be the next target for any crime that's going to happen in the country. I gave up after understanding she was paranoid for my safety. Not blaming her though.

It was only when she left for Baruipur, after settling me here, that I realized UPSC preparation can be quite monotonous. Study-eat-study-repeat. Sleep only when you can't stay awake any more. I simply couldn't keep studying all the time. I had to do something else to keep myself energized and also to earn enough to sustain my living in Delhi. Though ma was taking care of my stay and studies, as a twenty-two-year-old, one has (or should have) that ego of earning and sustaining all by oneself. I definitely did.

The Topsie Coaching Centre schedule used to keep me busy in the first half of the day. Then throughout the day, it was up to me when and how much I studied. Half an hour before I dozed off every night, I used to randomly surf YouTube videos. That's when I came across a video on mixology. The study of making cocktails.

Something about it was alluring in a different way. In the next two–three months, I used this half an hour slot to only study about mixology. Obviously, I never told ma about this. Sometimes, I feel the '80s and '90s mothers (women who conceived then) have this special talent of conveniently focusing on specific imagined possibilities based on certain keywords. For example, if I had told my mother about mixology and what it's about, I knew she would have forgone asking about mixology while giving her full attention to the word 'cocktail'. After which a barrage of questions would have hit me starting with, 'Shonai, have you started drinking? It's not good for . . .' Shonai, by the way, is my nickname. Every Bong has one. And mostly the nickname is their first embarrassment ticket for the world. Sorry, no digressing. So, then my mother's derivative way of thinking would take over. Cocktails are found in pubs. A pub is where Jessica Lal was killed. That too in Delhi. That's it. She would then tell me that if I pursued mixology, I would see her dead face. It would have been curtains for my new-found love for mixology.

Within the next six months, I finished an online course on mixology. I was studying as per the schedule of Topsie Coaching Centre, while I also took up work at a bar chain as a mixologist. My work was simple: to suggest new cocktails to the bar chain. I would be paid if the cocktail I'd suggested was approved and included in the menu. It wasn't necessary for me to physically go to the bars but at times when I was shit-bored at home, I did go there for a change of mind and mood. My flat had anyway become a dump-yard for alcohol. But I must say the bar chain themselves helped me with the alcohol for my mixes instead of me spending bucks on them.

During one of those nights when I was simply sitting behind the bar, trying to share my new drink with the bartender, telling him the portions that needed to be used, I saw him for the first time. Faizaan Ahmad.

'Do you have a cocktail for curing a heartbreak?' he asked. His eyes were on me. He looked lost. Maybe he thought I was a bartender.

'We have a lot of cocktails. Which one does what, is for you to sip and see,' I said, looking away from him. I was never into looking at strangers directly. One, I wasn't comfortable doing that. Second, I think it gives them unnecessary importance. To add to that, I have this special talent of becoming one with the crowd. I never stand out. Maybe that's because everything about me is average. Except my IQ perhaps.

'Any recommendations?' he asked. This time I looked at him. Being behind the bar a few times by then, I've had men—who had no other girl to go to—flirt with me. They had no interest in me. They only wanted a woman to whom they could exhibit their rotten sense of humour. What stood out in his query was that Faizaan sounded more serious than flirty.

'Let the gentleman try our new mix,' I told the bartender. He shrugged at me. I knew why. We weren't allowed to offer any drink to a customer till it was sanctioned by the owner officially and was in the menu.

'It's on me,' I told the bartender. He quickly mixed the drink—a new blend—and served it to Faizaan. I saw him take a sip, put the glass on the bar table, close his eyes and then ask, 'What is it called?'

I said, 'No name yet.'

'Let me name it then. *Miss Mixo*. The one you need if your heart is broken,' he said with an ironical smile like the one you give when you finally understand life is a bitch.

'So, it worked at the first sip?' I blurted. I don't know what made me say it. I didn't want it to become a conversation and yet . . .

'Oh yes, it's love at first sip for me,' he said. The seriousness had suddenly taken a sharp flirtatious turn.

'Good for you,' I said. Soon, I left the bar. I had to be home by 10 p.m. lest ma called and realized I was elsewhere.

I went into my daily routine and forgot about him. A couple of weeks later, when I went to the bar again, he was there as well. This time with legal papers.

'Damn, where were you? I have been coming here for a week now. I need your signature here,' he said.

I was taken aback. I gave the documents a quick read and realized they were for copyrighting my drink 'Miss Mixo'.

'I think you are doing it wrong. You are working for a bar chain and letting them pay you. I believe you should copyright your drink and charge royalties from every damn bar around who chooses to serve Miss Mixo to all the heartbroken souls,' he said, like a professional lawyer.

If that was his way of winning me over, I dare say he had my attention for sure. He must have picked on my smile the other night which I'd flashed before leaving the bar. On hindsight, I think I shouldn't have smiled. It encourages people. Definitely emboldened him. 'Smiles' in such circumstances, I feel, have brought more shit into one's life than any other expression.

Faizaan was constantly trying to converse with me. While I was doing my best to stop it. Somewhere it was giving me a kick. For the first time in my life, a guy was trying to fish for my heart. When ma called, I had to excuse myself and go to the washroom to answer her. I booked an Uber when I was finally ready to leave.

'What if I tell you I have a Ferrari waiting outside? I can drop you,' Faizaan said.

I smirked and replied, 'Intelligent girls like me aren't impressed with what you have outside. It's about what you have here.' I pointed at his temples to drive home my point. I flung my bag over my shoulder and went out. My Uber was five minutes away.

Faizaan joined me soon enough. As I expected him to.

'Ferrari is what I call my bike, actually,' he said.

'A footnote about me would be that I don't like people who keep one thing assuming it to be something else,' I said with a tinge of sarcastic amusement in my voice.

He seemed totally clueless with this comeback of mine.

'So, what kind of people do you like?' That was a give-up from him, I knew.

'Liking for me happens when the person stops being a stranger.'

'That will happen if we know each other better.'

'Precisely.' My smile stretched further.

'I'm Faizaan Ahmad, twenty-six years of age, stand at five-nine and weigh around seventy-five kilos,' he said in one breath.

'I'm Ekantika Pakrashi. Twenty-two, rise till five-seven and weigh fifty-nine kilos. And from Baruipur, West Bengal.' I followed his pattern.

He smiled, realizing he had to add the place part.

'From Delhi itself. But roots in Bhopal.'

'Live here alone or with family?' I asked, assuming that was pretty normal to inquire.

For the first time that night I thought he looked nervous and unsteady.

2

Let me be honest; before Faizaan, I've never come in close proximity, emotionally or otherwise, with a male specimen of our species. Like never ever.

I was born to a single mother. Ma earned for us, I later learnt, working as a surrogate for couples. After baba died, bad times had befallen us. Since ma wasn't well educated, she had nothing else going for her except her own body. It began by chance after she was approached by the head nurse of a clinic where she worked as a cleaner. The payment was good and it took care of us for two years easily without any extra income. Whenever she was gone, because she couldn't be seen pregnant in the locality in Baruipur, being a single mother, Nondar ma used to take care of me. She was an old lady who used to live alone in the same locality. Like us, she too hardly mixed with people. She was a professional nanny.

I had studied in a girls' school first, then a girls' college and only in Topsie Coaching Centre did I meet boys (some were men) as my batchmates. But that doesn't mean I have never observed men. I don't know how I should feel if I have to confess that I've always objectified men. Stripped them bare to analyse their anatomy. And in my mind, I have categorized men into three distinct types: the *looker*, the *choker*, the *gawker*. These categorizations are based on whatever my friends in school and college have told me. Some, however, I've seen myself, while some of it is based on my instinct.

The *looker* men are the ones who are best to look at from a distance. More often than not, they turn out to be just the kind of asshole you want to stay away from. They know they are good-looking and thus use it as an excuse to feel more superior to the people around. Especially in front of their female companions. They carry themselves in a way as if it's the female's good luck that they are giving them importance and have chosen her over others, otherwise they could have chosen anybody else. That way, they demand unspoken gratitude from them. They feel for females what the East India Company felt for Indians. And yet they need ordinary-looking females the most by their side. The hot ones have the same superiority complex as the men, while the average-looking female keeps fawning over these *looker* males.

These males make the 'average' women believe that they—the males—are the best part about them. All in an unsaid manner. I hate this category. Like, I can't stand them. Like, if I were allowed, I would kill them all. But this is also true that I objectify them the most. I mentally undress this category all the time. I told Faizaan about it later. So, every time a hunk kind of guy passed us, be it in a mall, or a pub or wherever, we did exchange a naughty look. He knew my mind. It was a thing between us. Looking at me, nobody would ever be able to guess I have such an almost-perverse mind. I look the studious (not nerdy) type. The kind, I'm told, guys eventually get married to. But nobody dates. Not when they have options.

Maybe that's why no guy ever approached me. Oh yes, except one. I remember this boy who used to come with his friend who was the boyfriend of the girl I used to accompany to my science tuitions in Standard Ten. He used to stare at me continuously, which used to irk me. I don't like boys who can't talk but only stare like creeps. One day after our tuitions, while the others went out, I stayed back for some time. Our teacher used to conduct these tuitions in his drawing room; now that the class was over, he'd gone to his bedroom. I quickly mixed some water from my bottle with the red paint I'd brought, used my ink pot dropper to place a drop of it inside my nose and then walked out. The boy was waiting for me. With my nose fake-bleeding, I looked straight at him for the first time and gave him my creepiest smile. He never stared at me again.

The *choker* type seems like the dream man but only while he is pursuing you. The moment you start dating them officially, they'll choke you with their junk chauvinism and nauseating gender-biased mindset. In the name of love, they'll imprison your freedom. Make you their property, supply you with emotional capsules every time you try to talk to them, convincing you that their possession of you is because of their love for you. Bullfuckingshit. But alas, you can't know whether a man is a *choker* or not till you get into a relationship with him. Unless you are clever enough to read the red flags beforehand.

The *gawkers* are the men who simply become your slaves. For anything and everything they have only one expression: to gawk. They have no alpha-ness. No guts. No nothing. They find this weird comfort in pacifying their female partners all the time. They do what they are told to do. They are non-chivalrous and use their love for their female to hide all their weaknesses. Point out to them their shortcomings and they will say, 'I love her, na, so . . .' The justification for being a hopeless, spineless being is always ready with them. Sorry, I can never respect such people.

When a couple of nights later, after I flashed that somewhat life-trajectory-altering smile at Faizaan, I was looking ahead to see if he would turn up the next day or not. He didn't. It was only a month later that I saw him again. He came straight to the bar counter and asked for me. Before the bartender could point to me, I approached him.

'Another legal document?' I wanted to make sure he knew that I remembered him. This much he deserved or so I felt then.

'I wish I could copyright you, but . . .' It was cheesy but because it was happening with me the first time, that a guy was using cheesy lines, I liked it. In fact, I may have blushed a bit too.

'I've already copyrighted myself for myself,' I said.

'Does the lady sip drinks or does she only mix them?' he asked. I knew it was a proposition.

'Not much into the drinks I mix. I'm good with Diet Coke,' I said. I was maintaining eye contact now.

'Two Diet Cokes, please,' he spoke to the bartender but was looking at me.

'You don't seem the soft drink type,' I said.

'I'm not. But Diet Coke and you is a hard combo,' he flashed his smile which, in his head I'm sure, was his Tom Cruise version. For me, it was Varun Dhawan at best. Cute in a desi way.

As our Diet Cokes arrived, I let my body language show that I was okay with standing behind the bar and not joining him at some table. Girls should be difficult, at least to begin with, I believe. Every soil needs a bit of toil.

'So . . . ,' he said. I intentionally kept quiet. I knew it would be problematic for him to continue the conversation. And that would be the moment for me to judge his intelligence. I was forever a sapiosexual.

'You don't look the Tinder type,' he said.

I knew what Tinder was, but I'd never tried it.

'What's the Tinder type?' I inquired.

'If I articulate it, you may get offended so . . .'

'But you said I'm not the Tinder type, so why would I get offended if you articulated something which I'm not?'

'But you sure look the type who gets offended easily,' he was trying his puppy face. It was somewhat working with me.

'And that would disturb your flirtatious vibe?' I quipped.

He smiled, sipping his Diet Coke.

'I myself don't know if I'm the Tinder type or not because I've never used it. It's a hook-up app, I suppose. I value bonding over hook-ups.' I didn't want to say that much but being someone who rarely talked with anyone, it all came out in a rush.

'Bonding takes time,' he said.

'Precisely. That which takes time to form, is intensified with time.'

'Are you a part-time sage as well?'

I couldn't help but smile.

'In the rules of dating, they say if the girl starts to smile, one has a chance.'

'My rules are different. I go by knowledge. That excites me. Not by someone's gym schedule.' I deliberately mentioned the latter because I noticed in Delhi, most of the young men walk the I-have-huge-biceps-so-I-walk-like-Robocop way.

'What do I do to appeal to you then? Recite the Quran or the Bhagavad Gita verbatim?' he asked. He had this constant I-am-trying-to-read-you gleam in his eyes. That was sure arousing in a platonic way.

'I'm not Arjun, nor are you Krishna. So, no! Tell me, what's Pink Tax?'

He looked as if he was waiting for a cricket ball to be thrown at him while I suddenly hurled a baseball. He frowned. I only kept waiting. I was sure he would not know what Pink Tax was. And with that, he would also realize I'm not only not the Tinder type but not his type as well.

'Pink Tax is a phenomenon arising from gender-based price discrimination for products mostly used by women,' he gulped his Diet Coke as if he had managed to hit the baseball with a cricket bat for a home run. Well, he had.

I gave him a surprised but acknowledging nod.

'Apart from passing random exams set by girls in a bar, I also prepare for the UPSC,' his voice had a hint of amusement.

For a moment, I heard my mother whispering to me that he was lying. Perhaps he had stalked me and now mentioned UPSC to find a common ground. He wanted to get into my good books and then . . . phew. I stopped my mother's voice from further poisoning my mind.

'Which institute?' I asked.

'Topsie Coaching Centre.'

My mother's voice had to be correct, I thought.

The First Kill
31 December 1992
Marine Drive, Bombay

Bombay was unlike *Bombay* that year. Especially in that last one month. Apart from being busy, it was slightly tense as well. There had been a few incidents of riots in its suburban pockets after the Babri Masjid demolition in Ayodhya earlier that month. Though no common man, who was only focused on earning his livelihood, was involved, the fear of repercussions hung over everyone.

It being the night of 31 December, people were looking forward to new beginnings, hoping the upcoming year would bring less bloodshed and hatred. Ankita was also among those few hopefuls. At twenty-three, she was a BSc graduate from Mithibai College who was there at Marine Drive with her fiancé. Pankaj had come up to meet her from Pune so they could spend the last night of the year together. In another twenty-eight days they were supposed to get married.

There were fewer people compared to the crowds on previous years' New Year Eves. Police patrolling vans were stationed at short distances with some officers active while others were bantering in groups of two or three. Pankaj had recently bought a Kodak camera with which he was clicking her photographs under one of the street lamps by the Marine Drive area.

'Come on, give me a good pose. Only four more clicks are left.' Pankaj said exasperatedly. He knew the hard copies of these clicks would be his only version of her till he met her again three weeks later. Ankita was in a different mood though. She indulged herself in tomfoolery, making funny faces all the time. It was her carefree laughter that caught *his* attention.

He was sitting by the cemented barricade lining the Queen's Necklace, another name for Marine Drive. In a taxi driver's khaki uniform with the first four buttons open, his laminated ID attached to his shirt's pocket. From the moment Ankita's laughter drew his attention, he kept staring at her with a scowl, as if he had a problem with her laughter. As if he didn't know what there was to laugh about in this goddamn city. As if he took her laughter as a personal offence. His stare was accompanied with a brooding frown.

Done with clicking photographs, Pankaj and Ankita started ambling, hand-in-hand, on the Marine Drive footpath. He too stood up, dusted his rear with his hands and then started following the couple. He didn't know why. He had never done that before. It was an instinctive thing.

Soon, the clock struck twelve. A barrage of rockets embellished the sky with various designs. It was 1993. He saw Pankaj hugging Ankita for the longest time. Then they stood by the road admiring the sky above. The reflection of the bursting of rockets highlighted the innocent smiles on their faces. A couple of minutes later, Ankita said, 'I'll have to go now.'

'I know,' Pankaj said and hailed a taxi.

He ran to his parked taxi. Started it urgently, put it in gear and went right behind Pankaj and Ankita's taxi.

From Marine Drive he followed them to Bombay Central station. Their taxi stopped. Pankaj stepped out. Then bent down a bit to put his face half inside the taxi's window to reach Ankita. Their hands clasped. A few seconds later, the clasp gently broke. As the taxi with Ankita in it drove away, Pankaj stood there waving at it.

Following Ankita's taxi, he saw her leap a little out of the cab's window and wave back at Pankaj till he turned to walk into Bombay Central station. *He* could feel the vibrant love between them. He found it abhorrent.

The taxi with Ankita drove further for another seven minutes and dropped her at a place in Tardeo. He too stopped his taxi at some distance from hers. After she stepped out of the cab, he switched off his vehicle's headlights first and then the engine. He became a part of the already foreboding silence around. Most of the people in the area were asleep. Some of the lights in the rooms were visible but nobody was at their window.

Ankita crossed the quiet lane quickly. She was careful not to step into any potholes with her new sandals. She had bought them because she was meeting Pankaj. As she disappeared into the side lane, he quickly opened the taxi's dashboard and took out a small Dettol bottle. He took out his handkerchief and, opening the bottle, dabbed its mouth on the cloth. He was a chronic insomniac. Till today he had used the chloroform, which he had stolen from a chemist's shop he once worked at, to put himself to sleep. Every night around 3.30 a.m. or so, when he knew that if he didn't close his eyes for some time, it would affect his driving during the day, he would use the chloroform to switch himself off from the world. When the effect wore off after a few hours, he used to wake up and get going with his daily chores.

He took a deep breath while locking his taxi from the outside. Then he tiptoed ahead only to take a left turn into the side lane, right behind Ankita. He managed to reach her in no time. Sensing someone behind her, Ankita turned but was cornered as he put the handkerchief right on her nose and mouth simultaneously. She fidgeted and tried to fight a little. Some muffled noise did come out but not enough to disturb the peace around.

A tad more than two hours later, Ankita came to her senses. The taxi's tape player was on. She could hear Kumar Sanu singing *'Maine pyar tumhi se kiya hai'* from the movie *Phool Aur Kaante.* Ankita tried to move, but couldn't. Her limbs were tied tight. She tried but wasn't able to see anything. She was blindfolded. She didn't know she was sitting on the passenger seat of his taxi.

He was sitting behind her. He had adjusted the rear-view mirror so that he could see her face properly in it. It wasn't long before Ankita realized she wasn't able to breathe either. There was a piece of cello-tape pasted on her nose. There was another, on her mouth, blocking both airways. As Ankita's body shuddered in desperation for oxygen, he sat behind her, watching her. Seconds passed. As Ankita inched towards her end, his brooding frown slowly kept changing into a smile.

Ankita's body stopped moving on its own. No fidgets, no nothing. He quickly opened his bag, where he kept his tiffin box, water bottle, a shirt and a Polaroid camera. He took the camera out and clicked a picture of the dead Ankita's face. Moments later, the machine pushed out an instant hard copy from its base. He removed the latex gloves he was wearing to hold the photograph in his bare hand.

For the first time in years that night, he slept without using the chloroform.

3

Our first outing together happened two weeks after our Diet Coke rendezvous. We went to watch a movie at a cinema hall in Connaught Place. He was the one who asked for it. We were going steady on chat. To be honest, I was hoping he'd say something so we could meet up. Thankfully he did bring up the movie thing.

I said yes to the movie proposal after doing some quick research about him. After all, I did agree with my mother when she said always beware of strangers. Faizaan was indeed studying in Topsie Coaching Centre but was three years my senior. He had attempted UPSC thrice and he passed the prelims once. My mother's hyper-suspicious voice took a deep breath in my head. Despite all that my mother had warned me about, it was indeed a coincidence that we met at the bar. After three years, he wasn't a regular at the coaching centre. He came only during the mock test sessions. And thus, we'd missed each other till then. Also, his subject was Engineering. Mine was Economics.

I understood the human tendency to compulsively flock into small like-minded groups and set up a symbiosis within the group for mutual benefits only after I joined Topsie.

In fact, one could spot a lot of UPSC aspirants in Karol Bagh itself. It was only I who couldn't find a partner/friend, let alone a group. I desperately wanted someone to approach me. I found it difficult to approach people or initiate anything because my mother had kept me in a fiercely protective cocoon throughout my childhood. Even during my girls' school and college stint, I could never make one single close friend. The kind to whom you can bare your heart.

I don't blame my mother entirely though. With baba's early demise, I was all she had. And she held me like her own heart. She didn't remarry even though she was only thirty years old when baba died due to a bad case of pneumonia. Even though I have never told ma this, one of my primary intentions to crack the UPSC exam is to make her feel somewhat empowered. All her life she has queued up for everything. With her daughter in a civil job, I want her to enjoy her life her way, feeling slightly superior to the rest.

When I told Faizaan that I too studied in Topsie, he started to frequent the coaching centre. He didn't come right into the premises. He simply stood by the nearest cigarette-paan shop, on his 'Ferrari' bike, sharp at 11.30. That's when my morning classes used to get over. The first day when I saw him there, I didn't want to make it obvious that I thought he was there for me. I simply smiled and responded to his 'Hi' while passing by the cigarette-paan shop. I made sure my 'Hi' wasn't an excited one.

'Hey!' Surprise first and then 'Hi.' Affirmative. The surprise was important so he shouldn't know conclusively that I was thinking about him too since the last meeting.

Trust me, it's both easy and important to fool guys. Or should I say, confuse them. In the beginning, at least. In their confusion, we girls need to understand their intent and vices. If Faizaan was an arrogant guy, he would have taken my surprise as vain and wouldn't have pursued me. Good for me. I never needed an arrogant chauvinist by my side anyway. If he was a creepy stalker, he wouldn't have said anything but would have continued to stalk me quietly. Hence, my 'surprise'. I'm like that only. I give a lot of thought to what I'm exhibiting. Perils of being a born introvert? Maybe.

'Where to?' he asked.

'Home. What are you doing here?' I asked. A little bit of interest was necessary, else he would have thought I wasn't into him at all. I didn't want that to happen because I was, of course, interested.

'To meet a few friends, exchange notes and all that, you know,' Faizaan said and then an awkward smile later added, 'Where do you live?'

'Close by,' I said.

'May I drop you?' He said it softly. In a non-authoritative manner.

I gave it a few seconds of thought and then climbed on the pillion.

For the next several days, this same moment seemed to happen in a loop with me coming out exactly at the same time from Topsie, seeing him waiting by the cigarette-paan shop. We used to chit-chat on the way till he dropped me home. We exchanged a few messages until night, whenever I was on a break from studying. Then the next morning again, the same routine. With him accompanying me, I didn't feel the urge to go out to the bar. I worked as a mixologist from home itself. After dropping me home for the first nine days, Faizaan finally hinted that he wanted to change the routine. That's when he asked me out for a movie.

I'm an introvert, not a fool. I've had classmates who have dated guys and have told me all that can happen inside a movie hall. I was ready. Not to challenge it. But to participate equally. I liked Faizaan. He came across as a guy who wasn't pushy for anything. If he wanted something, he would ask once; if I was game, he was happy. If not, he wouldn't bring the topic up again. He was non-intrusive and also non-probing. Both of which I believe is a rarity in men these days. You give them a little scope and they will start asking who's who on your Facebook, Instagram, who called you before I did, who is this friend of yours that you tagged and the like. And that cringe-worthy dialogue, 'What's your password, baby?' Huh! Faizaan wasn't like that. He heard whatever I told him but never asked for much. Probably he knew that if I thought he should know it, I would tell him. That kind of reliance is damn rare, trust me.

The movie was a long one, runtime-wise. I remember the seat numbers as well. It was screen 1, seat number N-34 and 35. And from the moment we settled down, I was aware of his every move, yet didn't make it evident. I was expecting him to hold my hand. He did after one hour into the movie. After that, I was constantly anticipating his next move, but it never came. The voluntary clasping of hands told me (and him too, I guess) loud and clear that we were in an unspoken relationship. That we weren't just friends.

During the interval, he asked if I wanted something to eat. I said no. And I kept giving him out-of-turn glances. Such glances are perfect signals for guys to know that we are ready, please proceed. But he didn't. Till the climax of the movie came. I checked my watch. Half an hour more to go. I had simply lost my patience. He may have kissed many girls, I didn't know, but for me it was the first chance to kiss a guy. And I didn't know when the next time would be if not this. I turned to him. He shrugged. I asked if he was thinking of kissing me and that he could. He immediately kissed me, then stopped and said, 'I wanted to do this since we sat down. Why didn't you tell me before?'

'Can we discuss this later? Let's kiss for now, please?' I gasped. Before he knew it, my lips were on his and I understood what it was like to engage in a sexual kiss with a male specimen. The rubbing of lips, soft bites on them, the touch of your tongue on his. I had my eyes open but saw his were closed, so I closed mine as well. The moment had unplugged the pleasure hormones inside me like never before.

I don't know why, but it didn't feel awkward as we found ourselves holding hands moving out of the cinema hall. We quietly walked to the point where his bike was parked. My phone rang. It was my mother. I didn't pick up.

'She keeps worrying about me all the time.' I gave him a little extra information.

He smirked in an I-get-that manner.

Then I casually asked, 'You never told me where you are from. About your parents. Any siblings?'

He let go of my hand suddenly. There was a certain restraint in his body language as he put on his helmet and started the bike. I sat on the pillion. I understood there was something in my question which deeply disturbed him. Like it had happened weeks before as well, when I'd mentioned 'family'. Was it the place part which turned him off? The siblings part? Or the parents part? I couldn't guess.

4

I never asked Faizaan again about his parents or siblings or anything like that. It was clear he wasn't ready to talk about it and I was ready to give him the time till he felt comfortable. You don't speak about something personal when the listener is ready. You do so when you, the speaker, are ready. A listener then simply appears. Or so I read somewhere.

One day Faizaan did hint about it in such a beautiful way that I started admiring him even more. That day, after my class, we drove on his 'Ferrari' to Connaught Place where we ordered two Starbucks coffees and were loitering around different blocks. I bought a couple of books on Economics from a roadside stall. It was then that he asked me, 'Do you know what Wabi Sabi is?'

I had read about it but it didn't come to my mind right then.

'Wabi Sabi is a Japanese view where people believe that real beauty lies in the transience and imperfection in everything. My family is imperfect and I used to hate them, but later I realized perhaps that's where its beauty lay. Perfection is anyway an illusion. All I can tell you is that I love my older sister. And I've told her about you.'

Though Faizaan said the last part rather casually, I felt little nervous.

'What did you tell her?' I asked.

'That finally I feel I have someone with whom I can go the longest,' he said looking around.

'And you have realized this so soon?' I couldn't hide my surprise.

He seemed to be lost in thought after which he turned towards me to say, 'I guess so. What, how and why you feel something, I think isn't a time function. It just happens.'

I couldn't agree more because somewhere I too was feeling the same but was afraid to put it into words. I had seen so many of my class mates swearing by their love in the first few months of their relationship and then they themselves told me they had started liking someone else.

'But listen, Mr Ahmad,' I said holding on to his collar, drawing him towards me a bit. He was taken aback as I continued, 'If you ditch me, I'll kill you for sure.'

He removed my hand and said with a smirk, 'We'll see who kills whom.'

We traipsed on. We both had stupid smiles on our faces. This time I had my hand linked with his arm.

The kiss in the movie theatre didn't change things much between us except that we started kissing more often. Whenever we got a chance. Not in public though. We also started to converse more. Since we both were studying for the UPSC, our talking topics were diverse. What I noticed was he used to mention his elder sister in almost everything. I understood she was close to him. But he never made me talk to her. To be honest, I stalked him on Facebook and other social media apps many times after we started spending time together, but couldn't locate anyone who could have been his elder sister. I could only decipher that his younger brother's name was Mohsin Ahmad and his mother was Saira Ahmad. No elder sister, no father. I assumed that since he had told his elder sister about me, it meant he was taking our relationship seriously. That's how it happens, right? A college batchmate of mine had once told me that when a girl lets a guy use her sexually with no questions asked, she is somewhere invested in the guy and trusts the relationship is for keeps. When a boy takes the girl to his family, more often than not, he is serious about the girl.

Something did happen for the first time, though, after our kiss. One night he messaged me saying he was getting bored after studying for five hours straight. I too had the same issue. We UPSC aspirants anyway have nothing else to do except study for as much time as possible. Self-discipline is of utmost importance. But yes, sometimes a little loosening-up is allowed. He asked me if I wanted to have some bullet coffee. I was game. I quickly wrapped up my daily call with ma, told her I was sleeping and got into my denims and kurti. That was my soul-dress. An old pair of denims and a cotton kurti. I think I have this weird problem of getting attached to my denims. I haven't thrown away any of my denims. Anyway, I was ready. But that's when it started raining. Blame it on the movies I have grown up watching but the moment a girl and a boy are about to meet and it rains . . . it's sexual encounter alert! Something about the possibility scared me. I was a virgin till then. Was this the night? I don't know why but I started to panic. I was constantly looking out of the window to spot him. I did call Faizaan but there wasn't any reply. Of course, he was driving to my place. Then I saw him park his bike outside my building gate. I wanted to shout from the window and ask him to go home but by then, he'd dashed inside.

I quickly called him on his phone but he was unavailable. There's never any network on the ground floor of my building. And before I knew it, there was the sound of the doorbell. I rushed to the door. Faizaan was standing soaked in the rain. He had a stupid smile on his face as he stepped in.

'What are you looking at? Where's the bathroom? Give me a towel, please,' he said.

I showed him the way to the bathroom, telling him that the towel was inside. As he went in, I found myself pacing up and down in the hall. He had not shown any inclination towards anything physical and yet my mind was scaring me. When he came out, he had the towel wrapped around his waist. This was the first time I was seeing him topless. Or any man topless for that matter at such proximity.

'We can still have bullet coffee. My version,' he said and ambled towards the kitchen. I kept wondering why he had no issue standing topless in front of me. Didn't he understand I would feel awkward?

Faizaan started making coffee, humming some old Hindi song while I stood by the kitchen door. That's when another 'filmy' thing happened. There was a power cut. Though it was a routine thing for the area, that night it all seemed like the universe was playing a role in helping me get rid of my virginity. For which I wasn't ready.

'Any candles or flashlight?' he asked, switching on his mobile phone's torch. 'I'm sorry but my battery will run out soon,' he added.

I stood still. Perhaps he sensed my dilemma. As he came close and held my shoulder, I don't know what happened to me. I simply held him and broke down. Tears welled up.

'Ekantika, what happened?'

'I was scared,' I somehow managed to speak.

'Of what?' Faizaan sounded genuinely concerned. He looked at me. I looked back at him.

'I thought tonight was the moment when we would end up being . . .' I took a few seconds before averting my eyes from him and said, ' . . . intimate.'

Faizaan remained silent. As if he knew there was more to come from me.

'And I didn't want you to see me that way.'

'Which way?' He almost whispered, hugging me.

'Na . . . naked.' I mumbled and sobbing further, added, 'I'm not perfect. I don't look great when I'm naked. I was scared you would lose interest in me. And leave me.' I kept sobbing, feeling at peace in his bear hug.

'Don't you remember Wabi Sabi? I'm not into perfect things,' Faizaan said. 'Moreover, we like each other beyond our bodies, I guess. Even I'm not a stud. So, how does the question of disliking you because of your body arise?'

'You aren't kidding me, right?' I asked, looking up at him. His face veiled behind my tears.

He started laughing. Suddenly there was a tinge of mockery in his laughter. I slapped him. He didn't stop. I punched him. His laughter became a roar.

That night we had his version of bullet coffee along with my version of Maggi noodles with onion and tomato. Later we cosied up in the balcony discussing our study notes, as it rained outside. It was our kind of romantic night. He could have touched me wherever he wanted to, but he didn't. In an unsaid manner he waited for me to give him the hint, knowing well even if he had touched me without giving any hint, I wouldn't have complained. A man who respects a woman's right to consent, is a man I had rarely come across. Or even heard of. Being sensitive to what you like or appreciate is an underrated emotion. I think that was the night I truly fell in love with Faizaan Ahmad.

Two days later, after my class at Topsie, he told me that he shared the rainy night incident with his elder sister as well. She told him that I was just the kind of girl he shouldn't let go of. I felt relieved to know that. Though it was only much later I came to know that he had no elder sister. He'd only imagined her all through his life.

The Fifth Kill
July 1995
On a New Delhi-bound train

It felt important to be featured in newspaper articles. First regional. Then after the third kill, national ones as well. Nobody had published any photograph or sketch of him, though. Nobody knew or had seen him yet. He was referred to everywhere by only a name. A name which only he knew had been coined for him by the media. *The cello-tape serial killer*. He wasn't in it for something as flimsy as fame though. There was a much deeper need at work which pushed him to kill. For the first time. And then four times more.

It had been two years since he preyed on his fourth kill. First it was a girl, Ankita Tamhale, in Tardeo. Then it was an elderly man, Ramesh Kulkarni, in Worli. The third was a teenager, Sachin Patel, in Colaba. While the fourth was a young pregnant lady, Sejal Shah, Borivli. All in Bombay.

Being in Bombay for some years now, he had had enough of the city. First he had worked at a chemist, then at a photo studio and then drove a taxi for the longest time. Same roads, same uniform, same traffic signals, same *pandus* (police constables) and, after a point of time, he realized even the passengers were all the same. Perhaps the only Indian city which was almost mythical to an outsider, but for an insider it made a mockery of life's value on a daily basis. The passengers, though, spoke in different languages but their problems were all the same. Love, money, property, health. Those were the four broad categories. When he had come to Bombay for the first time, the city used to talk to him. Especially after he gulped down one packet of desi alcohol. Slowly there came into being a stoic silence between the city and him. That silence bored him. And challenged his emotional inertia. He wanted to reach out. Wanted to make relationships.

Sahabzaade Samsher Khan had come to Bombay from his native village in 1989. An MA in Hindi, he was the only one in his clan and village to have studied this far. The one who inspired him to come over to Bombay was his neighbour in the village who spoke highly of Bombay every time he visited his hometown with gifts and cash for the family. With a big family to support, Sahabzaade thought perhaps it was a better idea to shift. Truth be told, he was suffocated in his own family. Every day someone or the other was sick. Or someone died. Or someone was pregnant again. He'd had enough, so he decided to stay in touch with them from a distance and live on his own. Having to live with nineteen family members in his small house made him start to hate the proximity of human beings. In his hometown also, he used to sit by a pond most of the time. Either lost in thought or reading a book. Every time he travelled to the closest town, he used to get as many books as possible from his cousin who was a *raddiwala* there. Reading had become his obsession. Anything beyond the pages he found uninteresting and futile. For books excited his imagination. Sahabzaade Samsher Khan was in love with his imagination.

When he arrived in Bombay, on the same train as his neighbour used to take, it wasn't long before he realized his neighbour wasn't some successful businessman as he claimed when he was in the village. He was a pimp. He tried to push Sahabzaade into the same profession, but he managed to scoot away at the right time. To sustain himself, he took up a job in a chemist's shop first and then at a photo studio in Colaba. From the chemist he had stolen a few bottles of chloroform for his own insomniac needs to begin with. He worked with them for a year each while learning to drive from his roommate in the chawl where he lived. Before leaving the job and becoming a taxi driver under his roommate's tutelage, he took the Polaroid camera from the photo studio, which fascinated him the most. One push of a button and a moment in life was captured. He used to clean the lens wearing gloves. The functioning of the camera was sheer magic for him. And with that Polaroid camera, he had captured the faces of the ones he killed. Four till then. And every time he killed someone and had the photograph, he used to spend months imagining a life with the person. With his first victim, Ankita, he used to imagine how she would be if she was his wife. What they would talk about and when. What would her weaknesses be, what he would teach her, what he would learn from her. This he did day in and day out till he was bored with Ankita. This was the time he used to sleep peacefully. Till his insomnia came back, he couldn't take Ankita's imaginary presence any more, and the brooding frown was back on his face. Then came Ramesh, who became his uncle in his imagination. Then Sachin became his younger brother, while in the last ten months, Sejal was his sister-in-law.

With Bombay becoming a bore as a city, and taxi-driving a monotony on a daily basis, Sahabzaade was wondering if he should shift place when luck struck as his mother (his father was dead by then) sent a telegram to his master's address calling him over for his own marriage.

A day after receiving the telegram, he gave his taxi keys to his master, swearing to give up driving, and took the first train to his native place. He sat up by the door, on the vestibule all day. Travelling without a ticket was the norm for him. Dangling his bag on his shoulder, sometimes he sat at the door of the vestibule talking to his imaginary sister-in-law Sejal, sometimes walked past different compartments casually looking at everyone on board. At night Sahabzaade started looking for any space where he could lie down for a bit. It was then that a man's cries caught his attention. He stopped, frowned. He looked down to see that the man was sitting in the space between two seats. Looked drunk. He soon stood up and went towards the vestibule.

Sahabzaade followed him. The man went and stood by the open door. The sound of the train told him it was running at its fastest. He held on to the two iron bars by the side of the door and popped his head out. A fierce wind hit him. He shouted out that he didn't want to live any more. That's when Sahabzaade approached him with the excuse of asking for a matchbox for his *beedi*. The man said he didn't have one. It took Sahabzaade another half an hour of constant talking to convince the man to not commit suicide. The drunk man, thanking him for intercepting him at the right time, excused himself to go to the adjoining toilet.

A few seconds later, Sahabzaade knocked at the toilet door ready with a handkerchief dipped in the chloroform and a roll of cello-tape in his pocket. The man opened the door. Sahabzaade pushed him inside the washroom. There was no sign of any anxiety on him. As if attacking someone was his everyday thing. The attack, however, took the drunken man by surprise. Before he could do anything, the chloroform's effect was triggered. He slowly lost his senses. Sahabzaade locked the toilet from the inside.

After three hours, he came back to where the man had been sitting. And somehow made space for himself between the two seats on the train's floor. The light and fan switches in the compartment were all on but none of the lights were functioning. As he held the photograph of the drunken man's dead face, he could barely see it in the darkness. Sahabzaade smiled, imagining the drunken man to be his servant. He soon dozed off.

5

No, Faizaan didn't suffer from any mental problem. Later, he did tell me about the reason behind his banter with his 'imaginary' elder sister.

His mother was pregnant once before he was born. She had told him that post-delivery, when his father learnt that it was a girl, he paid a nurse in the government hospital to kill the child. It affected his mother because she had done most of the shopping for the baby, and deep in her heart she knew it was going to be a girl child. Mother's instinct. When she got pregnant with another child, and later gave birth to him, a 'boy', he was 'allowed' to live, with his mother telling him about his elder sister all the time. Somewhere, Faizaan became so aware about it that he started addressing his elder sister, talking to her as if she was actually there. His imaginary elder sister became his confidante over the years with the practice only becoming intense with age. Should we call it a mental problem? Maybe medically it is, but I never saw him as a sick person. But that doesn't mean he wasn't dichotomous.

The same Faizaan who was always respectful of me, always talked without ever using an abusive word even as a figure of speech—unlike every other Delhi-ite around me—and who always kept my comfort as his priority, became a different person when we finally had sex.

It was around two to three weeks after that rainy night, that I went to his place for the first time. It was a half an hour bike ride from where I lived. It was a small one-room flat with an attached bathroom on the terrace of a house. There was a small bed and books everywhere. An old wooden wardrobe which belonged to the landlord. And an earthen jug from which he drank cold water. I'd seen ma using the same way back when I was a kid. Faizaan told me he was paying 5000 rupees rent to begin with but now was paying 7500 rupees for it. I noticed a heating pad with a pan on it. Around the pan were multiple packets of Maggi noodles. That itself was the kitchen.

'Have you opened a Maggi noodles franchise?' I asked. He chuckled and said, 'That's what is saving the majority of India's youth.'

'Especially the lazy ones,' I added.

As he picked up his deodorant bottle and sprayed it all over the room, I was amused.

'I'm sure it's stinking,' he said.

'Yeah,' I didn't want to lie, 'but deodorant is for your body, not your room.'

'Well, I can't make you wait here and go to get some stupid room freshener.'

'Yeah, yeah, I get that. But the stink is still there. What to do?' I said, making myself comfortable on the mattress. He came close to me and said, 'How about sniffing each other up?'

'Kinky but . . .' I couldn't finish my sentence.

They say it happens, when it is supposed to happen. I don't know what triggered it. We had been alone in close spaces before. We had been close to each other before as well. We had also smooched before. But when I felt his lips on mine at that moment, my gut knew something new was going to happen. The fact that his hands were trying their best to strip me while I was stripping him just sealed that gut feeling.

We were naked within a span of one minute. My first in front of a man. Our eyes were closed (at least mine were) till we stopped smooching. Sensing that he had moved out of the mattress, I opened my eyes and saw him approaching the door. His natural V-shaped back giving way to a supple bare butt was right in front of me. I felt like making doodles with my nails on them. He quickly closed the door of the room and turned. By then, my instinct made me pull the bedsheet from the mattress to cover myself up till my bosom. I was expecting him to jump on me but he opened the drawer of his study table and took out a plastic sachet. When he tore it open, I understood it was a condom. He wore it looking at me while I was looking at his erect penis. The condom didn't cover it completely. The thickness made me swallow a lump.

Faizaan came to me, and cuddled inside the bedsheet, kissing my breasts. I was somewhat embarrassed of his finger discovering that my juices were flowing. As he put his middle finger slowly inside my vagina, I could feel the pain. Impulsively, I removed his finger and hand. He kept it there again. I removed it again.

'Not now,' I rasped. But he didn't listen. Then what happened in the next one hour or so, was something for which I was neither emotionally nor physically ready.

When I looked into his rather claustrophobic bathroom mirror an hour later, I could see a girl with swollen lips, purple patches of bite marks on her arms, breasts, thighs and back, along with some deep scratches and spank marks on her butt which were still hurting. No, I wasn't beaten. But I was ravaged by Faizaan. I knew what he was doing but I didn't stop him during the act. I wanted to see if this was a real side of him. And if yes, then to what extent he could go without me having to pause or stop him.

I washed my face. Even took a shower. The touch of the soap created burning sensations around most parts of my body. Once done, I came out in a towel.

Faizaan was still on the bed, naked, with moist eyes. Frankly, I wasn't going to ask him anything about what we encountered an hour back. I thought of simply dressing up and leaving. And probably talk about it sometime later. But once again, something unpredictable happened. He leaped on to my feet as I came out of the bathroom, holding them tight and said, 'I'm really sorry. I don't know what happens to me in bed.'

That told me he had been so always. With women in bed. I, as a person, wasn't the trigger. I, as a gender, was.

'You have done this before?' I still preferred to fish for a verbal confession. And he knew I wasn't inquiring if he had had sex before.

He nodded, releasing my legs. His tears seemed genuine. I knelt down to come in line with his eyes. He understood it was a probing stance from my end.

'I've had three relationships till date. All of them left me because of this,' he said in a confessional tone. I didn't speak for a few minutes. Nor did he. We let the silence embalm our chaotic minds. In the end I had only one question for him.

'Is this why you took your time to be intimate with me?'

He slowly lifted his head up and looked at me. I thought it was a look of guilt but thankfully he contradicted my assumption with his words.

'I swear I was only waiting for you to be comfortable.'

'Hmm,' I said. That was the end of the conversation. I dressed up, took his handkerchief to cover my facial bruise and slight swelling and moved out. He did offer to drop me, but I didn't accept.

I didn't go to Topsie for a week. Nor did I meet him. We only talked over calls and messages. Of course, my mother knew nothing about anything. Not even the fact that I had a boy in my life. On the twentieth day when he was waiting for me in Topsie, assuming I would be there, I messaged him that I was at home. And I was pregnant.

He rushed to my place. I was sitting in the hall. When I opened the door, I still had the pregnancy stick with me in one hand. I showed it to him. He stared at the change of colour on it. And knew the obvious. I simply went and dropped back on the two-seater couch with a placid face. As if nothing mattered to me any more.

He slowly came up to me, kept the pregnancy stick aside and said, 'Listen, I will give up my UPSC studies and get a job. Something which pays me enough for us to have the baby.' A pause. Then he added, 'We can get married next month legally. I'll put in an application with the marriage registrar today itself. A friend of mine had once told me it generally takes a month.' Another pause. Then he said, 'I'll also talk to your mother.' Then he went quiet, realizing I wasn't saying much. He sat down on the floor with his head on my lap. Looking up at me, he said, 'Whatever it takes for me, I'll do it, but let's not abort this child.'

I was relieved to hear that. I wasn't pregnant. I'd mixed a little blood in my pee and fooled the pregnancy stick. I wanted to run this 'test' through him to know his reaction. Reactions are important in any relationship. It tells you about a person's core. Faizaan could have asked me the proverbial 'Who's baby is it?' which is often the first thought men in general have in such situations. I hadn't met Faizaan for a good twenty days. I could have had sex with someone before or after him as well. More importantly, he had worn a condom that time. But he didn't for once mention that. He simply trusted me blindly on this. As far as I was concerned, Faizaan had passed the test with distinction. I caressed his hair and then bent down to embrace him.

Before I broke the news of the fake pregnancy to him, Faizaan had mentioned something which I think is important for you to know. He had said that he had seen his father being irresponsible with his mother, and he had sworn to himself that he would give his family the first priority always. Come what may.

6

Two things which happened to me because of him, or should I say because of his presence in my life, were my addiction to cigarettes and alcohol. Within three months I was spending more on cigarettes than I ever spent on cosmetics. I basically wasn't a make-up kind of a girl. A little kohl in the eyes and a tinge of lip gloss, and I'm done. The alcohol part was always arranged by Faizaan though.

After my classes at Topsie, Faizaan used to be with me at my place. After studies, we started having a one-hour *sutta-daaru* session sitting in my balcony, watching the polluted Delhi city line. And after three pegs of Black Dog or Old Monk, we only had three gears in us: the nostalgic gear, the sentimental gear or the introspective gear. During one such session, Faizaan's nostalgic and introspective gears happened together.

'Has anyone ever ghosted you?' He asked.

I knew what he meant was ghosting in a relationship where your loved one suddenly disappears into oblivion without any intimation. Like simply disappears!

'You like me to emphasize all the time that you are my first, isn't it? Your male ego gets a hard-on,' I joked.

Faizaan smirked and said, 'Sorry. I forgot that. But I have been a victim of it even though I have only been once in a serious relationship out of three.'

'Your ex?' I probed but was careful.

He nodded. 'I don't know what happened. Everything was going so smooth between Nagma and me. Like it was all a dream. There were no complaints from my end. And then one day she suddenly disappeared.'

'What do you mean disappeared? You checked with her parents?' I found it hard to believe.

'I did. She was working here. She was actually from Allahabad. I have been to her place as well. But afterwards, I couldn't track her on her phone or even at her office or the working women's mess she lived in here, I called up her home. They too were clueless,' he finished his cigarette.

'Did you report it to the police?' I asked.

'I did. Along with her family. I remember her father was here. But there was no trace. One of the police officers at the station told me that generally if someone is kidnapped or murdered, sooner or later a trace is established. But the ones who go away willingly are the most difficult to trace.'

Looking at him I understood he was totally in his past at the moment. Probably thinking about Nagma and the moments they must have spent together. I felt slightly jealous too. I was even tempted to ask him if I could see a picture of Nagma. But I didn't do that. What if she was more beautiful than me? It would keep playing on my mind. I knew it. I kept mum.

After a thoughtful pause, two more gulps of whisky and yet another cigarette, he asked, 'Why do you think she would go away just like that?'

Honestly, there could have been several reasons. But that was not what I was thinking. I had a different question in mind. Blame it on the alcohol; I couldn't keep the question inside me.

'What would you do, Faizaan, if she reappears now?' I deliberately stressed on 'now'. *Now* was a different phase of life for him. I hope he knew that. In the last phase—the past—I wasn't there. *Now* I was. *Now* there was a different 'us' compared to Nagma and him. My question was surely legit. Especially when I heard the pain in his voice when he said she'd disappeared. That, however, I understood. He loved her and, of course, there would be pain if she disappeared suddenly. He hadn't had his closure with her. And emotional non-closures are worse than open physical wounds.

Faizaan's silence wasn't helping. I finished my cigarette and then lit another one feeling a certain nervousness. I was praying I wouldn't hear what I feared. Then he said, 'I'll just meet her once, probably, and ask her why.'

'If her answer satisfies you, you'll forget her?'

He nodded in agreement.

'What if the reason doesn't satisfy you?' If I wasn't three pegs down myself, I wouldn't have asked him this.

Faizaan again went into a thoughtful trance. After a long pause, he said, 'I won't mention her again. Doesn't matter how drunk I am.'

I beamed. Let out a deep relieving sigh. Gulped the remaining whisky from my glass and leaped on to him like a tigress. As I smooched him, I passed the whisky I mouthed into his. He gulped it, chewing on my tongue.

During another such session, we intentionally drank Miss Mixo together to celebrate six months of our knowing each other. We were in my balcony, naked under a blanket. While caressing my hair, he quipped, 'We shouldn't be like any other couple.'

'Of course we aren't.'

He smiled and said, 'Every couple thinks so.'

'So, what do you want? We dance naked in the streets?' I was still not three pegs down of Miss Mixo.

'You know, when I was in a relationship with Nagma, it was like a trance. Every day was like a lucid dream unfolding in the garb of reality. I was never scared then but now I am.'

The mention of Nagma made me uncomfortable though I didn't project it.

'Scared? Of what?' I asked.

'Of what the next day is going to bring into our lives. After my experience with Nagma, I now know every good thing ends. Most of the times, abruptly. And with that knowledge, an intense fear bites into you. These moments that we are consuming now, would be a matter of the past tomorrow. What then? Would we have better moments? Or would we be talking about each other to someone else, referring to ourselves as "ex"?'

For a moment I had moist eyes. I lifted my face, kissed his chin and said, 'Don't say that. Doesn't matter how cheesy it may sound, I love you too much to lose you and stay sane.'

'Same here. That's why the fear is ever so claustrophobic.'

'I always thought love happens at first sight. But I now know love happens every day as we immerse ourselves into the person bit by bit.'

'You're right,' he kissed my forehead.

'But your realization quotient is more than mine when it comes to relationships,' I said.

'Realization quotient? Is that even a term?' He sounded amused.

'Now it is.' I winked at him. He leaned forward and smooched me.

'Don't worry. I would keep sharing the realizations the way we share our UPSC notes,' he said and winked back.

We took the we-shouldn't-be-like-other-couples part a little too seriously. Let me tell you how. Once, I'd casually told him that the fact we stepped together into a relationship should be an event with its marks across the city. What Faizaan decided was every time we went out on dates to different restaurants, cafes, pubs or wherever, we would plant saplings in the area. That was our way of carving out time from the moment we were spending and making it a physical entity. Like people take pictures for their social media for preserving the moments, we planted saplings. And every time we were in the area we checked on them. When they would grow up, we discussed, we would cherish the moment we shared while planting them.

Another thing which we had in common was our fanaticism for the game of cricket. During IPL, we had our own bet on every match. The winner would command one act out of the loser which the latter had to perform. When

Mumbai Indians won the trophy that year, I was on the losing side. What he wanted me to do took me by surprise.

'Let's live-in,' he said.

Living-in was never a lifestyle choice a girl from Baruipur would have thought could be a reality. The same was with me. I was in love with Faizaan, was in a steady relationship, but never for a second did the thought of living together cross my mind. A girl and a boy live together only after marriage. Or that was what I had known since birth. Truth be told, I surprised myself by being a prude. I never thought I was one. I took my own sweet time to think about it. In the end I realized that except for sleeping in our respective places, we were anyway living-in.

I shifted to his place. Of course I didn't tell ma about it. This was probably the first time I had taken a big decision in my life without consulting or informing her. I felt guilty about it but later Faizaan explained to me that it was high time I took my own decisions. Moreover, ma would have never allowed me to live-in with a guy. She would have taken the first train to Delhi hearing this.

Late one night, soon after I'd shifted, I felt I wasn't able to breathe in my sleep. When I opened my eyes, I knew it wasn't a nightmare. It was real. Faizaan had clipped my nose with a clothes-peg. He was holding my hands tight, pressing on to my mouth. I swear every second seemed like a minute. Then an hour. I was losing myself. I fidgeted as much as I possibly could till I started feeling numb all over. At the very last moment, he set me free. I urgently breathed in, holding my chest, while he sat close by laughing his heart out like a psycho. Waiting for my breathing to come back to normal, I wondered if I had fallen in love with a devil.

The Eleventh Kill
October 1997
Mayur Vihar, East Delhi

By now Sahabzaade had stopped keeping a track of which newspaper was reporting him or which wasn't. He was bored because he knew he was too smart for the police.

Two years ago, on, reaching his native place, he read the *níkaah-nama*, trying hard to get a glimpse of his bride via the curtain but in vain. He wasn't given a chance to see his wife's face. Neither before the ceremony, nor during it. When the time came for the proverbial first night, he entered the room, and saw his new bride waiting for him all squirmed up on a rickety wooden bed. But he ignored her, lay down on one side of the bed and pretended to be asleep. After some time, he realized his bride had switched the lights off and had dozed off to sleep beside him. It was then that he turned and saw her face in the faint moonlight falling in through the window piercing the darkness. He thought how nice it would be if she were a photograph. Like the photographs he had in his bag of the dead people. He was almost lost in his imagination when his wife budged a bit. It made him frown. He understood in that moment, she was real. Not a dead body. He turned and dozed off.

Sahabzaade's new bride caught a viral fever the next day. The *daawat-e-valima* had to be cancelled. The couple couldn't consummate their marriage. And a week later, when she showed some signs of recovery, he had to leave for New Delhi where a friend from his village had set up a job at a new real estate project for him. He had been following-up with the friend for the past six months. He left the next day itself. But he found himself coming back home a year later.

It was a scandal which brought him back. His wife, Arfa, with whom he hadn't consummated his marriage (nor did he care) was found to be pregnant. His family's allegation was that the girl's family never told them she was pregnant before the marriage. When Sahabzaade learnt this, he fought with the entire family and asked nobody to say anything to his wife. He stood by her. Stayed with her for a month. And when she was comfortable, he left for New Delhi again. Nine months later when he came back to see she had delivered a girl child, he killed the infant and went back that night itself without telling anyone, never to return for a good two years.

There was something about mornings, Sahabzaade understood much later in life. They were underrated. He connected to a certain peace within whenever he stepped out of his small one-room place overlooking the Jama Masjid. He made sure he woke up before the daily azaan and went out for a walk. He had the photograph of a nine-year-old boy with him, his tenth victim, with whom he had imagined a father-son relationship. He had bartered a pair of Action shoes from a roadside hawker in Connaught Place for some *maal*, which one of his roommates had brought for him from Himachal Pradesh where the roomie worked in a seasonal resort as a waiter.

The shoes were comfortable enough as every morning he put them on and wandered around till it was time for him to go to office. He had been working as an office boy for a real estate firm in Delhi for the last two years. There was nothing much to do except greet visitors, offer them water/tea/coffee and keep the place clean. He used to watch the visitors closely. These were uber rich people buying posh flats and houses. Mostly it was an average-looking male accompanied by a gorgeous-looking female because he had money. He wished he had understood it earlier in life than now. Earlier, he thought education was the most important factor in life. Probably because he came from a shit hole of a place where the only thing that was allowed to be taken seriously was religion.

Looking at those rich people, Sahabzaade also wondered what could have been the basic difference between them and him. Why was he working and serving them water, while they were buying more and more houses? His conclusion was that life's all a matter of chance. From the time a sperm fertilizes an egg to your last breath; it's all a matter of chance. When you can't choose where you are born, to whom you are born, how do you choose to be who you are? People say hard work mattered. Perhaps, he thought, watching those rags-to-riches stories on television who gave a formula for their success. But if there was ever a formula, it should have worked for everyone. It's not that everybody who is a so-called failure doesn't work hard. In the end, Sahabzaade concluded that there was a conspiracy in the world to keep the poor poorer and turn the rich richer. For the rich fill the pockets of the conspirators while the poor provide the conspirators with power using their votes in democratic nations and subservience in other countries. It was a sham that nobody ever called off. Nor will. He thought and in the meantime, thousands of Sahabzaades would come and go, unnoticed. If a list of people or families had to be made, after our country's independence—Sahabzaade often told his imaginary son—who became rich from being poor, it would open up the working of this democratically run social scam.

During one of his morning walks, he had randomly discovered a joggers' park. It was a public park with no security guard as such. The trust which maintained it had a team, but they visited it during weekends. There was a group of old men who ran a laughter club there. There were seven of them. They used to constantly laugh for fifteen minutes before beginning their walk. That used to irritate him. Otherwise he loved the park. Especially for a peculiar bird that he had noticed when he went there for the first time. He didn't know which bird it was. It was small in size, had a yellow body and a beak which he hadn't seen on any bird yet. He started visiting the park exactly at the time it opened. 5 a.m. Sometimes he saw the bird, sometimes he didn't. The only time he used to smile was when he spotted the bird. He didn't express any emotion any time otherwise. Not even when he had poisoned his newborn baby's milk, two years ago. Only because it was a girl child. He didn't have anything against gender. His self-justification was that this society wasn't good for girls. Thus, the fewer the number the better. Following the death, his wife had gone into an undiagnosed depression. He couldn't care less.

Unlike other days, Sahabzaade had a companion in the park at 5 a.m. that morning. It was one of the older gentlemen who was part of the laughter club in the park. For reasons unknown to him, the old gentleman that day started laughing on his own without his group members. Sahabzaade walked a little closer. And stared at him with a brooding frown from some distance.

'You also want to join, young man?' the old gentleman asked.

'*Mujhe hassi nahi aati.*' I don't know how to smile, Sahabzaade said.

The old gentleman took it on himself to help Sahabzaade laugh like him. Three hours later, the old gentleman was found lying behind one of the many exotic bushes in the park. With a cello-tape on his nose and mouth. Body still. Hands tied. By then, Sahabzaade had long gone out of the park with a new relationship to obsess about in his mind. A father-son. Except, unlike the last time, in this one he was the son.

7

According to him, it was a prank. I felt sick to my stomach. He did apologize. And I took my own time to forgive him. He never tried another near-fatal prank on me again. I never understood the point of pulling a prank like that on anyone. Unless one is a sadist. Was he one? I can't conclusively state that. Neither then, nor now.

As time galloped on, I could guess Faizaan was losing interest in the UPSC. What infuriated him was the loop it had set his life into. Somewhere he desperately wanted to break free, while the fact was he'd invested some years in the UPSC exam. If he would have given in then, it would have been a sheer waste of four years of his life. I suggested he become a teacher at Topsie. He had enough knowledge. He was an engineer with a Masters' degree. Being a teacher would help him keep abreast with all his concepts, keep his mind well-oiled for the exams and, most importantly, break the monotony that had started to bother him. Faizaan saw sense in my suggestion. He applied and was accepted as a teacher at Topsie. But it had its consequences, which I wasn't expecting at that moment.

From the time Faizaan became a teacher at Topsie, I realized the girls, his students, were swooning over him. And why not? He was the youngest of the teachers. No paunch. He had piercing eyes with an alpha vibe oozing from his overall persona. Any girl would love to date him. Nobody in Topsie knew he was dating me. Not that any girl crossed any line but my problem was that I've forever been territorial. Blame it on my single child upbringing or whatever.

The first thing I did was slowly start sharing with everyone that Faizaan and I were dating. Then I intentionally spread it through the grapevine that he sucked in bed. That I was an emotional fool who loved her guy so much that she was ready to compromise on an important aspect of a relationship. I particularly picked upon those girls who swooned over him and told them his 'alpha-ness' was a defence against his bad bedroom performance. Everybody was shocked. Everybody sympathized with me. I could see their interest in Faizaan fading. But that was only my batch. Faizaan was teaching all the batches in Topsie. I couldn't do much about them. The helplessness made me wonder as to why I had this territorial tendency along with borderline trust and insecurity issues. It wasn't that Faizaan was even flirting with other girls. These things could make any healthy mind toxic. Then, some introspection later, I did get my answer.

You have to understand that I was raised by a single mother. For a single mother, this entire world is a jungle where her baby's protection is her only priority. It invariably sharpens the animalistic impulses a thousand times more because you have everything to lose all the time. Ma's protectiveness did two things to me. One, it made me less confident and second, I understood, at a subconscious level, perhaps protectiveness is the primal goal of any relationship. This understanding later branched out and became my territorial instinct.

Studying in a Bengali medium school and later on in a girls-only college, I remained low on confidence for many reasons. Ma never sent me to the grocery store alone so I never knew how to haggle with someone over the price of a product. That for me is any Indian's first training from childhood in developing the art of how to convince someone. Language was a barrier. I was fluent in Bangla but when I came to Delhi, I realized people were fluent in English, leave aside Hindi which was their mother tongue. Somewhere it made me believe I would never be special for someone because I grew up with a feeling that I had nothing special in me. I was average and average things would happen to me. It was a cardinal sin to think like that. Ma did try to make me feel otherwise but the more I went out, or watched television or interacted with people over the Internet, I understood ma's words were a fallacy. A mother's love for her child will always be special. When I met Faizaan I was actually surprised that he fell for me. Though I never told him this. Somewhere, Faizaan's presence in my life had also brought in the much-missed self-confidence in me.

When I stood outside his classroom in Topsie, waiting for him to be free, I could see fair girls, tall girls, well-shaped girls, gorgeous girls . . . everyone hovering around him to understand different concepts. These were girls not only from Delhi but all over India. The sight was a singeing one for me. Though I had upgraded myself emotionally with the daily dose of introspection, sights like these reset me back to my original self.

For a couple of weeks, I was also in denial about my own emotions. My instinct told me to stop the girls, whereas I simply went home after my classes. Faizaan joined me later. He did inquire why I wasn't waiting for him to which I made excuses. Till one day the denial bubble burst with a loud noise. Loud enough to squeeze some action out of me.

That day, after his class with one of the batches was over, I waited for him in the corridor. When he didn't come out after five minutes, I walked straight in. He, as usual, was explaining some engineering terms to the girls. I shouldered myself into the ring of girls to reach him. He looked at me with a stupid what-are-you-doing-here look on his face. I held his hair with both my hands and smooched him as wildly as I could. I could hear hush-hush 'OMGs' but those were sheer aphrodisiacs to me at that moment. I'd claimed my man in front of the world. Fuck you manners. Fuck you society. Fuck you everyone.

It was Faizaan who let go of me.

'What the fuck,' he was clearly not ready for this. As if I gave a flying fuck myself. Before he could say anything, I slapped him hard. And dashed off from the room like a tigress who came, who smooched and who claimed her prey as only hers.

Within a day, everybody in Topsie came to know that their Faizaan sir had a crazy girlfriend. And if that wasn't enough, she studied in Topsie itself. When danger is too close for comfort, it's only human to keep a safe distance. Or so I made it clear.

8

The authorities at Topsie let Faizaan go with a strict warning that day itself. Of course, he had to apologize multiple times. In particular, they were wary of the 'Me Too' movement and said the next time anything of this sort happened, he would be suspended. I wasn't sure if this was connected to 'Me Too'. Unless 'Me Too' was a gender-neutral movement. Here, a girl was invading the privacy of a man in public against his wish or knowledge. But such is the 'reverse sexism' in this country that they thought Faizaan must have done something to deserve the slap. They totally forgot that he was smooched first. I'm happy though. At least 'Me Too' has put some fear into men. Fear is important. Without that, the line between humane human and barbaric human blurs.

The real drama happened when Faizaan came home. He did look for me at the centre, but I was long gone from there after smooching and slapping him. While he went home, I was hogging some paratha from a nearby stall. Not finding me home, he called me. I didn't pick up. He called the second time. After which I switched the phone off to make him feel something bad had happened to me. I reached home late that evening.

'What the hell is wrong with you? First that scene in the centre and now coming home after seven hours? Where were you?' Faizaan blasted out on opening the door. It was the first time he was questioning me about something. I calmly stepped in, closed the door and then replied, 'I was with a few junior boys from Topsie. I was helping them out with some notes.'

'What?' Faizaan's expression told me he wasn't expecting this. Whenever ma was angry with me, I used to throw at her a situation which would trigger a dilemma. So, instead of asking me questions regarding the matter she was angry about, she used to first ask me questions regarding the dilemma. I was sure it was a good ruse for boyfriends too.

'But you were nowhere in the centre,' he said.

'Yeah, I was sitting at a cafe and answering their questions,' I said, keeping my bag on the couch casually.

'Which guy is it?' Faizaan seemed as if he'd like to knock his head off. I'd never seen him that angry. I felt a little pride sensing his jealousy.

'Guys! Plural, Faizaan sir,' I tried to mock the girls with the 'sir' pronunciation. Then added, 'I was with three guys.'

I think that's when he got why I did what I did. I was happy to know I wasn't dating and living-in with a dumb-wit.

'You could have told me you had a problem with the girls.' Faizaan came and stood right in front of me.

'I don't have problem with the girls. I have problems with the ones who swoon over you. Moreover, why else do you think I smooched and slapped you in front of them?'

'That's not the way.' His anger had subsided, I could tell. Now he was reasoning with me.

'Of course it is. It's Ekantika Pakrashi's way,' I said, drinking some water from the earthen jug.

'Talking is still a viable option between couples, if you don't know that already,' suddenly the pitch of his fight changed to a sophisticated one.

'I believe in action, Faizaan sir,' I mocked again. I slumped on the couch with the TV remote in hand.

'All right. You want me to apologize even though that was unintentional and pretty harmless from my end?'

'Do what you will,' I said, without looking at him.

'I'll apologize. But Faizaan Ahmad's way. With action.'

The next three and a half hours were the best sex of my life. Not that I had innumerable sex sessions. But from whatever I had, this was definitely the best. I came twice in the first half hour itself. And yes, I was slightly bruised by the end of it but I didn't complain. The way he consumed me, claimed me, convinced me with his heavy whispers to get rid of my insecurities was in itself orgasmic. It started as an 'apology' with him licking my right toe-thumb, but ended as a sheer conquering with him fucking me from behind, pressing on my breasts as we stood in the balcony. I stood on my toes so he could fuck me easy and proper. My calves hurt after a point. And nature was also not far behind as our act was punctuated with lightning and thunder from time to time but no rain. It rained only when I had gone to clean myself in the washroom and came back to cuddle in his arms. We lay on a mattress in the balcony inhaling the smell of the wet earth together, surrounding ourselves with quietude. Our fight was settled, my issues were settled, our love felt settled.

That year when Faizaan couldn't qualify for the mains, he finally gave up his dream of UPSC and took up a job in a start-up. I didn't motivate him to carry on either. I understood the most frustrating situation in life is to get caught between a dream and reality. Perhaps Faizaan was done chasing the dream of being an IAS officer. Perhaps he simply wanted to move on in life and earn properly and live his reality more. It wasn't that he was living on his family's money. He was living off whatever he had saved working as an engineer at an MNC for a couple of years while preparing for UPSC, and studying for his MTech on a distance course, until he resigned and went full time with his preparation.

We went for a road trip and trekking to Himachal on his 'Ferrari' a week later. As usual, ma knew nothing about it. While we were tenting close to Triund, he asked me, 'If you hear, smell, see and feel the same things all the time from which you derive comfort, will you be the same person ten years from now?'

I knew it was one of those rhetorical existential questions which didn't need an answer.

'I want to grow, explore myself and be a different man every ten years. I want to live a lot of versions of myself. This life, gifted to us, this body, this soul . . . I want to explore every inch of it,' he said.

I got my answer as to why he left UPSC preparation, if it was at all a question in my mind. But this confession of his also made me wonder: being a human, it's so difficult to let go of what we have secured in life. For some it's a home, for some it's a job and for some it's love. Sometimes what we've sought out with all our passion is also the thing which holds us captive forever. Or is it us who allow ourselves to become prisoners of what we seek? Maybe that's why it's imperative that we shrug off things which make us comfortable for too long and start afresh. Maybe not towards a new destination but with a fresh perspective towards the same one. Alas, easier said than done.

A month after Faizaan secured a new job, we shifted to a much better rented place in Gurugram. His friend was shifting to Dubai, so he gave Faizaan his car to drive as well. It was while packing our stuff that I came across a diary which I'd never seen before. When I casually flipped its pages, the one name which had multiple mentions in it was the cello-tape serial killer.

The Seventeenth Kill
January 1998
Dharamshala, Himachal Pradesh

Sahabzaade met his wife once in the last year and a half. And their interactions never happened through words. It was through his beastly grunts and her victimized shrieks. He fucked her. Slapped her. Tortured her. Left her all beaten and bruised. She was a toy in the hands of a brat.

Arfa was so ready for her first baby that she had made a lot of arrangements at a personal level. Her instinct made her complain about his role in killing her infant to his family, but it all fell on deaf ears. The big joint family she had married into had disintegrated after her father-in-law's demise. And those left behind didn't care about the others in the family any more. Even when they heard her weep in pain in the wee hours of the morning with Sahabzaade snoring away or when she was screaming for help being ravaged by her husband, they didn't bat an eyelid. Nuptial violence had been normalized long ago within their family.

A month after he left for Himachal for his new job as a waiter at a resort, he was informed that Arfa was pregnant again. Sahabzaade felt no emotion about it; he just shared it once with his imaginary sister—Gayatri Sinha—his sixteenth victim.

Being in Dharamshala, he found himself at peace, a sensation that he had missed in Bombay and Delhi. The resort he used to work in mainly had destination weddings, with a majority of honeymoon couples from the north pouring in. His immaculate behaviour with the guests earned him the largest monetary tips compared to his colleagues. Somewhere, the initial anger against the system, against life, against everything, had subsided. It was the acceptance phase Sahabzaade was going through. A phase where we accept the reality of life as it is. Where we tell ourselves, perhaps the child in us who dreamt of big things, that they are just . . . dreams. Now, it was that time of life where you opened your eyes and simply accepted life as it is. Without any fight. He understood he wouldn't be able to earn as much as the ones whom he saw buying houses and driving swanky cars in Delhi. Though he was technically educated, he had accepted that actually meant nothing. Educated poor was a concept that nobody talked about.

Something that happened for the first time in Sahabzaade's life was that a woman started taking an interest in him. She was a Dutch lady by the name of Tess De Vries. Though she spoke English well, he couldn't understand her easily because of her accent. She was a Dutch backpacker who was on a world tour. She was a practicing Buddhist as well, which made her visit Dharamshala. What made Sahabzaade interesting to her was his knowledge of things. She understood he had never been to any place outside India but he had read a lot.

Sahabzaade had never known a woman who was so carefree with herself. With the dresses she wore, the thoughts she shared, the way she walked, the way she behaved with strangers at the resort. Everything about her seemed to awe him. As if she had challenged all the definitions he had for women in his mind. He used to take her around, help her shop from local stores without being cheated by the owners, and stared at her when she meditated every morning in the open, looking towards the snow-capped mountains.

Once, he took her to a nearby village. For her, he even broke a pattern, though unintentionally. He photographed her, alive, with his Polaroid camera and kept the photograph with him.

'Where did you get this?' Tess asked, looking at the camera.

'My first employer gave it to me,' he said.

'You like collecting souvenirs?' she asked, amused.

Sahabzaade didn't understand what she meant. She chose to clarify.

'To keep something of someone that can remind you of the person or place later.'

He nodded. Tess leaned forward a bit and gave him a peck on his cheek.

'This one will make you remember me,' she said, flashing the most heart-melting smile as she walked away.

Sahabzaade didn't sleep that night. He shared everything in minute detail with his imaginary sister. Gayatri advised him to forget his wife and settle down with Tess in Himachal itself. Sahabzaade agreed with her. He was already imagining his family's reaction when they would see a white female as his wife. Even his present wife's reaction. And then he started imagining how contrasting red, purple and black Tess's skin would look against her natural white colour when he would abuse her in bed.

The next day, when Sahabzaade took Tess to another nearby village, she told him about her plans. That she was supposed to visit Delhi in a day from where she would fly to Australia to commence her journey to another part of the world. Sahabzaade remained quiet. He escorted her back to the resort. That night he tore Gayatri's picture and burnt it. He realized he didn't need a sister any more. He needed a wife. Someone who would understand him through and through. And someone who would not have plans of her own.

The next morning, Tess checked out of the resort. She took a bus for Delhi. She never reached there alive.

9

I didn't inquire about the diary immediately. I kept it exactly where I found it. Inside the last drawer of his study table. We shifted. Settled down at our new place. But I never forgot about it. It's not that I knew anything about the cello-tape killer but my only question was: what was a detailed account of a killer doing in Faizaan's diary? It stayed with me. One night when we went to Vermaji ke Parathe, after a long time, I ended up asking him about it.

'Oh that,' he said, sounding pretty relaxed. 'It belongs to one of my friends. We used to stay together at one time. Then he went back.'

'Didn't he call you for the diary? I mean, it seemed like a personal diary.'

'You went through it?' he asked.

'Na. Why should I? It looked personal. Diaries generally are.' I knew I lied, but I was helpless. 'But isn't it something that one may miss, all right, but won't forget about totally?' I made my point.

'He did call me once, telling me that he was coming to Delhi for some work, but then he never came from Patna.'

'Still in touch?'

'No. I think he changed his phone number as well. The WhatsApp messages don't go,' he took out his phone and showed me the chat window with the guy. I didn't register the friend's name but the messages from Faizaan to him were all single ticks. I was convinced with what he told me, so I didn't probe further.

Though we were already living-in before we shifted to Gurugram, I don't know why living together in this particular flat made me feel more like we were a couple. Maybe because the previous one was his bachelor pad. And in this one, we sorted out everything together, from the beginning. From the kitchen to the bathroom to the bedroom. In fact, we went shopping to get little things to decorate the place as well. We took off all the tube lights and in their place used a lot of tiny yellow and blue LEDs. It looked like a fairy tale when we made love amidst the hues surrounding our naked bodies like a surreal parameter.

This was also the time when I understood Faizaan much better. Especially the man that he was. Religion was something which never came between us. He did his namaaz but never asked me to consider it. While I did my puja and never asked him to participate in it. If either of us did participate, it was of our own volition. Our faith was our own private thing. Our own way to connect to that one supreme power.

We also did something truly innovative to understand our daily choices better. We kept Sunday as the day to play our you-be-me game. It was simple. Faizaan and I switched roles in the house. He did whatever I did throughout the week while

I did what he did throughout the week. Since we weren't earning a lot, we hadn't kept any maids. Cleaning the house and washing the clothes and utensils was my department. His look-out was to buy the groceries, vegetables, fruits or any kind of eatables, and cooking (because he was actually a better cook than me). On Sunday, we switched. Somewhere it helped us to see things from the other's perspective about the house we were running. And it wasn't *just a house* we were running. I realized when two adults in love run a house, they are also latently running their relationship. How smoothly they run the house, I feel, is in direct proportion to how well their relationship runs.

The one thing which we both were yet to do was tell our respective families about the other.

'What's the hurry?' Faizaan asked. I agreed. On a few counts. First, I was sure he had major family issues that he never told me about. And I never asked. This was the time I understood the elder sister he talked about was actually imaginary. I know most would label him a 'weirdo', but I didn't. We all are weird, trust me, in our own way. We only need to choose if we are okay with someone's weirdness.

Anyway, we were young. We had time. And we had the advantage of experiencing one thing that our parents never did. We could actually experience how 'sure' we were of the other. Nobody before our generation had this option, I think. This was one reason why I didn't tell ma about Faizaan as well. I had seen college mates sharing information about their boyfriends with their family quite early in the relationship and when it didn't work out, their family forced them to get married quickly for they lost trust in their own child's choice. How unfair!

Everything between us was going smooth and steady. I had passed my prelims as well that year and was preparing hard for the mains, till we went to watch a movie that night. I didn't know that an hour after the movie was over, I'd lose Faizaan forever. It wasn't that I lost him. It was similar to what happens in the game of Jenga. You pull out a wooden block and everything comes crashing down. God had pulled that one block out for me.

10

As I pressed the stop button on the recorder given to me by assistant sub-inspector Preeti Jangra, I realized in the last few hours, while narrating Faizaan's and my story, I've lived a life through all those memories. I felt a sudden vacuum inside me. It was time for reality. And everything around me would push me into thinking that moving on from the past, from Faizaan, is my best bet to live my life from here on. The question is, will it happen that easily? When you spend so much time with another person, like every second of each day you are with him, it feels like we aren't two people but one with two minds. It feels like something from me has been snatched away suddenly and now I'm expected to live with that deficiency and call that incompleteness within, my whole.

Every place—from our rented flat to Topsie Centre to all the places we used to frequent for our dates—flashed in front of my eyes. And I could see myself alone everywhere. Like a plant that was ready to flower but was subjected to being in the shade forever from now on. For a moment I couldn't even move. I heard assistant sub-inspector Preeti come in and say, 'You are done. You can leave now. We will transcribe the statement and take your signature later.'

Leave? Where to? By then, I'd made up my mind not to go to the rented flat immediately. Maybe I would go to a cafe. One which I hadn't been to with Faizaan. Sit there. Talk to ma. Don't know if I would be telling her anything. Should I? Where would I begin? No, I won't tell her. Then by the end of the day, I'll go to . . . I realized it didn't matter how much I tried; I wouldn't be able to escape what was waiting for me. Can anyone?

I moved out of the interrogation room. Preeti secured my recording and made me sign a few papers before that. When I came out, I noticed Inspector Gagan talking to someone. He looked like his senior. He glanced at me, and said something to Gagan who moved away quickly. The man then approached me.

'ACP Pradeep Ahlawat,' he said.

'Ekantika Pakrashi,' I said.

'Tea?' he asked. He had one cup in his hand.

'No thanks.'

'My wife prepares this amazing ginger tea,' he said.

I gave him a tight smile. Just a hint that I wasn't in the mood for any small talk. I had lost the love of my life, for fuck's sake.

'Did you by any chance know Faizaan's parents or siblings?' he asked, sipping his tea. His lips had lost their natural colour, I noticed, probably due to heavy smoking.

'No. I never met or talked to them. I did bring up the topic a few times but Faizaan never seemed comfortable. All I know is his mother's name is Saira and his younger brother is Mohsin Ahmad. Why do you ask?'

'We got in touch with them. The mother, I mean. But she was acting . . .' he paused, ' . . . weird.'

'Weird? It's her son who died, goddamnit,' I knew my pitch was raised.

'I know.' The officer was unmoved. Probably in his line of duty he had come across much too many cold reactions like that.

'I'll assign an officer to you. She will be in plainclothes and keep an eye on you.'

'What for?'

'As Gagan must have told you, something happened which led us to think perhaps you were the intended victim, not Faizaan.' He'd finished his tea by then. As I contemplated what I'd heard, he went to throw the paper cup into a nearby dustbin.

I didn't know what to say next.

'Anyway,' he was back facing me, 'take care. I'll let you know if you need to come here again.' ACP Pradeep Ahlawat was about to walk away when I stopped him.

'Why did Inspector Gagan say that the killer was after me?' A legit question. I thought it was better to ask than ponder over it all day.

'Did you ever meet Faizaan's former lover? Her name is . . .'

'Nagma,' I completed. He nodded. I shook my head in the negative and said, 'Never. Didn't even see her picture. But he did mention her. He said that she'd disappeared one day just like that. Untraceable.'

'Well, she didn't just disappear. She was killed.'

'What?' I had a feeling something sordid was coming.

'We recovered her dead body late last night. She was killed and dumped inside a pipe at a deserted construction site in Gurugram. The pipe was blocked with soil from both ends.'

My throat went dry.

'The interesting part, though, was . . .' ACP Ahlawat paused and then added, ' . . . she had a cello-tape pasted on her mouth and nose. Same dimensions as that used by the cello-tape serial killer with all his victims. Including Faizaan.'

I wasn't able to think clearly. I heard him say, 'That's why I believe you are definitely on the hit list. You stay safe.' The officer walked off.

I stood still.

The Twenty-Fourth Kill
May 2000
Lucknow

The grief of Tess's death was too heavy for Sahabzaade to find any joy in life. Though he had killed six people after Tess, he had never clicked their pictures. Or formed any imaginary relationship with them. It was Tess. His beloved, whose dead-face photograph he had still kept with him even after two and a half years of her death.

In his chaotic mind, he had accepted Tess as his wife. He used to converse with her in broken English for the first few months after killing her. The police had come to the resort. Everyone had been interrogated. Especially him, since his colleagues knew he used to take Tess out to the local villages. But Sahabzaade had his alibi ready for everyone. He was in his room with a bad stomach ache. He had not reported to work that day. One of the waiters confirmed it as well. That he was inside his room. Only, nobody knew that for six hours that day, Sahabzaade was not in the room. He was busy following Tess and later killing her when the bus stopped at a roadside motel for snacks en route to Delhi. The fact that the death didn't happen in the resort and she had checked out ensured the police didn't come back.

Months later, he even tried learning Dutch so he could converse better with Tess's photograph. It gave him peace when he was able to do so. He could see Tess smiling in the photograph where her nose and mouth were taped with cello-tape. But a year later, he started feeling frustrated. He wanted to hear her talk, he wanted her to give him pecks, he wanted her to take his name. All that she used to do when she was alive. It irked him that the photograph wasn't able to do so. He decided to move on from Tess. He killed six more, but Tess never left him. Slowly, she became more intrinsic to him than his own wife, Arfa.

Sahabzaade decided to move. He was bored with the mountains, snow and hilly roads. Using a contact from one of his relatives, he secured a job in Lucknow's prestigious Clarks Avadh hotel as a waiter in the Falak Numa restaurant there.

In his thirteenth month of working there, Sahabzaade noticed a woman who looked older to him. She was part of a family entourage who had come from Jaipur for a marriage to be held in the hotel. Sahabzaade overheard her name—Vanya—while serving the group lunch one day. She seemed to be forty years of age but had maintained herself well. Sahabzaade never saw any man or child around her, which told him perhaps she was single. Not that he was interested. But what interested him was the fact that Vanya looked interested in him. She always used to give him meaningful glances. She particularly mentioned his name during her in-room dining service calls. When he took her signature on the bill after he served her food in her room, she used to come dangerously close to him.

So much so that he could now tell which perfume she used if he knew the brands well.

During the cocktail party when the entire family entourage was at the banquet, Vanya was getting drunk by the bar counter. She noticed Sahabzaade going around with a tray serving starters. She gestured for him to come over.

'What do you have to offer?' she asked, looking at him like a huntress. Sahabzaade extended the tray, knowing well she wasn't looking at it.

'Listen, you want to earn extra bucks?' She asked, sipping her drink with a constant lewd smile on her face.

'Sure, ma'am.'

'Then come to my room in five minutes,' she said, putting her drink on the bar counter and strolling towards the elevator. By now Sahabzaade knew what her room number was. Five minutes later, Sahabzaade stealthily made a move towards the emergency stairs. He went to the second floor and in a few seconds, found himself standing in front of Vanya's door. He knocked.

'Come in,' he heard her say. He pushed the door and stepped in.

'Lock the door,' she said. Sahabzaade did as asked and then turned to see her in a transparent negligee. Her nipples were starkly visible. She was holding a bottle of vodka.

'Did anyone see you coming?' she asked.

'No ma'am,' he said.

'You know how to give a body massage?' she asked, drinking from the bottle.

Sahabzaade nodded.

'Good boy. Don't waste time now,' she said and went to lie down on the couch. She had her eyes closed. Looking at her curvaceous, almost bare body, Sahabzaade wondered how it would be to have a 'keep' in one's life. Like the ones rich men had. Who would go to any derogatory extent for them because she wanted to experience the riches herself. His village people used to call such women, bad women. He suddenly felt an insane urge to have a bad woman by his side. That would be a first for him.

'Give me five minutes, please,' he said. And exited the room. Vanya looked irritated as she gulped more vodka.

Sahabzaade was back with a cello-tape, a Polaroid camera and some chloroform in a bottle.

In the wee hours of that night, as he put Vanya's dead-face photograph in his pocket, he was able to burn Tess's photograph. Love wasn't for him, Sahabzaade concluded. Lust fitted more into his scheme of things. For it was temporary. Like life.

BOOK 2: CRIME AND SOME LOVE

1

Night Delights was a small hotel in the Paharganj area of New Delhi. It remained busy mainly with small-time businessmen, foreign backpacking tourists and horny couples. One couldn't guess its expanse standing outside. But once you were in, you couldn't help but appreciate the smart work done by the architect. The hotel had been structured internally for maximum rooms and one bar-cum-restaurant.

The hotel had a total of three floors. The last room on the first floor, overlooking the entrance, was morally owned by Assistant Commissioner of Police, Pradeep Ahlawat. Morally, because he had raided the hotel thrice, years ago, and had caught drug peddlers. Even exposed a sex racket there. None of it went into the police files. Pradeep took 30 lakh rupees in cash from the owner and a permanent room for his recreations. And recreations for officer Pradeep Ahlawat meant making dirty love to assistant sub-inspector Preeti Jangra.

Preeti belonged to the same village in Haryana as Pradeep. That was the common ground that made them converse outside their work for the first time. Unlike other men, he was proud a woman from his village had made it this far.

Three years ago, Preeti was stationed in his circle. Identifying her investigative prowess, Pradeep kept her under his tutelage during different task emergencies. Neither of them knew exactly when they had crossed the line that one should adhere to when working professionally.

Room 1071 was the best kept room in the entire hotel. Instead of LCDs, as in other rooms, it had an LED smart television. The AC was from a branded company unlike the local assembled ones in other rooms. The electricity was connected to a separate generator so the power never went off in this room. Also, this was the only room with a mini bar, a wardrobe with spare towels and a washroom with all the toiletries. These too were part of the luxury demands from Pradeep.

And every time he felt horny, during work hours or after that, or sometimes, before that, Pradeep would WhatsApp Preeti to meet him here in room 1071. Preeti would invariably reply with an 'Ok'.

To begin with, Preeti thought Pradeep genuinely loved her. It was the classic 'I have a bad marriage' sob story that Pradeep had told her. But the more she talked to him, after their fucking sessions, the more she realized that, after making his wife pregnant three times in the last few years, all he needed was a tight vagina. And a woman who played along with his perverse sexual demands. Preeti had never met his wife. She'd just seen her picture in his wallet along with those of his three daughters. As far as she knew, Pradeep's wife was a coy housewife who considered her husband to be from the same gene pool as Lord Ram.

Today was no different. Another perverse sexual demand had to be fulfilled by Preeti at his behest. She was going to lose her anal virginity. The unsaid process that had come into being since they started frequenting room 1071 of Night Delights was simple. A couple of days before Pradeep's 'Come to 1071' message would arrive, he would start sending her porn videos with some specific fetish. When they met, he invariably lived the fetish out with her. This time he had been sending her anal porn. Preeti had an inkling of what was going to happen the next time they visited room 1071. After securing Ekantika's audio statement, she came here prepared with KY jelly. And lunch. Pradeep loved the food she prepared.

It wasn't that Preeti didn't understand Pradeep had turned her into a fuck-toy in the garb of the 'I love you' he used to message her every now and then or whisper into her ears while thrusting inside her. But the situation had become slightly tricky. With time she'd realized how fragile Pradeep's male ego was. If she said something to him now, which had the scent of a complaint, or even the slightest hint that she wasn't interested in the fuck sessions any more, he would not let her progress in her career. Pradeep loved to screw people up as a hobby. And the way he boasted of it in front of Preeti made her realize that loving Pradeep had become a quicksand of sorts, of late. From the time she began at a lower rank, Preeti understood it quick enough that it wasn't only your professional work that gave you a promotion irrespective of your gender. It was about how deep one remained in the good books of the seniors. A bitter truth, but truth nevertheless.

After close to two hours of sexually surrendering herself to Pradeep, who had emptied the tube of KY jelly by then, Preeti went to the washroom to clean herself up, only to see Pradeep come in. They showered together after which they had lunch. Preeti had prepared his favourite mutton biryani.

'You would make an ideal wife. The biryani is better than what I've had anywhere in Delhi.' Pradeep said, sucking on a mutton piece. Preeti smirked, wondering how deep patriarchy was hardwired in men. He had never told her how she could become a great police officer even after doing her bit in several cases. And yet, every time she brought him lunch, it was the same thing she heard. *Ideal wife*. Preeti didn't want to be an ideal wife.

Pradeep's wife called as they were eating. As Preeti watched him talking to his wife, she had a faint smile on her face. The way he talked to his wife before and after they had sex was distinctly different. And that's where she knew lay Pradeep's lie. He didn't love her. He only loved his lust for her. She put more biryani on to his plate.

Pradeep finished the call with his wife and picked up his plate again. He bit into a succulent mutton piece, chewed it for a bit and then gulped half the glass of Pepsi kept beside his plate. A burp later, he said, 'Preeti, I have something for you.'

Preeti looked up expectantly. She stopped chewing her food.

'I could have put anyone with that girl whose statement we recorded.'

'Ekantika Pakrashi?' Preeti asked. She could visualize her face clearly.

'That's correct. I'm putting you, not anyone else, with her.'

This too was Pradeep's way of passive-aggressively stamping his ownership on her, Preeti knew well by now. He could have easily told her that he was putting her with Ekantika. Instead, he first mentioned what he could have done, if not this. He then said, 'Right now, all you have to do is station yourself at her place in Gurugram,' as he picked up another meat piece.

'Why do I need to be with Ekantika?' Preeti asked and waited for Pradeep to finish the mutton he was chewing on.

'I believe her life is in danger,' he said, followed by a prolonged second burp.

'And I think being on the case would help you in your career.'

For the first time that day, Preeti smiled from the bottom of her heart.

2

As the distance from the police station to her society premises kept reducing, Ekantika's body kept getting warmer. She could feel a knot in her stomach tightening with every passing second. Soon she would reach the place which Faizaan and she called home. But from now on only one of them had to live in it. Talk of life being unfair, Ekantika thought and wiped away her tears.

She preferred to leave her Uber outside the society premises and walked in. She thought perhaps the cramped AC space inside the cab was making the situation worse for her. And a little walk in the open would help her breathe properly. She was wrong.

'Madam,' she heard the security guard shout from behind her. She stopped, turned. He came running to her with a packet.

'This came for you,' he said.

It was a parcel. She'd ordered a couple of coffee mugs for Faizaan and her with their pictures on it. She took the parcel with a heavy heart.

Ekantika passed by the parking lot where she had found Faizaan's dead body a night before. A certain nervousness gripped her as she almost scampered into her wing and inside the elevator. It was as if she was wary of Faizaan's ghost catching up with her. She wouldn't have minded that except that too would have proved, like everything else around, he was no more.

As she unlocked the door to their rented flat and stepped inside, she wondered how quickly life had changed. The last time she was in the flat, Faizaan was downstairs. He was alive. Now he wasn't. She closed the door. She felt an emptiness within and all around. As if the walls had stepped further away to visually prove to her that Faizaan had left a lot of space for her that was impossible to fill.

Every time she came in from outside, she would shout his name out. Still holding the parcel, she ambled to the balcony deck and stood there looking out at the bustling morning traffic of Gurugram. Her world had come crashing down, but nothing had changed outside. The usual traffic, the usual horns and the usual bustle. Ekantika sat down on the deck, drew her legs close to her chest. She tore open the parcel and took out the two coffee mugs. Their best smiling pictures were on both of them. She put them on the ground. The next instant she started weeping uncontrollably.

With the police coming in, the investigation was triggered immediately. Ekantika had no time to even grieve properly.

With her face deep in her lap, she could sniff her own perfume which immediately unlocked playful memories. Faizaan never used a perfume or deodorant. He always used to spray hers. It used to infuriate her. And that's what he liked. There were times when she used to hide her perfume bottle but he somehow managed to find and use it. His logic was simple.

'Let's smell the same,' he used to say.

She always made a face, showing him the middle finger as a response. Now all she could do was weep. The scent was there, the person wasn't. She wept on. Suddenly, her phone rang. She glanced at its screen. It was her mother. It was time for the routine morning call. Ekantika knew if she didn't take it, her mother would keep calling. Then would become anxious. But was she ready to tell her mother about all this?

'Hello ma,' she said, trying her best to beat the clog in her voice.

'Shonai, *ki hoyeche? Shob thik ache toh*?' What happened? All good? Her mother, Charulata, asked.

'Yes ma, all's well. Just couldn't sleep properly last night. So I'm feeling sleepy.'

'Why?'

'I was studying.'

'Why don't you make a time table . . .' Charulata went on and on. Ekantika kept listening and then agreeing to whatever her mother said, and ended the call with an excuse that she was going for a shower. Then kept weeping again till she actually lifted herself up for a shower hours later.

Sitting on the bathroom floor, with the shower water cascading on her naked self, reality started punching holes in her emotional bubble. Faizaan and she had shifted to this Gurugram flat because he had a job to pay off the rent. With the month nearing its end, Ekantika knew she would have to find a new place for herself that she could afford without raising her mother's doubts. The excitement behind the job as a mixologist had faded away with time. Mainly because of the pressure of studies. She had given it up a long time ago.

This year's prelims were also around the corner. Within the blink of an eye, two years had gone by. And why not? Time seemed to be sprinting with Faizaan around. Now suddenly it was crawling. It seemed to her that days, and not hours, had passed between last night and now.

Ekantika heard the sound of the doorbell. She didn't care to budge. A few seconds later, the doorbell rang again. This time in a series of two. Irked, Ekantika stood up, quickly put on a dress, tied a towel around her head and went out.

She opened the door with the intent of shouting abuses if it was a salesman.

'Hello. Remember me?' Assistant sub-inspector Preeti Jangra said with a smile. The smile was more friendly than professional.

'Of course, officer Preeti,' Ekantika said. She recollected being told about a police personnel being sent for her, but it had escaped her mind.

'Please come in.' Ekantika opened the door a bit and stood to the side. Preeti stepped in and Ekantika closed the door.

Seeing Preeti go inside, the killer stood still inside the elevator. And then pressed the 'G' button on it.

3

The TV reporter's voice had hit a high pitch as he shared the details of the killing of Faizaan Ahmad, while the red ticker below flashed in a bold white font: *The return of the cello-tape killer*.

It had been two days since the police handed over the body of Faizaan to his family after the post-mortem. Ekantika had been to the funeral at Anjuman Baghiya. Though uninvited. She stood there helpless with moist eyes as Faizaan's body was buried. She did notice his mother and younger brother. He was consoling the mother. She wanted to approach her but decided otherwise in the end. What would she tell her?

Sitting in the hall of the rented flat now, Ekantika was staring at the TV. She was sucking on the fifth cigarette of the morning. Since Faizaan's death she'd found his cigarette carton and emptied one pack. The second pack was nearing its end as well. And right beside her was a glass of Miss Mixo. The drink that she'd prepared exclusively for Faizaan when they'd first met. Keeping the cigarettes and the drink close made her feel Faizaan was somewhere close. So what if he wasn't visible? She did try to distract herself with studies but couldn't. Ekantika knew in another day or two she would have to go back to studies in a proper way.

There was nothing new that the reporter was talking about except for the two murders that had rocked Delhi-NCR overnight. Faizaan's and Nagma's. Along with the mysterious Monkey Man episode in New Delhi and the Stoneman murders which had happened in Mumbai and Kolkata, the cello-tape killings were the ones that had remained unsolved for over two decades. The cello-tape serial killing, though, didn't get as much media coverage as the other two. One of the reasons was the lack of leads in the case. Nor any public hullaballoo. The police of the respective states were criticized when the killings happened for their failure to catch the killer, but then the media hopped on to other things quickly enough.

'You had never seen her?'

Ekantika averted her eyes to notice Preeti come out of the kitchen with a cup of tea for herself. She had asked if Ekantika wanted one as well but she wasn't in the mood.

She glanced at Preeti, then at the TV which was flashing Nagma's picture. She understood what Preeti meant.

'No. He didn't show me any pictures, I didn't ask.'

'I understand. Love is a tricky thing,' Preeti said.

Indeed, Ekantika thought but remained quiet.

'What's that you are drinking? Whisky?' Preeti asked. Ekantika wanted to tell her the personal history of Miss Mixo and how it came into being. When a person is gone, you want get hold of someone, anyone, and tell them stories about the deceased. Especially when the person was as close as Faizaan was to Ekantika. In the end, she only nodded and said softly, 'Yes.' End of discussion.

'That's such a different colour. Must be imported,' Preeti said.

Ekantika nodded again. As she continued watching the news channel, taking large drags on her cigarette, there was a sudden crease on her forehead.

'They aren't going to flash my name, right?' Ekantika asked. There was a tinge of fear in her voice.

Sipping her tea, Preeti glanced at her and asked, 'They shouldn't. Why? Scared?'

'My mother follows crime stories all the time. Like it's her favourite hobby,' Ekantika said, taking a sip from Miss Mixo.

'Is she in the police?' Preeti asked.

Ekantika shook her head in the negative and answered, 'When a woman raises another woman, she should be aware of the shit that men spread.' She stubbed the cigarette in the ashtray.

A smirk later Preeti said, 'You'll be surprised to know how much crime is planned and executed by women in India.'

'Maybe, but who is going to explain that to my mother?'

Preeti smiled, getting the drift. *I wouldn't know though*, Preeti thought. She was only delivered by a woman. But grew up amongst men. The ones who considered women as an object, a burden on their shoulders, a child-bearing machine, a . . .

'The way this news is picking up, I'm sure my mother will know about it soon.' Ekantika's voice brought Preeti back to the moment.

'Will there be any damage if she gets to know?' Preeti asked.

'She is a BP patient. Knowing that a killer is perhaps stalking her daughter, as officer Pradeep said, would definitely affect her. And whatever affects her, affects me.'

'Don't worry. Your name won't come up. Not so easily,' Preeti said and turned towards the TV. There were attempts from a few journalists to reach Ekantika for a news bite, considering she was the girlfriend of the deceased, but Preeti, on Pradeep's orders, told them they weren't getting anything.

Preeti had been living for a little more than two days with Ekantika. She knew that to be associated with a big unsolved case like this was certainly going to be a chance for her to hop ahead in her career. She was grateful to Pradeep for this opportunity. It didn't matter how ego-laced his statement was, but he could have asked anyone to be with Ekantika.

This was also the first time Preeti was staying with a female. She stayed alone in her small rented flat in Hauz Khas. Pradeep had made sure she had to give only half the rent there. In her village in Haryana, Preeti had her father and six brothers and their respective wives and children. She was the youngest. Growing up, she saw many feminists and women's rights activists on news channels and social media voicing what they voice best, but Preeti understood while living within the cocoon of patriarchy that chauvinism leading to toxic masculinity wouldn't be weeded off only by women and girls fighting back their male counterparts. If someone had to uproot this, it had to start from how a mother parented her son. And looking around, she knew what a vicious circle this was. A girl, all her life, was subjected to mean gender roles and gender definitions till she became a mother and taught her son the same roles and definitions. After a point in time, Preeti was simply frustrated realizing perhaps this was a fight that had no end. A pessimist surged up within her but alongside, an escapist, too, popped up its head. She understood that if a girl wanted to live her life the way she wanted to, she didn't necessarily have to fight the system. She had to manipulate it smartly. Preeti fooled her entire family to arrive in New Delhi fanning her zealous independent spirit.

Over the years, Preeti had saved up some money from the tuitions she gave to kids in her village. She gave the money to a boy, Sudheer, whom she met on Facebook. They went to her elders and confessed they were in love. With Sudheer being from their own caste, Preeti's family didn't have a problem. With their father no longer alive, the brothers wanted to get rid of their brotherly responsibility of getting their only sister married.

They got the two married, agreeing to give dowry according to the ongoing rate in the village to Sudheer's family.

After marriage, both Preeti and Sudheer came to Delhi, telling everyone that Sudheer had a job here. Then they mutually separated as per their deal, with Preeti giving him half of the jewellery she got in the marriage from her brothers, while she took the other half. She used the money she got after selling the jewellery to sustain herself in Delhi. Simultaneously, she took up a job as a primary teacher in a school while studying for the SSC Police Recruitment exam.

Sudheer convinced his parents that Preeti wasn't the girl he thought she was, and invested his share in his dream business. That was the deal they'd struck on Facebook.

Preeti's brothers were told the separation happened because she was infertile. It was a lie propagated by Preeti herself. She hit them where it hurt; the fake family honour. The family knew a second marriage would be impossible after this news reached everyone in the community. They slowly stopped caring about her, while Preeti carried on with her career, living alone in Delhi. A woman with a plan of action is too lethal an entity a man, or men, can handle.

Done with her tea, Preeti stood up and sauntered to the kitchen. She came back to stand beside the sofa on which Ekantika was sitting.

'From where do you buy your undergarments?' she asked.

For a moment, Ekantika thought she hadn't heard her correctly. She turned to look at her. Preeti had a casual expression on her face. As if they used to talk about intimate things all the time.

'I order them online,' Ekantika said, turning back to the TV again. She didn't want to initiate a conversation with any 'Why are you asking?'

'Which website?'

'Zivame,' Ekantika said, without looking at her this time.

'Thanks. I get mine from Sarojini Nagar market. They look so cheap compared to yours,' Preeti said.

When did she check out my undergarments? Ekantika felt weird even thinking about a visual where Preeti was going through her undergarments. She gave her a lame smile.

'I saw them on the rope in the balcony,' Preeti clarified. Ekantika understood she was talking about the ones she'd put to dry after washing them. She could feel a certain awkwardness brewing up. Fortunately for her, Charulata called up.

'Hello Shonai, done with your breakfast?'

'Hello ma, long back. Wait, network is a little weak here.' Ekantika made an excuse about the network and went to her room. She closed the door behind her.

Preeti understood it was still not a good time for any ice-breaking conversation. But she also knew Ekantika had invaded her mind and heart like no one before. There was an alluring aura about Ekantika which she wanted to explore. Preeti felt she was the one who would understand all her pain with merely a hug, and would unlock the highest kind of unprecedented pleasure with a touch. Sometime later, she switched the TV off and went to her room.

That night, after Ekantika dozed off to sleep while checking out all the pictures in her phone of Faizaan and her, she suddenly opened her eyes feeling uneasy. Something was wrong, she felt. Half a second later, she realized she wasn't able to breathe at will. There was a tape on both her nose and mouth.

4

The immediate instinct for Ekantika was to use her hands to remove the cello-tapes from her nose and mouth. That's when she realized her hands were tied. It increased her urgency. And filled her mind with an acute fear of death. As she rolled on the bed, she realized her feet were free. She stepped down from the bed. *How could she alert Preeti?* Ekantika thought. She had locked the room from the inside. With her breaths becoming shorter with every passing second, she glanced at her phone on the bed. It was impossible to call Preeti with her hands tied. Ekantika scampered to the room's door and hit her head on it to make some noise. She realized if she repeated this, it would hurt her more than it would alert Preeti. Ekantika turned and collapsed on the floor. With the rise in heartbeats, her breaths were becoming all the more rapid. She lay down with her legs facing the door. And then she started kicking the door with all her might.

Preeti woke up with a jolt. Since her police training days, she always slept lightly. She rushed to Ekantika's room, following the sound of kicks on the door.

'Ekantika, you all right?' Preeti asked. All she could hear were muffled noises. Preeti understood she wasn't. She tried to unlock the door from the outside but it didn't open. With every kick, Preeti could make out Ekantika's energy was going down.

Inside the bedroom, Ekantika's breaths had nearly slowed to a stop. She could see nothing but blackness in front of her eyes. Her lungs were closing down. A countdown to death had begun in her mind. She had to summon all her might to keep her eyes open. In her mind, she was kicking the door but in reality, she wasn't able to kick it any more. Preeti went back to her room, came back with her service revolver and aimed it at the lock.

'Ekantika, I'm shooting the lock open,' she said and fired, breaking the lock.

As Preeti entered the room, she found Ekantika by the door. She wasn't moving. Preeti quickly removed the cello-tapes from her nose and mouth. She soft-slapped her cheeks a few times.

'Ekantika? Ekantika, speak up. Can you hear me?'

No response. Preeti checked for her pulse and heartbeat. Both were still present. She slapped her again, calling out her name a bit loudly. That's when Ekantika drew in air from her mouth, coughed, choked and came to her senses. She looked at Preeti with bewildered eyes. She couldn't believe she was alive.

After Preeti put Ekantika on her bed, she searched the house for any intruder. Finding nobody, she called up Pradeep.

'Yes?' Pradeep's groggy voice came on the call. It was 3.47 a.m. His two daughters were sleeping in their room while the third was lying between his wife and him. He hadn't even cared to see who was calling before taking the call. Hearing Preeti's voice, he sat up on his bed.

Within an hour, Pradeep visited the society with two constables and Inspector Gagan. By then, Preeti had calmed Ekantika down.

'Did you see him?' Pradeep asked, once he had settled down on the sofa in the hall, opposite Ekantika. She shook her head in the negative.

'All I knew when I woke up was that I wasn't able to breathe normally. Then . . .' her voice trailed off as she wiped the tears from her eyes.

Pradeep seemed lost in thought for a moment. He stared at the forensics team, who joined them half an hour later, going about their job with aplomb. Nothing had come up yet.

'It's clear that he must have used chloroform on you before pasting those cello-tapes,' he said softly, as if he was talking to himself.

'The fact that I woke up tells me he used the chloroform only on her. Not me,' Preeti said.

'Why would he use it on you if I was the target?' Ekantika asked.

'He must have known I'm also here in the house. The most obvious thing for someone in this situation is to negate the only help that you may have,' Preeti said. It made sense to both Ekantika and Pradeep.

'Or maybe he is too confident of himself,' Inspector Gagan, sitting beside Pradeep, said.

'With Ekantika alive, his confidence should be dented. She is the only victim of his, in twenty-one years, who remained alive after he tried to kill her,' Pradeep said in his introspective tone.

Ekantika picked up the bottle kept on the table and gulped down half the water in it. She looked visibly scared.

'Who is he? What does he want? Why did he kill Faizaan? Why is he after me?' She asked in a flurry.

'That's what we are trying to find out,' Preeti said.

'But you told me the cello-tape killings have been happening since the nineties. Then, what's the motive now? Where do Faizaan and I fit in?'

'And Nagma. Let's not forget her,' Pradeep looked up at Ekantika as he said this. After a pause, he continued, 'No motive was ever found in the twenty-six killings that have happened over the years. That's why the killer wasn't caught either. It was always random. Or so it seemed.'

'Sir, maybe the last two are copycat murders?' Inspector Gagan spoke up.

'Copycat murders?' Ekantika asked.

'People often copy famous serial killers for various reasons,' Pradeep said and turned to Gagan, 'Hmm, could be. But we need evidence to arrive at that conclusion as well.'

A constable entered the flat. He stood at attention in front of Pradeep.

'Sir, I checked the CCTV cameras in the society. They aren't working.'

'From when?' Pradeep asked with a tinge of irritation in his voice.

'Yesterday. They have raised the issue with the company.'

'A coincidence?' Gagan asked. Pradeep nodded and said, 'Interesting. The killer didn't toy with the cameras when he was about to kill Faizaan. But now . . .'

Pradeep's talk was cut short by one of the forensics team's members.

'Except for a tiny hair strand on the wardrobe, we have nothing. I haven't seen a cleaner crime scene before. Even the cello-tapes are clean. Just like Faizaan Ahmad's tapes. We'll run a DNA check on the hair strand. And match it with whatever we have on record from the previous killings,' the forensics guy said.

'At least we have something. Let me know the results,' Pradeep said.

The forensics guy nodded. His team started packing their stuff and then left. Pradeep turned to Preeti and said, 'I think it's better you two shift someplace else.'

'How about my place?' Preeti said.

Both Pradeep and Ekantika glanced at her together.

'Good idea. I don't think the killer would try and invade a police officer's place. Some killers take it as a blow to their ego if the victim survives,' Pradeep said, standing up. Ekantika shared a worried glance with Preeti.

It took three days for Ekantika to pack her stuff and shift to Preeti's flat in Hauz Khas. She took some money out from her account to pay off the last month's rent. Her mother received an SMS of the withdrawal and immediately called her.

'Shonai, all good? You withdrew so much money at one go.'

'All good, ma. Doing a short course. Had to pay the fees,' she lied.

'Oh, all right. I was worried,' Charulata said.

Though Preeti's flat was too small for two people, Ekantika knew it was a stop-gap solution. Soon the killer would be caught. She would shift and start living alone like old times. Or so she thought.

As Ekantika's routine life began, she was accompanied by Preeti, in plain clothes, to Topsie Coaching. It was particularly painful for Ekantika since every corner of Topsie used to remind her of Faizaan. She decided to take a month's break from going to Topsie and study only from home.

Ekantika remained at home while Preeti used to go out for her police duties at times. At night, when Preeti returned, she always used to bring some snacks for Ekantika and herself.

For Preeti, there was someone to go home to now. This was unprecedented for her. She felt excited while leaving her office and travelling in the auto rickshaw and then the metro to reach home. She felt like both a provider and a nourisher, two of the most archaic human roles. And she was enjoying this abrupt change that life had brought in the form of a case.

Preeti placed the egg rolls on the small dining table attached to the wall in the hall once she was back that night. Then she went to the kitchen, brought two quarter plates and placed the rolls on them, one each, and took it to Ekantika who was studying in another corner in the same room.

'Take a break now,' she said.

It broke Ekantika's trance. The one reason she seldom used to take a break was because she wanted to avoid thoughts of Faizaan. Seeing Preeti there, Ekantika smiled at her. She saw the egg roll on the plate.

'Ma makes this at home. You have to have them once,' she said.

'I would love to. Egg rolls are my weakness anyway,' Preeti said. She hadn't changed out of her police uniform yet. She noticed Ekantika looking at it while taking a bite from the roll.

'You always wanted to be a police woman?' Ekantika asked, unwrapping the egg roll a bit.

'No. I just wanted something to do with power.' There was a certain melancholy in Preeti's voice.

A silence followed. Both hogged on the rolls. Ekantika suddenly spoke up.

'You don't have a boyfriend?'

'I had one during my training. We were serious about each other. But his parents didn't want a daughter-in-law who was in the police.'

'Why?'

'That only they know. What I know is my guy didn't want to go against his parent's wishes.'

'But he must have known his parents didn't want a police woman for a daughter-in-law. Then why did he get into a relationship with you?' Ekantika sounded offended.

'One of those men,' Preeti said, finishing her egg roll. 'I didn't feel like having a serious boyfriend after that. So much of emotional investment and when it doesn't work out, for whatever reason, it's too much to handle,' she said, licking a little sauce from the corner of her mouth.

Ekantika knew how that felt. Especially when a relationship didn't go the distance without your involvement. It probably takes years to come to terms with that. Or probably the coming-to-terms never happens. And when it doesn't, the mind starts its favourite sport: denial.

Ekantika took another bite from the egg roll and after a moment said, 'I saw officer Pradeep looking at you like . . .'

'Your observations are sharp.' Preeti looked surprised.

Ekantika smiled, finishing the food in her mouth.

'It started with love, now we just have sex occasionally. That's all,' Preeti said. Ekantika could judge it wasn't the truth. It was said as if it was the residue of a bigger truth that Preeti didn't want to talk about.

Ekantika finished her roll quietly. Preeti later changed and started checking out YouTube videos on her phone with her headset on so Ekantika could study in peace.

Around 10 p.m., after her mother's phone call, Ekantika pushed her study chair back, stood up and, stretching her body a bit, went for her night shower. It was a routine, Preeti had noticed, since she started living with her.

Ekantika went inside the bathroom, unaware that Preeti had put a hidden camera inside whose live feed was appearing on her phone.

As Ekantika undressed and started her shower, Preeti tugged her shorts down till her knees, along with her panties, and started touching herself. Her eyes were filled with not just raw lust but also genuine admiration for Ekantika.

5

Hari Prasad Mishra had been the environment minister of India for the last four years. Looking at some old party pictures on his tab, he completed a nostalgic trip sitting in his office. His party was ruling at the Centre. He'd joined it during his college days as a feisty, honest young student leader. Now, only the leader part somewhat remained true.

Today had been a little less busy than normal for him. He had only one meeting over a proposed sports project on forest land somewhere in Himachal Pradesh. This was the third time he was supposed to meet the parties and understand their revised plan after he had rejected it twice. He wouldn't have given them a third chance had they not come with a reference from the home ministry.

The meeting started on time. Hari Prasad was convening it, staring at the large projector that illuminated his otherwise dark conference room. The projection was suddenly interrupted as the main door of the room opened slightly. Hari Prasad glanced up to see his secretary, Dinesh Sahu, hurriedly coming towards him. While the presentation continued, Dinesh leaned slightly to put a slip of paper in front of Hari Prasad. He looked at the name written on the paper. *Saira Ahmad.*

'You all have to excuse me.' Hari Prasad stood up immediately. The presenter tapped the space bar of his laptop and the PowerPoint projection stopped.

Hari Prasad walked out hurriedly. Dinesh stayed in the room. He smiled at everyone present.

'Sir will be back shortly. You need anything else? Coffee? Tea?' Dinesh asked. With that, everyone in the room knew this would take time.

Hari Prasad entered his room and saw Saira settled on the couch. She looked stoic. He made sure he locked the door before turning towards her.

'I think we were clear that you'd come here only when there was an SOS,' he said, going straight to his chair. Saira stood up and came to sit on the chair opposite him.

'Faizaan has been murdered,' she said in a voice filled with foreboding. It hit him in the gut, though he didn't show it. The news of a son's death is sheer tragedy for any father. He had read about it already but wanted Saira to reach out to him. The veteran politician that he was, Hari Prasad knew this wasn't the only reason that had brought Saira here.

Hari Prasad and Saira's romance began in the late 1990s when he was a hotshot promising spokesperson of the party while she was an air hostess in Damania Airlines. Soon the airlines had to change its name to Skyline NEPC. It was on one such flight, 35,000 feet high up in the sky, that the two had met for the first time. She was a vivacious twenty-year-old who was the only earning member in her family. Saira came from a humble, conservative Muslim family in Bhopal. Had the family of twelve not been hard-pinched for money, they wouldn't have allowed their daughter to doff her burqa and serve strangers food and water with a smile. It was during one of his flights from Delhi that Hari Prasad, then thirty-two, noticed Saira for the first time. He was already married then. He couldn't take his eyes off her. Though twenty, Saira had the gait and growth of a lady. It didn't take long for him to woo her with costly gifts and incessant pampering. He was the first man in her life. Eventually, she said yes to his proposal, knowing well her family may not agree to the relationship. But Hari Prasad wasn't only a politician by vocation, he was one from his mind as well.

He slowly took over Saira's family problems. Helped every sibling to have an above average life for themselves. In short, he made the family indebted to him. In return, he asked Saira from them. They didn't have a problem. A nikaah took place between the two with Hari Prasad secretly adopting Islam but Saira never became his wife publicly. The reason why Saira never complained and Hari Prasad never ignored her was the same. They loved each other. Genuine, unconditional love.

He gave her whatever a man could provide his woman in a nuptial set-up except for the social identity of a wife. When she was twenty-two, he made her pregnant with Faizaan. Then two years later with Mohsin. Hari Prasad's social wife, Vandana, had an inkling about this but she was clear in her mind. Saira was her husband's *keep*; it didn't matter how much he wanted to embellish the relationship in private. And she was the wife. Till her fortress—her bedroom—wasn't taken over, she didn't care much. With her, Hari Prasad had one son and one daughter.

'Murdered? The last thing you told me about him was that he was living in Gurugram. What happened?' Hari Prasad looked genuinely concerned.

'The police are saying it was done by some cello-tape serial killer,' Saira said. As she spoke, Hari Prasad noticed that, at forty-three, she still looked a stunner. He could fall in love with her again.

'Let me check from my end. I wasn't aware of it at all. Don't worry, the killer will be caught soon.'

'I'm not here for that,' she said. Her tone made Hari Prasad uncomfortable.

'Then?' he asked after pushing his glass of water towards her. She didn't take it.

'Faizaan and Mohsin are my security,' she said.

Five years after Mohsin was born, Saira understood what Vandana had already known since the beginning. She *was* his keep. It hurt her self-respect. The innumerable promises that he would divorce Vandana and announce Saira as his legal wife to the world started to stink by then. It was time, Saira knew, that the love she had for him should have some conditions. She was also ageing. What if he stopped his money? Where would Saira and her sons go? She pressed him for contacts and reinitiated her work life as an air hostess in Air India. But Hari Prasad was the possessive kind. Without telling her, he got her fired from the very job he helped her get. From then on wherever Saira applied, she was fired within six months. She was forced to stay put at home and accept the money Hari Prasad used to deposit in her account. Faizaan and Mohsin grew up. Both kids had their own lives. But now, with Faizaan's death and Saira's menopause knocking at her door, she knew if there ever was a time for a perfect *retirement plan*, it was now.

'I want you to take Mohsin into your political party and give him a good position,' she said. Hari Prasad's first instinct was that someone was influencing her. Never before had she made a flimsy demand in such a naked manner.

'Of course Mohsin is in my priority list,' Hari Prasad said. This was the time for the carrot, not the stick. And he was an expert at when to use what.

'It's now or . . .' Saira tried her best not to make it sound like a threat but the pause took away the pretence.

'I'll have to come out clean in front of the media,' she completed.

'Clean about what? Have I raped you?' Hari Prasad leaned forward.

'About the fact that I too am your wife.' Saira made sure the last few words came out clear and with the proper effect.

Hari Prasad knew where this was going. A moment later, a smile appeared on his face.

'Let's not jump the gun here. First things first. Let me see who's behind the killing of Faizaan.'

'That's second. First is Mohsin getting a ticket,' she said as if she meant business. By now she knew if a family had to eat well all their life, one of the members had to have a good job. But if generations wanted to eat and live well, one of them had to be a politician.

'He is only twenty-two. The party isn't my property. I will have to answer to a lot of people,' Hari Prasad argued.

Saira sat still. Her unmoved poise was also her stand for her demand.

'Okay, let me see what I can do. And next time you come here, drop me a message first.'

Saira left. Hari Prasad had a feeling that probably Faizaan was killed so that Saira could get to this demand and not the other way around. Was it someone from the opposition? Or worse still, his own party?

Seeing Saira walk out, Dinesh, who was waiting right outside Hari Prasad's cabin now, knocked and went inside.

'Get me the Gurugram police commissioner,' Hari Prasad ordered him immediately. A minute later, Hari Prasad took a brief about the cello-tape serial killer from the commissioner. Two minutes after the phone call, the commissioner called up ACP Pradeep Ahlawat.

'Yes sir,' he said. Pradeep was being driven home. At first he took the call on the speaker of his phone, a second later he transferred it to his Bluetooth headset. He repeated the same 'Yes sir' a few more times, listening intently to all the orders. As he ended the call, Pradeep understood Faizaan's death wasn't just another case. It had the making of a big one from which the smarter ones would benefit. He put his phone aside and took another look at the DNA report sent by the forensics team from the hair strand they had picked up at Ekantika's place.

The hair strand belonged to Preeti.

6

'Yes ma, studies are going fine.' Ekantika said on the phone, carefully blocking her yawn. Last night she'd slept at the study desk itself.

It was Charulata's morning call that woke her up. She tried her best to sound fresh. The everyday schedule she had told her mother that she followed was totally different from what Ekantika actually used to follow. For Charulata, her daughter woke up at 6 a.m., did yoga before preparing some green tea, studied a bit, then ate breakfast and then went to Topsie. Then, after coming back in the afternoon, she took a bath, had lunch, had a power nap and then studied till late evening before it was time for dinner. She took a shower, talked to her mother after which she studied again till midnight. This was the schedule Charulata knew that her daughter was following since she left her alone in Delhi. She didn't know that in the last two years, her daughter had grown up and how, Ekantika thought.

'When is the main exam this year?' Charulata asked.

'I don't know, ma. The prelims come first. If I qualify, then the mains. How many times do I have to tell you this, ma!' Ekantika sounded irked by the time she finished.

Charulata never understood or remembered this. All she knew was that her daughter was preparing for an exam, and after passing, she would get a high position that would make her proud.

'All right, then let's talk about something for the first time,' Charulata said.

'What?' Ekantika was fighting herself not to yawn again.

'You remember Shukla *maashi*?'

'Who?'

'Shukla maashi? She used to live in the same locality here with us. Then her husband got a transfer and they left? You were quite young then.'

Ekantika had a faint idea about the woman Charulata was talking about.

'No idea, ma.' Ekantika hoped that would discourage her mother from telling her more about this Shukla maashi. She was wrong.

'Doesn't matter. So, all of a sudden I get a call from Shukla maashi yesterday. And . . .'

She knew her mother, like always, was off on a verbal marathon. That was the time when Ekantika used to switch off her attention. After a minute, she brought her attention back to what Charulata was saying, as for the first time in their telephonic conversation history, she had mentioned a man.

'Whom are you talking about?' Ekantika asked, clearly having missed the major part.

'Taksh Shukla. He is Shukla maashi's son. He also lives in Delhi. I have given her your number. She will give it to him and he will get in touch.'

'What? Why? I can't guide anyone around here right now.'

'No Shonai, he is . . . *eyi re*, I forgot what Shukla maashi told me, but he has a settled job and has been in Delhi for the last ten years.'

'Ten years? He must be some *kaku*-type someone. Why did you have to share my number?'

'Lately, I have heard of a lot of crimes happening in Delhi. There should be someone to go to in case of an emergency. I can't come down from Baruipur to Delhi that quickly.'

Ekantika rolled her eyes. How could she tell her mother that there indeed was someone for her all the time? Just that now he was dead. She was about to say something when she noticed Preeti looking at her expectantly. She shrugged, muting her side of the phone.

'Pradeep sir wants to meet you at the police station.'

Ekantika nodded and after a few minutes, agreeing to whatever Charulata said, ended the call. A couple of hours later she found herself sitting in front of Pradeep in the Gurugram police station.

'Is there an update?' Ekantika sounded eager. Her body language, as Pradeep noticed, was tense.

'There is. This isn't a small case.'

'As in?' Ekantika frowned.

'I heard your audio statement again. You said you never met or knew Faizaan's family. But you knew his mother's and younger brother's name.'

'That's true. Faizaan seemed slightly disconnected from his family every time I brought the subject up.'

'Does the name Hari Prasad Mishra ring a bell?'

Ekantika thought hard. Then she said, 'He is our environment minister.'

'Apart from that?'

'Apart from that, nothing. How on earth will I know a minister personally, if that's what you are asking me? I come from a humble background.' Ekantika's voice told Pradeep she found this absurd.

'Hmm. I want you to now think hard and tell me if Faizaan ever told you about politics or about Hari Prasad,' he said. When the commissioner tells you that the environment minister is looking into this matter personally, there had to be a link, Pradeep thought.

Ekantika thought for a moment and then shook her head, 'No. If he did, I would have mentioned it in my statement.'

As Pradeep kept probing her about Faizaan's family, unbeknownst to them, the killer was inside Preeti's flat. From the way the killer was looking around it was clear a desperate search was on. It took twenty minutes to finish the search.

Ekantika went to Topsie for a mock test after her casual interrogation at the police station. She had gone to meet Pradeep with a lot of enthusiasm but realized it was a pointless summons. She came back home from Topsie by lunch time.

As she came in, one look at her desk and she knew it had been touched. Preeti came out from the other room, holding her head, as if it was aching. Ekantika was taken by surprise with her presence because it was her duty hours.

'You didn't go today?' Ekantika asked.

'I overslept.' Preeti said, groggily still holding her head.

Ekantika turned her eyes back to her desk. She looked at every object on the table meticulously.

'Did you touch my desk by any chance?' she asked in an accusatory tone.

Preeti shook her head in the negative.

'Then I think someone was here. Faizaan's friend's diary is missing.'

7

It was only the second time Pradeep had come to her flat. The first happened when Preeti had rented it after becoming an assistant SI.

Pradeep looked tense. Anyone looking at him could tell the killer had outsmarted him. Preeti and Ekantika stood in front of him. They had told him what had happened. Faizaan's friend's personal diary, where he had supposedly chronicled a lot about the cello-tape killer, was missing. How could he have missed it? Ekantika had clearly mentioned the diary in her audio statement. He should have asked for it immediately. Pradeep sighed. *What has happened, has happened,* he told himself.

'Didn't you hear anything?' He looked up at Preeti. She shook her head and reiterated what she had told him before, 'I was asleep.'

'But your sleep isn't that deep, usually,' Pradeep said. Preeti was tongue-tied.

Ekantika remembered Pradeep had told her that the DNA report stated the hair found at her place belonged to Preeti. She brushed off the thought of Preeti having a role to play in this, since she wasn't aware of any motivation. Not yet.

'It's clear the diary had something important in it which could have nailed the killer.' Pradeep spoke softly and then, looking up at Ekantika, said aloud, 'Did Faizaan ever tell you why he maintained the diary on a specific killer?'

'No. In fact, he didn't know that I knew about the diary's content. And he'd said it wasn't his. It belonged to one of his friends, who used to live with him once.'

Just like she'd mentioned in the audio statement, Pradeep thought remembering the mysterious friend part.

Ekantika said, 'I understood it was something personal. And sometimes it's better to wait for the person to open up about something like that than probe him face to face. I did wait. But he never talked to me about it.'

'That's what is confusing me. We maintain diaries about someone when we have a personal axe to grind with the person. How is Faizaan's friend related to the killer?'

'If the actual killer of the nineties had turned up, then what would his age be now?' Preeti asked.

'A conclusive age profiling is difficult as the case never had much success. But he won't be young for sure.' A pause later, Pradeep added, 'Are you saying this friend of Faizaan was the killer?'

Ekantika swallowed a lump while Preeti was quick to respond, 'Maybe.' She turned to Ekantika and asked, 'Did he mention how old this friend of his was?'

Ekantika slowly shook her head in the negative.

The women remained quiet. Preeti suddenly scampered to the kitchen sensing the milk had boiled. She was preparing tea for Pradeep.

'My assumption was wrong. I don't think you are on the killer's hit list,' he said.

Ekantika didn't know if she was supposed to be happy or sad hearing it.

'Does that mean we won't ever catch the killer?' she asked, sounding low.

Pradeep took his time before speaking. By then, Preeti had come into the room with his cup of tea. He spoke a sip later.

'Of course we will hunt for him. Our jobs are on the line,' he took another sip and then added, 'Ekantika, you may shift if you want to. Even if the killer wants to attack you, he won't do so here. If he had to, he would have done it. That I'm sure of.'

Preeti clenched her jaw holding her cup of tea. She didn't like the idea of Ekantika shifting.

Four hours after Pradeep left, Ekantika found herself waiting in a cafe near Topsie. The inevitable had happened. Taksh Shukla had messaged her. He was the one who fixed the time and place, based on Ekantika's convenience while being late himself. She tried to check his face out but his WhatsApp DP was that of Tom and Jerry. She had no clue what this guy looked like. She tried Facebook and Instagram with no success. She knew she had to go through this meeting and be done with it to avoid her mother giving her a lesson on her security, using emotional blackmail.

Four minutes after she messaged him that she was waiting in the cafe, she noticed a tall man coming in. He looked thirtyish. He had black carbon-frame specs, a two-day-old stubble and a chiselled jawline. His hair was short and neatly parted. And she realized she had seen him somewhere but couldn't recall where.

The tall man looked around; then spotting her, flashed a smile. She responded with a faint smile. He came and pulled out the chair in front of her.

'Hi, I'm Taksh Shukla.'

'Ekantika Pakrashi.'

He settled down, looked at her coffee cup.

'How is the coffee here?' he asked. He had a manly voice. Sharp, heavy and arousing, Ekantika noted. Faizaan's was more friendly.

'Small-talk sucks,' Ekantika said. Taksh looked at her and smiled.

'I don't know why my mother keeps giving me phone numbers of girls and asking me to meet them,' he said.

'And you actually end up doing so? Quite a mumma's boy, I must say.'

Taksh gave her a sharp glance. She realized the sarcasm was unnecessary especially when she had just met him.

'I can't hurt my mother. Or anyone for that matter,' he said, keeping the laminated menu on the right, neatly. Ekantika wondered if he too had some OCD like Faizaan.

'You know what they say about people who can't hurt others?' she asked.

'That they hurt themselves the most,' he said with a been-there-done-that smile.

Ekantika nodded with a wry smile.

The one thing that struck her was his congeniality. The ease with which she was conversing with Taksh, someone whom she had seen and met just now, was happening for the second time. The first was with Faizaan, she thought. Or was her mind playing a trick on her? Did she want him to be like Faizaan? Would she compare, from here on, every guy she met with Faizaan? And obviously when they'd fall short in the comparison, she would negate them in her mind. But negate for what? This wasn't a probable matrimonial meeting going on. Ekantika controlled her mind and focused on the moment.

Their conversation lasted over two cups of coffee. All through she had a feeling she'd seen Taksh somewhere, but couldn't guess exactly where. When Ekantika was waiting for him, she had her dialogues for the meeting preset. All she wanted to tell Taksh was that, unlike what her mother thought, she didn't need any guardian in the city. But in case she needed one, she would get in touch. She would then make an excuse and leave. It was to be a meeting that would last ten minutes max. It had gone on for an hour.

'I'm presuming your mother gives you the phone numbers of girls because she wants you to get married,' Ekantika said, finishing the complimentary cookie that came with every cup of coffee one ordered.

'Of course, I know that,' Taksh said.

'Then what is stopping you?'

'I'm in love with someone,' Taksh said.

'Okay. So, introduce the girl to your mother,' Ekantika said. She thought Taksh was sounding like a sixteen-year-old who loved someone but didn't know how to go about it.

Taksh added some sugar in his coffee and stirred it. She noticed that he didn't pour the entire sugar sachet in at once.

He poured some sugar, then drank a bit, then poured sugar again. She found it odd.

'Sorry, I'm just wondering how to say what I have in mind so that it makes sense to you,' he said, still stirring.

'Don't take too long, please.'

'I've realized it's not necessary that you have to get into a relationship with a person whom you love. That love and relationships are two different things,' he said.

Ekantika took some time pondering over it and then said, 'But getting into a relationship with the one you love is the most obvious desire, and step, isn't it? That's what we want all the time, right? That, when it doesn't happen, gives rise to heartaches, no?'

The fact that she asked three questions told Taksh that perhaps she hadn't understood what he'd said though he had tried his best to keep it simplistic.

'That's right,' he began, 'what I mean is some people are meant to be loved only from a distance. The moment you get into a relationship with them, their flaws slowly come into prominence and then there's a chance that those flaws may outweigh your love for the person.'

'In that case, nobody will ever be in a relationship! Everyone has flaws; major, minor or whatever.'

Taksh smiled in an amused manner and said, 'Not really. Now let me answer why I didn't take the girl I'm in love with to my mother and tell her that I want to marry her. Because I just want to be in love with this girl. And marry whoever and get used to the person's shortcomings like she would get used to mine.'

Ekantika took her time to digest it, then spoke up with renewed brio.

'Fuck, that's screwed up, no?'

Taksh laughed out loud. The relationship conversation carried on for another half an hour. Ekantika wasn't sure why she stayed on, though. Was she craving for a male companion, an emotional rebound of sorts or was it that Taksh indeed was interesting enough as a human being to allow him the extra time? He definitely seemed like someone with whom a clean, platonic friendship could be maintained. Someone who would pick up your call at 3 a.m., not complaining about the loss of his sleep, and would hear you out patiently. Someone who wouldn't be frustrated if you didn't let him get inside your pants.

Finally, it was time to leave. They went Dutch on the bill. While the waiter was getting them the change, Ekantika suddenly slapped her forehead. Taksh shrugged at her.

'We discussed probably everything except what we are doing in Delhi. Maybe ma has told Shukla maashi about it,' she said.

'Oh yes, ma told me you are pursuing UPSC prep here,' he said.

'My mother didn't say what you do though.'

'I'm in the forensics team with the Haryana and Delhi police.'

And that's when Ekantika knew where she'd seen Taksh before. He was the one who collected the hair sample from her place after she was supposedly attacked by the cello-tape serial killer.

8

'Why didn't you tell me before?' Ekantika asked as they stepped out of the cafe.

'Tell you what?'

'That you were there at my place the other day with the police.' Ekantika sounded borderline angry.

'Look, I did recognize you from the time I entered the cafe. But this wasn't a professional meeting. I thought perhaps telling you about that would make you uncomfortable. And you may think of me as a creep.'

Ekantika felt frustrated because he had a point. She didn't show it though. She took a deep breath which partially took care of her impulsive anger. Before taking an auto rickshaw to the nearby metro station, she said, 'Listen, please don't tell my mother I'm living in Gurugram.'

'Don't worry. Our lives remain strictly ours.'

She gave him a smile of relief.

'By the way, I'm also heading towards the metro station. Mind sharing the auto?' he asked.

The next minute they both travelled to Karol Bagh metro station.

'Isn't Gurugram far from your tuition centre?' Taksh asked.

Ekantika didn't tell him much about her relationship with Faizaan, nor the fact that she'd shifted with Preeti to Hauz Khas. Instead she said, 'Yeah, that's why I'll be shifting soon.'

'Let me know if you need any help.'

'Sure.'

When Ekantika asked for a ticket to Hauz Khas at the metro station ticket counter, Taksh did notice it but he didn't probe. Soon, both took two different line metros.

Ekantika didn't know she was being followed by Preeti. She'd noted that the forensics guy on the case had met Ekantika over coffee. She couldn't hear their conversation as she didn't step inside the cafe lest she was spotted. But this was not a professional pursuance. Only Preeti knew it. Ekantika wasn't just a case any more for her. She was a subject of special interest. After both Ekantika and Taksh took their respective metros, Preeti took the one heading to Gurugram.

Ekantika reached Preeti's place in Hauz Khas and was about to go for a quick shower when Pradeep called her up.

'Someone wants to meet you,' Pradeep said.

'Who?'

'Hari Prasad Mishra.'

'He wants to meet me? Why?' Ekantika had a bad feeling about this.

'I'm afraid I don't know that. Just be ready. I'll pick you up in an hour,' Pradeep said and ended the call.

Ekantika went for a shower and spent some time wondering what the reason for the meeting could be. It was clear to her that Hari Prasad was somehow linked to this case, otherwise there was no motive for him, a minister, to meet her. She called Preeti and relayed the information to her.

'I'll be there soon,' Preeti said. She was in the police station at the time. As she turned, she noticed Pradeep moving out in a hurry from his room. Preeti sauntered up to him.

'Why is Ekantika meeting Hari Prasad?' she asked. Pradeep paused, giving her a look, 'Are you her girlfriend or what?' Pradeep said in a mocking tone.

Preeti ignored the jibe. 'Is there something I don't know yet?' she asked.

'The hair strand belonged to you, the DNA report stated. What were you doing at Ekantika's bedroom wardrobe?' Pradeep asked.

'It's just a girl thing. I was checking her clothes out,' Preeti lied.

'Seriously? I stationed you with her for protection purposes. Not for doing some silly girly things together.' This time his pitch was high enough for everyone around to hear.

'Sorry sir,' she said aloud, then whispered, 'but am I not being informed of something? I thought I too would gain something out of this case and . . .'

'This case is bigger than before.' Even Pradeep's voice was low now. 'The environment minister called the commissioner about this. There has to be something. I will keep you updated.'

'Hmm. Sure sir,' Preeti said. After that conversation, she knew she couldn't rely on Pradeep much. And she also knew when cases came with big connections, the lower rank officers were either ignored, or became the bait or worse, the victim of some senior's fault. She had to be extra alert from now on if she wanted some professional mileage out of it, Preeti told herself, settling behind her desk.

Ekantika could guess it was a political party office. There were party posters, standees with party leaders in boisterous poses with party flags all over. Pradeep escorted her inside a room where she saw a few men were already sitting. She had seen Hari Prasad Mishra's face on news channels and in newspapers a few times. She knew she would recognize him if she saw him in front of her. Dinesh came up to Pradeep and Ekantika. He asked Pradeep to wait, and escorted Ekantika into a cabin further up.

'Hello, young lady.' Sitting behind a huge wooden table, Hari Prasad sounded warm and amicable. Dinesh ushered Ekantika inside but stood by the door.

'Hello sir,' she said, feeling a tad nervous. She was taught in Topsie about IAS stress-interviews but this felt worse. She still didn't know why was she there.

'Please sit down. You want anything? Tea or coffee? Cold drink?' Hari Prasad asked.

Ekantika sat down on the chair opposite him and shook her head, 'No sir, thank you. I just want to know why I'm here.'

Hari Prasad's face stretched into a smirk.

'I'm told you are preparing for UPSC. If you keep your attitude to the point like now, you'll surely achieve higher laurels in administrative services.'

'Thank you, sir.'

'Talking of to the point, I know you lost your boyfriend, Faizaan Ahmad, recently. My condolences.'

'Thanks,' Ekantika said meekly, still looking expectantly at Hari Prasad.

'You see the person standing there?' he asked, raising his hand. Ekantika turned to follow his gesture. There indeed was a man standing in a corner of the room. She hadn't seen him while entering the room. She nodded.

'He's the one who killed your boyfriend,' Hari Prasad said conclusively.

9

Ekantika looked at the man attentively. He looked like a daily wage labourer. Unshaved, with an uncouth half-drunk look in his eyes, badly dressed, unkempt. *Was this the cello-tape serial killer? The one whom the police of five states had not been able to catch in twenty-eight years?* Ekantika wondered. She turned towards Hari Prasad.

'What's the proof, sir? Did he confess?' she asked.

'Leave the proof and all to Pradeep. He will arrange a press conference for you tomorrow. All you have to do is tell the media that you saw this man leaving the parking lot where Faizaan was found murdered. The rest will be taken care of.' Hari Prasad said it in a conclusive tone bereft of the initial warmth which he exuded. His plan was simple. If Faizaan was killed and Saira had been influenced against him, the first thing he would do was close the case ASAP. Then focus on influencing Saira back to normal. With the case open, it would incline towards Saira and the one who was responsible for killing Faizaan. Or so he thought.

He glanced at Dinesh. There was a slight nod from him. It meant Hari Prasad hadn't missed any point.

'But I never saw anyone. I have said this to the police.' Ekantika's voice was filled with bewilderment. She understood the man Hari Prasad had pointed towards was a scapegoat. What she didn't understand was, why was it necessary?

Before Ekantika could think clearly, Hari Prasad chose to speak up. This time the warmth was back again.

'It's a request. That's all. You will be a very credible eyewitness. If you choose not to say so, we will have to create an eyewitness.'

'Like you have created a killer?' she said softly, feeling a knot in her stomach.

Smirking, Hari Prasad said, 'Best of luck with your studies, young lady. Let Pradeep know of your choice by tonight. Nice to meet you, Miss Pakrashi.'

'Likewise, sir.'

Ekantika stood up and left the room. Pradeep was immediately called in. Before going in, he asked Ekantika to wait for him outside. But she didn't. She took an auto rickshaw from outside the party office to the nearest metro station. She took the metro to Hauz Khas and walked down to Preeti's flat. The latter was at home.

'What happened?' Preeti asked, the moment she opened the door. Ekantika came in, quiet, and sat down on her study chair across the room. Preeti locked the door and stood beside her.

'They won't catch Faizaan's real killer,' Ekantika said and started sobbing. Preeti held her in a consoling manner. It was a shock for Preeti as well. In between her sobs, Ekantika told her what had transpired at the minister's office. But Preeti's mind was elsewhere at the moment. She could feel Ekantika's breasts pressing into her stomach. It was sending waves of arousal within her. She felt like tearing her clothes off and making love to her. Woman-to-woman love. And in her sexual trance, she didn't realize she had been actually caressing Ekantika's back a little too obviously. Ekantika suddenly distanced herself from Preeti, feeling awkward. Then stood up to go to the washroom. She locked herself inside.

Preeti let out a deep sigh. She was in love with Ekantika from the night she had seen her, when they'd brought her into the police station. The way she was trembling, that look of vulnerability on her face, that vibe that she needed someone to allay her fears . . . it all aroused Preeti emotionally. She had decided she would be that person for Ekantika at that very moment. She would be her provider in every which way possible.

Later that night, Saira Ahmad was at a department store, shopping for groceries, a kilometre from her residence. The house had been given to her by Hari Prasad himself after their nikaah. She did hear that Hari Prasad was making sure Faizaan's killer was caught soon but that didn't make her any happier. It wasn't why she had gone to him. Catching the killer wouldn't bring her son back to her. Moreover, she never had a cordial relationship with Faizaan. It was Mohsin whom she loved dearly. And knew it was high time she too tasted the very power using which Hari Prasad had become the architect of her life. And leave a legacy of that power for her much beloved younger son. Mohsin would just be a pawn. She would be the one who would control the decisions from backstage. History was proof that people remembered the king, but the ones who ruled longest were the kingmakers. She would be one soon.

Mohsin, her younger son, was still studying in Jawaharlal Nehru University (JNU). He had made some headlines in the local newspapers during the last JNU elections. He lived with Saira but Faizaan, after he had caught her in a sexual act with Hari Prasad, had given up on her. From then on, he always lived on his own.

Saira finished her shopping, pushed her trolley towards one of the cash counters, paid in cash and then walked out to the parking lot.

She reached her car quickly. It was late. There weren't many vehicles in the lot at the time. She loaded the packages in the car's boot. Then moved to open the driver's door. She climbed inside, started the car and was about to release the brakes, when she heard a knock on the window. She turned to her right, and pressed a button so the window came down.

'*Parking ticket bahar lete ho na?*' Saira asked. Looking at the person's uniform, she assumed he was there to ask her about her parking ticket.

The person standing outside the car gestured to Saira to look down. Curious, Saira poked her head out of the window and looked down. Before she knew it, a wet-handkerchief-laden hand pressed against her mouth; another hand opened the driver's door. The person didn't stop till Saira became unconscious.

After that, it was the usual modus operandi. One 3.3-inch cello-tape for her nose. One 6-inch cello-tape for her mouth. And a rope to tie her hands.

10

Pradeep was having problems thrusting himself in and out of Preeti. He used his saliva a few times. It remained easy for a few minutes, then again the friction hurt him.

They were in Hotel Night Delights. They had first feasted on some kebabs prepared by Preeti, and a couple of beers, after which Pradeep got in the mood.

Midway, feeling the friction of his penis in her vagina, he stopped and looked down. He pulled out, touched her vagina and said, 'What's wrong with you today? You are so dry.'

Preeti remained quiet.

'Not in the mood?' he asked.

Still quiet.

'You could have told me earlier. I would have brought the jelly with me. It doesn't feel good this way.' Pradeep moved away from her and lay on the bed. He covered his hard-on with the blanket.

'I'm sorry. I don't know why this is happening. But let me not spoil it for you.' Preeti slowly tugged the blanket down and took his erect penis in her mouth. She gave him what she was an expert at: a pulsating blowjob. She knew his pressure points. It took a few minutes before his semen came out in a rush. Preeti cleaned it with a tissue paper. And then excused herself to go to the washroom, naked, with her mobile phone.

Inside, she threw the napkin in the bin and sat down on the toilet seat. She unlocked her phone, and from her photo gallery, opened Ekantika's nude bathing video she had secretly filmed. She held the phone with her right hand, while with her left she started playing with her labia. In half a minute, she was dripping wet. Another minute later, while she was stroking her clit and knew an orgasm was around the corner, she heard knocks on the door. It broke her spell. On instinct, she removed her hand from her vagina.

'Be quick, Preeti. Commissioner has called. I need to go,' she heard Pradeep say from the outside. Preeti reluctantly stood up and opened the washroom door to see that Pradeep was already in his uniform.

'What happened?' She asked, quickly picking up her panties from the floor and wearing them.

'There has been another killing.'

'What? Is Ekantika all right?' She was now hooking her bra around her.

'She is okay. The killing happened in Delhi.'

'But that's not our jurisdiction,' she said.

'It's the same cello-tape killer apparently. And it's Faizaan's mother this time. Saira Ahmad,' Pradeep said, buckling his belt around his waist.

'I'll see you later.' Pradeep opened the door and moved out. Preeti sat down on the bed in her undies, still feeling wet between her legs.

Pradeep could see a horde of journalists around the parking lot.

'Motherfuckers,' he murmured under his breath as his vehicle reached the place. He stepped down at some distance where other police vehicles were parked. Somehow, he managed to squeeze himself through the media assemblage and went into the police cordoned area. He met Inspector Lallan Dhariwal who went into an attention stance seeing the extra star on his uniform.

'Sir,' he saluted.

Pradeep saluted back saying, 'I'm looking after the recent Gurugram cello-tape murders.'

'Right, sir.'

'What's the update here?'

'Prima facie looks like another of the cello-tape killer's victims. Everything matches.'

'Where's the body?' Pradeep asked, looking at the car which was still parked and a bodyline sketched in white inside it where the body had been found.

Inspector Dhariwal pointed behind Pradeep, who turned to see a body wrapped in a white cloth with the Delhi police seal on it.

'We are sending it for post-mortem after forensics are done.'

'Did forensics get anything?'

'They didn't say much.'

Pradeep looked around to spot a few CCTV cameras.

'Collect all the camera footage.'

'Already asked for that, sir.'

There was nothing much Pradeep could do on the spot. He looked up at the journalists creating a ruckus. It surprised him. It wasn't this menacing when Faizaan was killed.

'What do they want? Why so much of uproar?'

'It's about the chat, sir.'

'What chat?'

'Someone mailed all the leading media houses a WhatsApp chat with pictures and videos of the deceased Saira Ahmad and environment minister Hari Prasad Mishra.'

It was then that ACP Pradeep Ahlawat realized he wasn't only standing at a murder spot but also in the middle of a scandal. He had a deep frown on his face. The only word that stood out was . . . Ahmad . . . Saira Ahmad . . . Faizaan Ahmad. Now he guessed why the commissioner was suddenly interested in the case and Hari Prasad wanted to meet Ekantika. His frown changed to a faint smile which pronounced the fact that he was right. This case was big.

'All right, if there's any update please let me know. Nobody talks to the media unless asked to. These are orders from the Gurugram commissioner,' he said.

'Right, sir.'

'Also, ask the forensics team to call me if they get anything.'

Inspector Dhariwal nodded.

Pradeep quickly took out his phone and tapped on one of the news portal apps to listen to the live breaking news, as he walked to his vehicle.

At the home minister's residence, an emergency meeting was called with Hari Prasad also present. The moment Hari

Prasad and Saira's chat had leaked in the media, the ruling party high command had figured that the media would give the matter of Saira Ahmad's murder prime time importance while the Opposition would paint it in the religious colour that would affect the party's image for the assembly elections scheduled to happen in four months.

Hari Prasad thought he would be let off with a warning, but when he met the home minister, Jatin Shah, he didn't know the party had already decided on the course of action.

'Hari Prasad ji, you will have to immediately resign from your post. Let the law take its own course and when you are cleared, if at all, we will see what we can do,' the home minister said. He was holding a glass of ORS. He had been under the weather for some time now.

'But sir, I have no involvement in this. Why do I have to resign?' Hari Prasad wasn't the kind to go down without a fight.

'Then why were you doing something as stupid as trying to create a fake killer? To score brownie points with Saira Ahmad?' The home minister was furious.

Hari Prasad had only hoped that part wouldn't have reached everyone.

The home minister continued, 'The chat clearly mentions Saira Ahmad was pushing you for a seat for her son. And the next day she is found murdered. You think the Opposition is going to let this go? I already have information that three top news channels of the country are going to feature this as tonight's prime time debate. With you offering your resignation, at least we can contend you are innocent until proven guilty and it projects our party's face in the public as a fair one,' Jatin Shah said, sipping his ORS in between.

'But sir . . .'

'We don't have any interest in your personal life. Whether you had one or two or three sons with Saira is none of our business. But nobody will look at it personally. Everyone is going to treat this politically. So right now you have two options: one, sit in on the press conference we are arranging for you in an hour and resign from your post, claim innocence and fight on legally. You will have our full backdoor support. Or else, we officially throw you out of the party till the matter is resolved, which you also know may take years.' An ORS sip later, he added, 'Who is this *madarchod* cello-tape killer, anyway?'

Every other person in the room was as clueless as him.

Looking at Jatin Shah, Hari Prasad knew there was no way he could convince him out of the decision. He folded his hands and quietly moved out.

An hour later, a press conference was arranged at the party head office where Hari Prasad said exactly what he was asked to.

Saira Ahmad's killer, meanwhile, was also watching the news. It had gone exactly as planned. Now the case had become big. The state of affairs was such in the country these days, the killer thought, that without involving the media, one couldn't do anything on a massive scale except for a scam. With Saira Ahmad gone and Hari Prasad Mishra cornered, the Haryana police would have to go after the real cello-tape serial killer like hunter dogs now.

And the killer was confident they would reach nowhere.

11

It was just a casual message from Taksh that led to his coming over to Ekantika's place to help her with the shifting. Taksh had uploaded a picture of a glass of *khus ki sharbat,* which he'd prepared for himself, on his WhatsApp status. Ekantika responded with a '*Where did you order this from?*' message.

I prepared it myself. I didn't tell you but I've this keen interest in cooking. These days I'm researching lost food recipes of India and preparing them. Taksh responded.

You prepare them and have them all alone? What an insult to the food. It was cheeky on her part.

Haha. No, no. You are most welcome to taste it.

I sure will, thanks. Looks awesome. But right now need to shift place.

That was it. He offered his help. She didn't refuse it.

The first thing, though, Ekantika told Taksh after she opened the door of Preeti's Hauz Khas flat was, 'Please don't tell ma or Shukla maashi that I lived here or I shifted from here.'

Taksh smiled and said, 'Don't worry. I'm not a mumma's agent. As I told you the other day, nothing that transpires between us goes there.'

'Thanks,' she said.

Since she had hardly any time, Ekantika had decided to hunt down a place through a realty website. It took her two hours to select a new place, checking out all the pictures posted by the owner. The place was in Old Rajendra Nagar. Another hub for UPSC aspirants in Delhi.

'That's it?' Taksh asked, seeing her luggage. He had expected there to be more.

'I sold off most of my belongings,' she said and hoped he didn't ask why. The explanation that it would demand, if he asked, would take her to the point which she was evading. The reason behind selling half of her belongings was Faizaan's death.

Initially, Ekantika wanted to keep them, thereby keeping alive the spiritual proximity with Faizaan. Then one night she realized any tangible thing that connected her to Faizaan was frivolous compared to how much her soul was coalesced with his. She understood this was another façade that the mind helped create. To 'hold on'. You don't hold on to someone who is there within you, has become a part of your core. Till you are, he will be. Till she was, Faizaan would be, Ekantika thought. Thus, she put everything up on OLX and later sold the lot. Except 'Ferrari', his bike. At first, she thought of giving it to his family. But as nobody came to ask about it, she decided to keep it for herself. She would ride it one day.

Taksh helped Ekantika with the little luggage she had. He even booked an Uber for her. They were waiting for Preeti. Ekantika wanted to talk to her before leaving. She'd understood somewhere while living together with her, Preeti's concern was not limited only to her duty.

Preeti arrived half an hour later. Though she knew Ekantika was supposed to leave, she wasn't aware she would leave that day itself. Taksh excused himself, realizing the two ladies wanted to talk in some privacy.

'Thanks, Preeti di, for the care you have shown all these days,' Ekantika said, referring to her as 'di' (elder sister) for the first time. She gave her a bear hug. Preeti responded by tightening her arms around her. Ekantika had been a human vacation for her which she was desperately longing for. A *vacation* which made her look beyond any social validation.

'Boyfriend?' Preeti asked.

Ekantika smiled and said, 'Just a friend. I don't think I can handle anything of that sort for some time now.'

'I know you have gone through a lot. Losing someone close is devastating. You know, no one can ever take someone else's position in our heart. And sometimes we yearn so much that we create a place within ourselves for a person not knowing if he or she deserves it.'

Ekantika had never heard Preeti talk so deeply with her before this.

'But girl, always beware of men. We'll always be like cigarettes for them. They come to us, convince us that they are here for us. That's actually an illusion they create for us. Once they puff us off, they stamp on us so nothing remains of us. Only then you'll realize they weren't here for us. You'll know they had come to us only because they wanted to have us. It was always about them. We curse one specific man or we curse all men but I think the problem lies within us. We women are suckers for illusions.'

'Basically you are saying all men are bastards?' Ekantika asked.

Preeti smiled a little and said, 'All I'm saying is,' she came close to Ekantika, with her right hand moved a strand of hair on her face and caressing her nape, added, 'Men don't necessarily have the answers to all our queries. Sometimes a woman satisfies a woman on a deeper level than a man can. Or will ever reach,' she gave Ekantika a peck.

Preeti could feel Ekantika had instant gooseflesh.

'Keep in touch,' Preeti said. The eye lock remained for a tad longer than usual.

'I will,' Ekantika said. Preeti saw her move out of the door. She closed it and wiped her moist eyes. She wished that society had less stringent rules. And allowed genders to flourish openly than be limited within themselves.

The next day at the police station, Preeti spent the whole day studying the CCTV footage from the parking lot of B-Mart where Saira was shopping before being killed. Pradeep, in particular, had asked her to do so instead of Inspector Gagan.

She was pausing, magnifying frames, rewinding, forwarding, trying to figure out if they could capture a glimpse of the cello-tape killer. Five hours later, nothing concrete surfaced. After a short break, Preeti once again started going through the footage from the beginning.

She noticed that, in one of the frames of the parking lot, a staff member abruptly came out of a dark corner. Preeti had missed it before. She asked the person, who was helping her with the footage, to take her to the frame where the staff member went towards the dark alley. There was no capture for the person going into the corner. Preeti stood up with excitement.

She beamed as she asked the helper to freeze the image of the supposed killer. In two decades, she was the first one to capture a glimpse of this killer. Finally, her career would fast-track from here, Preeti thought, cracking her knuckles in excitement.

12

The police commissioner of Gurugram, Dhirendra Singh Goni, was present alongside Pradeep and a few other officers, briefing the media about the cello-tape serial killer case. They were in the media room of the commissioner's office. Preeti stood in the corner by the room's door. Keeping an eager eye on the enthusiastic journalists, especially the men, and thinking one day she too would brief them individually. They would ask her questions and she would have the right to reject or answer them as she wished.

The moment the image of the cello-tape killer came on the projector screen, everyone looked up. The room was blanketed with silence for a moment. Then the buzz returned. It was a heavily pixelated image where one could only understand there was a man in the parking lot in a staff uniform. Dhirendra played the short video clip as well and one could see he walked with a slight limp. The same clip and image were shared with the media so it could be played on their channels.

'We have officially reopened the cello-tape serial killer case since the last killing in 2000,' Dhirendra said on the mic.

'Sir, any idea who it could be?' asked the journalist of a Hindi newspaper.

'If we had an idea, then we wouldn't be sitting here with you guys showing his picture and video.'

'Are the killings still random like they used to be back in the day?' This journalist appeared to be senior.

Dhirendra glanced at Pradeep. The latter chose to speak.

'Not that random as before. There's, of course, a relationship between Saira, Faizaan and Nagma's death. They were related.'

'How was Saira related to Nagma?'

'Saira wasn't. Faizaan was. Nagma was Faizaan's former lover. What needs to be noted is even though the randomness isn't there, the last three deaths were done with the same modus operandi of the cello-tape serial killer.' It was Pradeep again.

'But could it be copycat murders for some other agenda?' asked Kisha Bhargav, who was a crime journalist with India's number one Hindi news channel.

'We haven't ruled that possibility out,' Dhirendra replied.

As the press conference continued, Ekantika was watching it live sitting in her new 1BHK in Old Rajendra Nagar. The television was drilled on the wall while she was on the couch facing it. It was a modest semi-furnished flat. Taksh came out from the kitchen with two glasses of *khus ki sharbat*.

'Khus or vetiver is here to refresh you,' he said, putting both the glasses on the centre table. He noticed Ekantika was teary-eyed.

'What happened?' he asked. She simply leaped towards him and hugged him tight, sobbing.

'I thought I would never know who killed Faizaan. I was asked to choose a fake killer. Now, they have reopened the old case,' Ekantika said as her body shuddered against his. Taksh was in two minds. He wanted to console her but he was wary of touching her against her wish or permission. He let the moment be.

There was awkward silence between the two. Taksh could hear and see the press conference on the television. Suddenly, Ekantika let him go.

'I'm sorry,' she said, realizing what she had done in an emotional impulse.

'Who asked you to choose a fake killer?' Taksh sounded puzzled.

'Hari Prasad Mishra. I'd messaged Pradeep Ahlawat sir that I wouldn't be able to cheat my beloved. I wouldn't be able to choose a random man as the killer. I want justice.'

A silent pause later, she added, 'I thought they would have presented the killer today in front of the media but with Faizaan's mother getting killed . . .'

'Faizaan's mother has also been killed?' Taksh asked. As a forensics guy, he only focused on the work which came to him. He wasn't in the team which had made the forensics report on the findings in the parking lot where Saira was found dead.

Ekantika nodded, wiping her tears. An advertisement started running on the TV. Taksh picked the remote up from the centre table and switched it off. He put back the remote and looked at Ekantika. She was back on the couch, reclining, looking at the ceiling and trying to get a grip on herself.

'It's good to see you loved him so much. These days we rarely experience such love when we are alive. Forget about someone loving us like this when we are no more,' Taksh said.

Ekantika picked up one of the glasses and sipped the sharbat.

'This is so damn tasty,' she said, knowing it was best to change the topic lest it became too emotionally claustrophobic for her. 'Better than what ma makes.'

'Thank you. I'm glad you liked it.' Taksh too picked up his glass.

'Lucky whoever will marry you. There's something sexy about kitch-men.'

'Kitch-men?' Taksh looked amused with the word.

'Men who rule the kitchen. I just made up the term.'

'Like you made Miss Mixo?'

Ekantika threw an incredulous look at him. She'd never shared this with him.

'How do you know about Miss Mixo?'

Taksh made a guilty face and said, 'I checked your social media.'

'Ah, before meeting me or after?'

'After.' It sounded like a confession.

She gave him a nervous smile. Suddenly, the 1BHK seemed smaller. It was obvious why he had checked her social media after meeting her. The same reason why she lamented he didn't have active accounts on it. Both had found the other interesting enough. Both wanted to know more without the other knowing it.

'So, who is that girl? The one you are in love with but not in a relationship?' Ekantika asked. She realized he knew more about her than she knew about him. It was time to square-off.

'She is where she was. Happily doing her journalism with a news channel. She doesn't even know I intentionally made sure our relationship faded.'

'What?' Ekantika said, swallowing a sip of the sharbat hurriedly.

'So my love for her remained alive.'

'Sorry for saying this, but don't you think you are a little too complicated?'

Taksh laughed out loud.

'If you say so. I don't know. A complicated person won't understand his complications much. For him, it's just how things are or should be.'

'But seriously, there's no one big reason for you to leave your ex?'

'There is. I wanted to love her more. For longer. If I stayed with her in the relationship, I would have fallen out of love with her.'

'Dude, please make some sense.'

'All right, we met online. Had some common friends. I liked her DP. She was looking gorgeous. So sent her a friend request. She accepted. Then sent her a 'Hi' on the messenger. She replied. Before we knew it, we had exchanged more than ten thousand messages. Then we decided to meet. We were like a house on fire. There were so many things we both felt passionate about. So many things to talk about. It was obvious that we had to be in a relationship because we were spending more time with each other anyway.'

As Taksh talked, images of Faizaan and herself kept flashing in her mind. Every exclusive love story is so universal in its core, Ekantika thought, as he continued.

'Everything was awesome till I slowly started understanding one small difference between us. She was self-centred as a person while I was the opposite. I'm not saying she didn't keep me as a priority. She did. But after her own self. Unlike me. I'm also not saying that's a bad thing. But because of that trait, she wasn't able to meet some of my expectations that I thought were important if a relationship had to go the distance. I started developing a detachment towards her. Maybe because that side of her was eclipsing the love I had for her. And I didn't like it. That's when, during one of my introspective sessions with myself, I realized that sometimes, to protect and preserve your love for someone, perhaps you have to avoid being in a relationship with the person. Then I intentionally started giving her less time. And she interpreted it as my lack of interest in her, just as I had thought she would. We broke off. But till this day I love her the way I did in the beginning.'

'And she thinks you hate her?' Ekantika asked. She was finding it difficult to believe what she had just heard.

Taksh nodded and said, 'Worse. She thinks I'm over her.'

There was silence. Ekantika had nothing to say. Her phone showed a notification. It was a message from her Topsie study group. She picked up her phone and checked it out. Taksh sipped his sharbat with his eyes on her.

'May I say something?' he asked.

Ekantika looked up at him.

'Sure.'

'You have a beautiful smile,' he said, knowing well she could have misinterpreted it thinking he was trying to lead the situation to something.

'Thanks. It's all because I'm really happy right now. Finally some lead in Faizaan's killer's case,' she said.

'Then allow me to celebrate this happiness of yours. Dinner prepared by me?'

The passion with which he said so, Ekantika couldn't say no. 'But here, please. I'll order whatever items you need to cook.'

Ekantika didn't want to go to his place just yet. Taksh agreed. Ekantika's mobile phone started ringing with an alarm. She stopped it.

'Sorry, my study alarm,' she said, looking at Taksh.

'In fact, I'm sorry. I should let you study now, rather than talk about smiles.'

Ekantika smirked, saying, 'I have my prelims in two weeks.'

Taksh had his eyebrows raised as she continued, 'And only I know how unprepared I am.'

'Just give it your best shot.'

Ekantika gave him a tight smile. He finished his sharbat in one gulp and said, 'Tell you what,' he said, 'you focus on studies. I'll go to the market and get whatever I need to prepare the dinner.' She gave him an acknowledging nod. She knew she had found a much-needed friend.

Preeti was given the task of following-up with all the victims of the cello-tape serial killer over the years across states.

'If you want a promotion out of this case, just dive in now,' Pradeep told her.

First, she contacted the families of the victims from Delhi. Sixteen of the twenty-six killings had taken place in Delhi. Next, she found herself taking the Lucknow Express where two killings had been reported. In Mumbai, there were four victims. Then she went to Dharamshala, Himachal Pradesh, for two victims, including a foreigner. And finally to Bihar as one of the victims was found dead on a train.

Wherever she went, Preeti talked to the local police stations, checked the records, talked to the victims' families or friends, recorded their statements and asked them to be alert, updating them about the reopening of the serial killing case. She located the foreign victim's mother in Delft, the Netherlands, with whom she did a video call to update her. Two weeks went by in all this at the end of which only the last, the twenty-sixth, victim was left. Though he was killed in Lucknow, he was from Bihar.

Once in Baheri, near Darbhanga, Bihar, Preeti contacted the local police and located the victim's house. She discovered that the last victim's family home had been turned into a cowshed owned by a local goon. Preeti asked around if anybody knew where the family had gone. Everyone said the elders of the family died while the wife and the little son vanished into thin air after the man of the house was killed by the cello-tape serial killer.

13

The shrill alarm rang for the third time. And Preeti knew this time she had to get up. The train had brought her to Delhi at 3.30 a.m. The last two weeks had been exhausting. Constant travel, bad food and new places to sleep every few days. Preeti had this weird habit of not being able to sleep if she was anywhere other than her home. Even at Ekantika's place, she couldn't sleep peacefully.

Preeti sat up on her bed at once. Her head felt heavy, and her eyelids were dropping shut. But she reminded herself that professionally it was an important day for her. She was ready with her report, which she had prepared in the train itself last night, on her way back from Bihar. Pradeep would be happy with the report and she would inch a step closer to becoming an inspector. As a child, Preeti had seen how much her brothers and father used to respect an 'inspector' in the village. She had never seen them bow down to anyone but a police inspector.

Preeti reached the Gurugram circle office on time. She went in and submitted her report to Pradeep. He did notice the dark circles under her eyes, but didn't inquire about them. Alternating between sifting through the report and sipping his ginger tea, Pradeep said, 'You found anything untoward?'

Preeti shook her head, saying, 'Nothing. Of the twenty-five families I got in touch with, sixteen have moved on while the other eight wanted the killer to be caught and punished with a death sentence.'

'That's twenty-four. What about the remaining family?'

'I couldn't track the family.'

'Dead?'

'Can't be conclusive. Wife and son missing, though no missing report was ever filed. Other members died over time.'

'Hmm, all right.' Pradeep pressed a bell. A constable hurried in.

'Saab.'

'Send Inspector Gagan in.'

'Ji saab.'

The constable went out. Seconds later, Inspector Gagan came in.

'Sir.'

'This is Preeti's report about the family members of the victims of the cello-tape serial killer. Go through it and prepare a report detailing the similarities with the recent killings. We need to submit it to the commissioner tomorrow.'

'Right, sir.' Inspector Gagan took the file from Pradeep and moved out. Preeti stood dumbfounded. There was no response from Pradeep.

'We are finished,' he said curtly.

'I could have made the report for the commissioner as well,' Preeti said, shocked.

'I know. But if I bypass Gagan and go to the commissioner with you, he'll know the obvious.' Pradeep sounded matter-of-fact.

'Then you could have asked Inspector Gagan to go after all the families of the victims. Why me?'

Pradeep took his reading specs off and gave Preeti a mean look.

'Let me decide that.' His voice was stern.

'Sir,' Preeti said. She was extremely hurt as she knew what would happen after this. The case would never come to her. And the seniors would take all the mileage from it on the basis of her hard work.

Preeti went to the washroom, locked herself in and cried her heart out, while sending a flurry of punches hard into the wall.

Ekantika's prelims centre was in a school in Saket. She came out feeling numb. This was her third attempt at the UPSC prelims. As she reached the main gate of the school, she spotted Taksh on the footpath on the opposite side. He flashed a smile at her. He had accompanied her to the exam centre. As she reached him, she broke down. Taksh's smile dried up.

'Hey, what happened?' he asked.

'I had a blackout. I couldn't answer anything. All I could see in my mind was Faizaan's face,' she said. Taksh realized there was nothing he could have said that would have helped her then, so he just let her be.

For ten minutes neither talked. She kept walking. Taksh walked beside her. Ekantika got a call from her mother.

Charulata inquired about the exam. Ekantika lied that she did her best. As she talked to her mother, Ekantika recovered her poise. She was yet to tell her that she already had a friendship with Taksh. For Charulata had been told that they had met only once till now. After she was done with the call, Ekantika looked at Taksh and said, 'Let's go somewhere.'

'Sure. Where?' he asked.

Ekantika took Taksh to a cafe in Hauz Khas where she had been with Faizaan before. Ekantika checked out the plant that they had planted outside during one of their dates. It had grown a bit. She took a water bottle out from her bag and watered it. Then she went inside the café with Taksh.

'Do you stalk your ex still?' she asked, settling down in the cafe.

'She has blocked me.'

'Ah, is that the reason why you aren't active on social media?'

'Guilty!' he said and then added, 'Though I have a fake profile only to check on her whenever I miss her.'

Ekantika laughed.

'Such creeps we all are.' Taksh joined in on her laughter.

Preeti had skipped her lunch. She was still burning with anger. Pradeep behaved as if nothing had happened. To push her anger further into a rage, he shared a porn video on WhatsApp with her. It was an FMF threesome. It was clear Pradeep wanted to try that out during their next hotel escapade. Angrily, she messaged that she was uncomfortable doing a threesome though she wanted to type 'fuck off' in caps. Pradeep read the message but didn't respond. Right after lunch, he came to her and said, '4.40 this evening, hotel.' And went away. As if she was his paid whore. Preeti was so angry that she could have killed someone.

Pradeep left on time. She also left the office so she could reach Hotel Night Delights on time. But today there wouldn't be any sex between them. Preeti knew what she would do. Once they were naked, there wouldn't be any senior-junior between them. She would then talk it out straight with Pradeep.

Everything is based on takeaways, she thought, sitting in the metro, which was taking her to the New Delhi stop. If Pradeep was fucking her because he didn't have the kind of wife with whom he could live out his perverse fantasies, she too was fucking him, after knowing this wasn't about love, so he could be of some help when needed and not just throw her out after verbally appreciating her hard work.

Preeti reached the hotel five minutes late. As she walked past the reception, the manager handed her the key. As always.

Preeti stormed to the room, unlocked the door and was about to step in but stopped. Pradeep was standing in the middle of the room holding the hair of a woman. She didn't know who. They were naked. The woman was sucking his penis. For a moment. Preeti was tongue-tied. She couldn't hide her shock. Pradeep looked at her and said with an evil grin, 'I called you here to tell you to fuck off. Never dare to say no to me; otherwise I will make sure you are the youngest one to retire from our force.'

Preeti's entire body was shaking. Her eyes were moist. Nothing made any sense. She seemed to have lost the strength in her knees. A moment later, she quietly closed the door. Gingerly walked down, handed the key to the manager and moved out. She stood under a street lamp, then threw up.

Before reaching her home, Preeti purchased a bottle of whisky from the nearby wine shop. At home, she finished half of it, neat, pretty quickly. She was gulping some more when she heard the doorbell ring. She went to open the door. Her face stretched into a smile seeing the person there.

'Arrey, sexy. How come you're here?' Preeti asked. Ekantika could smell the whisky on her breath. Preeti moved aside; Ekantika stepped in. One look and she knew she was correct. There was a bottle of DSP Black on the table, where she used to study, with a plate of chips beside it. And a glass with whisky in it; neat. She chose not to mention it.

'I was in the area so I thought of visiting. Any update on the case?' asked Ekantika.

'Yes. A very big update,' Preeti said with a diabolical smile.

Ekantika looked inquiringly at her.

'You want to catch the killer desperately, isn't that right?' Preeti asked.

'Yeah, I do. I don't think either Faizaan's or my soul will rest in peace till he is caught.'

'And I want to teach someone a lesson just as desperately,' Preeti said.

A moment later, Preeti added, 'I have a plan.'

14

'What are you saying?' Ekantika was shocked to hear of Preeti's plan. She had been at her flat for some time now. Preeti was about to respond when Ekantika's phone rang. It was Taksh. He was waiting outside. Ekantika had told him she would take a couple of minutes. She had taken twenty.

'Yeah, Taksh.' Ekantika said on the phone.

'All good?' he asked.

'Yeah, yeah. I think I'll take some more time. You getting late?'

'Not really. Felt like checking.'

'I may take some time more,' she said.

'Cool, no problem. I'm here,' he said and ended the call.

'I think you should go now,' Preeti said.

'What? Why?' Suddenly Ekantika had too much to think about after hearing Preeti's plan.

Preeti came close and held Ekantika's shoulder saying, 'Go home and sleep over what I told you. Nobody should have a suspicion that we are up to something. Not even Taksh.'

Ekantika took half a minute to understand what Preeti had said. Then she left.

All through the journey back to her flat, Ekantika remained quiet. Though Taksh asked her a couple of times if all was okay, she put the blame on a non-existent headache. Taksh dropped her home and left.

Ekantika couldn't sleep that night. Preeti had told her how the Haryana police had not reached anywhere. That she felt, because the case had a political angle to it, there was a chance that it would go under the carpet soon. Or in the garb of employing a bigger agency like the CBI, the politicians would take control of the case. And to keep the urgency of the case alive against the will of the politicians, they had to do something big. Preeti's idea of what the 'big thing' should be definitely startled her.

'We will fake my killing,' Preeti had said. Ekantika didn't know how to react then; she didn't know how to feel now.

'You will be here with me. Help me get the tapes on. We will do everything exactly the way the cello-tape killer does. Then you will save me when I'm about to become unconscious. And immediately call Pradeep. If a police officer is almost killed by a serial killer, it will break the case open once again and the police will be under greater pressure to solve it. The media won't let them sit in peace.'

What Preeti didn't tell Ekantika, as she sat sipping the last peg of the night, was that it would put Preeti in the centre of the action. The Haryana police would have to consult her and keep her within the realm of their investigation since she would be a survivor victim for them. And not just an assistant SI who worked on the case to begin with. Her importance would immediately double. And she would be able to show

Pradeep the middle finger without really showing him the finger.

While Ekantika's mind was oscillating between whether she should be a part of the plan or not, Preeti, in her flat, was totally drunk as she lay on her bed smiling, with Pradeep's WhatsApp DP open on her phone.

'Never fuck with a woman who wants to make it big,' Preeti mumbled before passing out.

The next morning, Ekantika called Preeti and said she was on. They would execute Preeti's plan together. She, too, wanted the case solved quickly and the killer arrested. After her classes at Topsie, Ekantika made her way to Hauz Khas. She kept calling Preeti, updating her about her location. After she had reached the cafe where they had decided to meet, Ekantika waited for Preeti to come in from her duty. They had chosen this particular cafe because it had CCTV coverage. The police would check Ekantika's alibi and they would know she was sitting here alone before going to Preeti's flat. In case anyone questioned their story.

Preeti met her outside the cafe, at a corner which wasn't under the arc of the CCTVs. She gave her the flat's spare keys, matched the time on their phones and then went home. A quick GPS survey showed Ekantika that the flat was a three-minute-walk from the cafe. Ekantika was supposed to move out to Preeti's flat at exactly 8.35 p.m. Once there, she would come in using the spare keys and save Preeti. Then Ekantika was supposed to call the police and tell them she was in the area and thought of returning the spare keys of Preeti's flat, which she had been given when they were staying together. She would say she saw Preeti in trouble, supposedly attacked by the cello-tape killer. She had saved her and called the police. They would make sure the marks of the cello-tape were on Preeti's face when the police came. So they acted out the story as if it was happening for real. There didn't seem any loophole in the plan. Neither to Preeti, nor to Ekantika.

At 8.35 p.m., Ekantika moved out of the cafe. It took three minutes for her to reach Preeti's flat. She took a deep breath and used the spare keys to get in. She saw Preeti lying in the hall with her nose and mouth taped. Only her hands weren't tightly tied. There was a twinkle in Preeti's eyes seeing Ekantika. The latter did the obvious. She tied Preeti's hands a little tightly so they left their mark. A moment later, Preeti's breaths started becoming shorter. Her body started fidgeting. She thought Ekantika would remove the tapes any moment now. She started gesturing to her with her widened eyes. But the moment never came. There was an expression of bewilderment before Preeti's body went quiet.

Assistant SI Preeti Jangra was dead.

And seeing that, Ekantika Pakrashi let out a sigh.

BOOK 3: OF LOVE AND CRIME

1

If there was someone who was an expert at living a monotonous existence without complaining, it had to be UKC. The man who helped the Delhi and Haryana police solve complicated crime cases.

Living in his GK-1 house, with only a girl Friday called Neema—a middle-aged lady from the north-east, trained in various martial arts, and who made the world's best chicken soup, according to UKC—monotony was his comfort zone. Any kind of experiment or adventure seemed pointless to him. It was for those, UKC believed, who thought human beings were here on Earth for a greater purpose. For him, human beings were here on Earth to eat, fuck, reproduce and die. End of story.

He was wheelchair-bound due to a serious accident, which had paralysed his body from the neck down. The accident, however, took away the most pertinent part of his existence: his pregnant wife. He was the one driving that night. They were going for their babymoon to Manali. But 100 kms before Manali, a truck had rammed into their car.

After coming to his senses, UKC realized he would have to live with the guilt that he was responsible for the death of his wife and his unborn child. Everyone told him it was the truck driver's fault. But he thought otherwise. However, the accident couldn't touch the most important part of him: his brain. Living with the guilt, which led him to maniacal depression and acute suicidal tendencies, would have turned him hollow from within if a particular murder case hadn't rocked New Delhi at the time.

As a defence mechanism against his depression, UKC diverted his entire focus to the murder case as an outsider who had nothing to do with the case nor had he been asked to. He had been an avid reader of crime novels since his teens. And he wasn't just a reader. After reading every novel, he wrote an alternate ending and an alternate possible murderer, squeezing out from within the story a motive for the character who had been proven innocent in the novel. It was his only hobby. Professionally, he worked in a private equity bank and was in love with the monotonous routine it gave him, before the accident derailed his life.

Within three months after UKC concentrated his attention on the murder case, he had 707 paper cuttings of the case from numerous local and national dailies, along with several recorded news channel clips reporting the murder. In the fourth month, he pulled off the impossible. With those newspaper cuttings and channel clips, he found out who the murderer was. This was something that the Delhi police couldn't do even with first-hand information about the case.

ACP Abhay Pratap Singh was handling the murder case then. UKC sent him an email with his findings and deductions. He also mailed him a flowchart depicting the plan of action for the Delhi police. Abhay followed it, the murderer was caught, he confessed and the Delhi police were hailed in the media everywhere.

When Abhay told his seniors about UKC and his role in solving the case, the word went up to the then home minister who called up UKC and requested him to continue his complimentary services for the police force in general. UKC agreed. A small stipend was given to him by the government for his services. UKC didn't need it per se, but he didn't refuse it either because without the stipend, he wasn't a professional. And he wanted to be a professional resource for them. It was the same ACP Abhay who had brought him Ashvamedha Chauhan's case earlier, when he helped the Delhi police. UKC was still in touch with Sanisha Singh and was following the court proceedings regarding the matter.

Not only was he wheelchair-bound, but UKC had this peculiar phobia that if his skin was exposed to natural light, he would have continuous lifelong itching. It was a phobia he developed because of his depression. He remained locked up in his house 24/7/365 days, with the curtains shut and the doors and windows closed. The lights of the house were on during the day as well. He wore a rain poncho whenever Neema opened up the house to the sunlight once a week.

That night, while Neema helped him sip his favourite Scotch, he was lost in the latest thriller he'd heard about, in the form of an audio book. In his mind he was trying to select a different murderer, keeping the sanctity of the story intact. That's when the landline phone in the house rang. It disturbed his focus.

'Which moron doesn't sleep at this hour?' UKC said. Neema sauntered to the landline in the room. She picked it up. And listened intently for some time. Then she said, 'It's ACP Pradeep Ahlawat.' Neema said, 'He wants to meet you.'

'I'm with my Scotch now. Ask him to call in the morning,' UKC bellowed.

2

Though the idea of a possible attack on her was Preeti's, the death of a policewoman in the attack, that particular twist, was Ekantika's brainchild. Merely an attack by the cello-tape killer on Preeti wouldn't have made the cut. It sounded too soft to Ekantika. A serial killer, who had been on the loose for twenty-nine years, coming back to kill a policewoman who was investigating the case was just the kind of flesh the ever-so-hungry media would have devoured. And it made it personal for the Haryana police as well. Now, Ekantika knew, they wouldn't sit tight on the case, letting it turn cold even for a day. One of *them* had been killed after all.

Ekantika stuck to the post-attack plan as Preeti devised it. She had immediately called Pradeep and told him what had happened. That she had come to give Preeti the spare house keys. But Preeti didn't open the door even after she pressed the doorbell five or six times. Then she called her on her phone. The missed calls were noted by Pradeep and his team when they secured Preeti's phone. The first thing Pradeep did was check the phone for any of his messages or photographs before handing it over to the forensics team first and then the cyber team. Taksh was part of the forensics team that came in.

The post-mortem of Preeti's dead body told Pradeep that she was already dead for an hour before Ekantika made the SOS call. They didn't know she was simply waiting beside Preeti's dead body with the timer open on her phone. The moment it struck one hour, she stood up, went outside and pressed the doorbell five or six times so that her fingerprints were imprinted on it. Then she came in again using the spare keys and pretended to discover Preeti's dead body. She screamed and dialled Pradeep.

The media across India went berserk on the latest development, highlighting the killing of assistant SI Preeti Jangra. Numerous women rights' activists came together and initiated a rebellion on Twitter demanding the resignation of the police commissioner. Their plea was simple: if a woman in uniform isn't safe, then which woman is? The murder, according to them, had stripped the government of the sham they were carrying out in the name of women empowerment and development.

Some of the journalists reached Preeti's ancestral home in her village and interviewed her brothers. They spoke highly of their sister, even though that was the first time they learnt that Preeti was serving in the police force.

Even Ekantika was approached for an exclusive interview, but she told them categorically she wouldn't speak to them. It was a police case and whatever she had to say she had already said to them. She was happy. Preeti's death wouldn't go to waste, or so she thought. The cello-tape serial killer would be caught soon. And that's what she wanted doggedly from the bottom of her heart.

Two days later, when the media frenzy had subsided a little, Ekantika messaged Taksh in the morning to check if he was free to teach her how to ride a bike. He was. Two hours later, they were at it.

Ekantika fell off the bike for the fourth time that morning. She was learning to ride Faizaan's Ferrari. Taksh came running to her.

'You rode a good distance this time,' he said encouragingly.

'Yeah, 50 metres,' she said and laughed. She was able to balance the bike but she was finding it difficult to master turning it.

'That's all right. If you keep riding, you'll get better,' Taksh said, picking up the bike. And then helping Ekantika to get up as well.

'I think I'm done for today,' she said and looked around. They were on the lane of her place in Old Rajendra Nagar. She spotted the roadside juice-wala she had taken sugarcane juice from, a day before, while returning from Topsie.

'He makes some amazing juice. Want to try?' she asked Taksh. He nodded. He went to park the bike inside Ekantika's new apartment premises while she ordered two glasses of fresh sugarcane juice.

By the time Taksh came back, the sugarcane juice was ready. They took their glasses.

'Awesome,' Taksh said, gulping half of it at one go. Ekantika gave him an I-told-you-so smile. Once they were done, Taksh reached for his wallet but Ekantika stopped him.

She paid. They started walking slowly towards her building gate, when she spoke up.

'I thought about what you said; that being in love is more important than being in a relationship.'

'I'm glad. Though that makes me sound like some preacher whose words you remembered,' he said jocularly.

A smile later, Ekantika said, 'While wondering about your one-sided love . . .' She saw Taksh giving her a sharp glance. She chose to clarify, 'It's one-sided right now because your ex doesn't know you intentionally engineered the drift. Now she hates you, probably.'

Taksh nodded in agreement.

'Initially, when you told me all this, I was apprehensive. I wondered if what you said made any sense at all. But then I realized people often say one-sided love is bad. But what's worse than one-sided love is a one-sided relationship.'

Taksh glanced at her. There was a look of wonder on his face as he hadn't thought of it that way.

'True. People think love is overrated. I think relationships are overrated. They say humans are social beings. Perhaps that's why the urge to be with someone supersedes the urge to just be where you are and love the one you want to,' Taksh said.

'Not that I entirely agree with it and I would love to continue this conversation, but I have to go now. Study time,' Ekantika said.

'Take care of yourself. The assistant SI's death was pretty startling,' Taksh said. Ekantika nodded. She knew he was involved in Preeti's case as a forensic expert but she intentionally didn't ask him anything directly lest he became inquisitive. Ekantika went up to her flat. Just as she was freshening up, she heard the doorbell ring. She went to open the door and saw a young girl with an expressive smile standing by the door.

'Hi, I'm Kisha Bhargav,' the girl said.

'Okay. Do I know you?' Ekantika asked.

'Ekantika Pakrashi, right?'

Ekantika nodded. She felt she had seen her somewhere. And before she knew it, the girl introduced herself.

'I'm a crime journalist. Working with *Aaj Tak*. I'm here to inquire about assistant SI Preeti Jangra's death. May I please ask you a few questions?'

'Look, I've already said no . . .'

'A few basics. That's all. Won't trouble you much.'

'It's not a video thing, right?' Ekantika asked, falling for Kisha's pleading voice.

Kisha looked a little unsure when she said, 'It is,' she turned towards her cameraman who came up to stand behind her now with a friendly smile.

'I'm sorry . . .'

'Don't worry, we will blur your face if you prefer,' Kisha cut her short.

'No. Sorry . . .'

'We will only use your voice then? No video,' Kisha seemed to be agreeing with what Ekantika had asked first.

'The least we can do as citizens is to keep the urgency alive so no more murders happen,' Kisha said.

Ekantika looked at Kisha, then at her cameraman and thought the moral pitch was certainly a trap, but she also had a point. She was the first one to find Faizaan dead and then Preeti; her interview on TV would definitely keep the news hot. And that's what she had to do till the original killer was caught. The only thing was, what if her mother saw the show?

'You're sure only my voice will be used?' Ekantika asked.

'Absolutely,' Kisha said with confidence.

The next half hour passed with Kisha recording Ekantika's version of the events. When it was telecast later in the evening, Kisha introduced her as the deceased Faizaan's live-in girlfriend. As promised to Ekantika, she blacked her face out and didn't mention her name, but the fact that she was pursuing UPSC in Topsie and was from Baruipur living alone in Delhi was mentioned without Ekantika's permission. And one of the several lakh viewers of this exclusive and hyped telecast was Charulata.

She immediately called Ekantika.

'Shonai, what are you doing?' she asked.

'I'm home, studying. What happened, ma?' Ekantika could sense something was wrong.

'Just put on the television. *Aaj Tak*.' Charulata said. And Ekantika knew what had gone wrong. She pushed back her chair, stood up. She went and picked up the remote and switched the television on to the *Aaj Tak* channel.

'Let me explain, ma,' she said.

'You were living-in with a guy? You have disappointed me, Shonai.' Charulata said in an emotionally choked voice and ended the call. Ekantika called her back a few times but there was no response.

As Ekantika went back to her study table and sat down holding her head, her phone rang with Pradeep's number.

'Yes sir.'

'Please be free tomorrow evening at four.'

'Sure. What happened? Any breakthrough?'

'Hopefully soon. Just be punctual tomorrow as the person you will meet is unpredictable with unpunctual people.'

'Whom am I meeting, sir?' Ekantika asked.

'UKC.'

3

'You know, Neema,' UKC said, 'what's the best thing about humans?'

'I thought you were a hardcore misanthropist. Is there anything good about humans for you?' Neema said in her usual stoic manner. She was helping UKC have his chicken soup.

UKC had a hint of a smile on his face. A rarity with him.

'Humans have no role in the best thing about humans. It's just the way they have been created.'

'And what's that?' Neema dabbed his mouth twice with the napkin.

'The capability of creating memories,' UKC said and continued, 'I remember when the cello-tape killer's name first appeared in the newspaper, I was in Standard Ten. My father was posted in Pune. I never knew how to live without ma and baba back then. And I believed that once they died, I would also die. But see, here I'm still living after so many years of their death. We all adjust to what is; doesn't matter how difficult the situation.'

'Right. Life goes on no matter what.' Neema added her bit of wisdom. UKC nodded.

There was a prolonged silence after which UKC spoke.

'There are four types of serial killers. The ones who commit murders because they believe a greater power is making them do it. Then the ones who do the killings to attain some kind of pleasure; physical or otherwise. Thirdly, the ones who take killing as some sort of mission. And lastly, the ones who love to exert power and control to such a psychotic level that they go on to kill people. And that's where the cello-tape killings were different.'

Neema kept quiet. Though she was done helping him with the chicken soup, she still stayed there, listening to him.

'I'd read whatever material we had on the cello-tape killer over the years and then the file ACP Pradeep Ahlawat shared. One of the reasons why the police of five states couldn't catch this killer was the lack of any concrete motivation. They couldn't guess it. If you get a series of mutilated bodies of prostitutes or raped females or young people being killed, a possible motivation could have been figured out and then a profiling would have followed. But here, all twenty-six victims—excluding the ones who died recently—were different and thus seemed random. The victims weren't of the same age, or from the same place, or of the same sex or economic status. There was no similarity or pattern except the modus operandi. Also, all the murders didn't happen in one place alone. That would have made things easier. And since this happened in the 1990s, we did not have the technology or medical skills to pick up the minor forensic evidence he left behind. There was no intention communicated either. Like the Zodiac killer loved to challenge the police by reaching out to them. There was one such case in Delhi also. But our killer here was definitely not after any challenge game or even fame.

'We can't say he was an angry or frustrated soul either because the murders weren't brutal. In fact, from what I know, these could be the most neatly done serial killings across the world. So he could be a minimalistic guy in his everyday life. Happy or content with simple things maybe. Even the gaps between the murders were not small and definitely random. Twenty-six kills in seven or eight years. That's not something from which we can conclude he was itching to kill people. So, there wasn't some 'mission' he was following. The question remains . . . why was the cellotape killer killing people in the first place? Motivation is everything. It leads to the murderer.'

'Killing as a sport maybe? Maybe he killed for the first time by chance. Then when he wasn't caught, it gave him a thrill?' Neema argued.

'Even if we consider kill-because-of-thrill as a motive, then psychologically speaking, the numbers should have been higher. It should have been fifty-plus victims in eight years in that case. I don't think if someone follows killing for real, he would be bored, ever.'

There was silence again. The big pendulum wall clock in the hall struck the hour. It was 4 p.m. The doorbell rang. Pradeep and Ekantika had arrived earlier, but waited outside the house because UKC loathed people who came earlier or later than the time he had given.

Neema came out into the hall and opened the door. She ushered Pradeep and Ekantika inside. They had taken their seats. UKC was already in the hall in his wheelchair. He glanced at Ekantika once from his high-powered specs and then at Pradeep. The latter introduced her.

'Nice to meet you, sir.' Ekantika said. There was a pungent smell, the kind when a house remains closed for a long time.

'People rarely say that to me. Unless they want me to think well of them beforehand,' UKC said with a straight face.

Ekantika couldn't guess whether he was joking or serious. She threw an awkward rescue-me glance at Pradeep.

Then UKC quipped, 'I hope my joke didn't poke.'

Pradeep gave him an awkward smile and said, 'You mentioned that you had something to ask Ekantika.' Pradeep knew UKC preferred people getting to the point fast.

'Any idea about the friend Faizaan had?' UKC asked. It took Ekantika by surprise. That's what UKC wanted. How people answered queries that they least expected said a lot about them.

'Which friend, sir?' Ekantika asked. She was taking her time to think of a response.

'The one you mentioned in your audio statement. Someone from Patna. According to what I heard, the diary, which was stolen by the killer or so I'm told, belonged to Faizaan's friend.'

Ekantika swallowed a lump. Her throat was bone dry. She had to answer quickly, and answer correctly, for Ekantika knew she was being judged. The truth, as only Ekantika knew, couldn't be told.

For Faizaan had no such friend.

Ekantika: 4–7 Years Old

It was a rented house whose owners lived in Kolkata. The bare-looking house just had a ground floor and a half-constructed terrace. It didn't have a boundary wall except for some tin barriers. But it was still good for Charulata. She had got it for half the ongoing rent in the locality. That night, after Ekantika's fourth birthday, there was the *Kaal Boishaki*. These were fierce winds along with deafening thunderstorms, followed by torrential rain. It looked like there wouldn't be any tomorrow. As if Mother Earth had decided to filter out some amount of life from the world. It was doomsday-like-scary to say the least.

Charulata wasn't at home. It was her second surrogacy. Unlike the first, this time the money was better. It was for a Marwari family in Kolkata. According to the deal, she had to stay in Kolkata for the entire nine months under the supervision of the family. It was this clause in the verbal contract that made Charulata increase the money. The family agreed after doing all the necessary medical tests. Charulata was the healthiest of the lot they had zeroed in on. It was the hospital itself, where Charulata worked as a cleaner, which had introduced Charulata to the family. Nine months meant staying that much time away from her Shonai. She made sure she paid Nondar ma well to take care of her baby. After all, she was doing it all for her child. Money would make sure they could live in a better house and she could put Ekantika in a private school. She'd learnt the private schools gave better education than the government ones.

Nondar ma was an old nanny. Everyone called her by that name while nobody had ever seen or known who Nonda was. That night when nature went wild outside, she held on to a scared Ekantika as they stood against the window of their hall. The power had gone long ago. The entire locality was blanketed in darkness interspersed with the lightning. And in that flash of lightning little Ekantika could clearly see the neighbours on their well-sheltered terrace. The neighbour girl was the same age as Ekantika and just as scared. Yet she had someone telling her not to be afraid of nature. Someone whose hand she had held tightly. *Was it why she wasn't scared like her?* Ekantika wondered as she looked at that someone. The person didn't look like her mother. He had a dense growth of hair under his nose, he looked broader, his hair was also much shorter than her mother's. It wasn't long before little Ekantika knew what this someone was called. *Baba.* That's what the neighbour girl was calling him as he made her touch the raindrops outside. The father and daughter were having a good time between them. As if the strong wind or the thunder didn't matter to them. Instead, they were enjoying themselves. Ekantika muttered under her breath for the first time in her life . . . *baba.*

When Charulata came back after ten months, Nondar ma told her that Ekantika had stopped going to school for the past month. She had gone up one grade by then.

'What happened, Shonai? School will help you do whatever you want to later in life. It's important.'

Seeing her mother after many months, she couldn't help but press her face to her bosom and cry her heart out.

'I know, Shonai must have missed her ma,' Charulata said, caressing her child's back while feeling the jab of guilt right in the middle of her heart. 'Ma won't go anywhere.' The money the Marwari family gave her was enough to last three or four years for Ekantika and her. She would put it in a bank and then take up a job as a house help to sustain their daily life. Her plan was simple: she would go for the surrogacy two or three times in the next six years and save up all the money. Charulata had understood if the family was wealthy, she could leverage her position for good money. The expression on little Ekantika's face broke her trance.

'Everyone laughs at me in school. I won't go there ever,' she said. And dug her face in her mother's bosom again.

'Laugh at you? Why, Shonai?' Charulata looked worried.

'I'm the only one without a father. They say the one without a father is a bastard child.'

Charulata's core was shaken hearing the swear word from her child.

'Don't I have a baba?' Ekantika asked. Her innocent eyes almost crushed Charulata's heart. She knew she couldn't tell her the truth. She smiled at her instead, and said, 'Of course you have a baba. He is in a faraway land.'

Ekantika looked up, not believing her ears.

'When can I meet him?' she asked.

'Soon Shonai, very soon,' her voice clogged while saying it.

But the soon never came. Charulata made sure she started sending gifts to Ekantika and pretended they were sent by her baba.

Ekantika, now six, started interpreting what her baba would be like from the gifts given to her. It became her favourite pastime. Other kids played during recess in school; she talked to her baba. She even stopped praying to God. Her talks with her baba were far more interesting than her prayers to God. Before she knew it, her baba had become an obsession with her. And she couldn't wait to meet him. Every time Charulata told her he would be coming home, she would be on her best behaviour that day only to later learn that his ship had not arrived. Charulata had told her that her father worked on a ship, hence remained on the sea for the longest time. The last time he was with her was when she was two years old and thus she didn't remember it. That too was a lie.

A year later, while cleaning the house, Ekantika found an old black-and-white photograph of a man. She took it to her mother.

'Whose photo is this, ma?'

Charulata took the photograph from her hand, looked at it as if thinking of something and then said, 'That's your baba.'

She had never seen her daughter's face exude the kind of happiness that it did in that very moment.

4

'I have no clue who the friend was, like his name or native place or anything.' Ekantika had told UKC. The latter didn't fire many questions at her except for certain confirmations like where she was when Preeti died. A retelling of Faizaan and Preeti's deaths. UKC only wanted to check if there was any apparent mismatch of details between what Ekantika told him compared to what she had narrated in her statement. There weren't any. Before letting Pradeep and Ekantika leave, UKC asked Pradeep to share with him all the forensics reports and also the supposed killer's video which they had captured from the CCTV footage of the parking lot where Saira was killed. The police had given up on it since the image hadn't led to any concrete face. UKC also asked Pradeep to track down this 'friend' of Faizaan's. According to him, if someone's personal diary was stolen, not many people would know about its existence. Perhaps the friend could throw some light on why he was maintaining a personal diary which, as Ekantika said, had all the information regarding the cello-tape serial killer.

When Pradeep dropped Ekantika back home, she had already made a decision. She understood UKC was far more intelligent than anyone around. And that Faizaan's friend, who actually didn't exist, had to be found by Pradeep so UKC would know once and for all that whatever Ekantika had told them was the truth. But he couldn't be found alive. By the time she entered her home, she'd Googled which trains reached Patna from Delhi the quickest.

That evening itself Ekantika caught the Sampooran Kranti Express, which was supposed to take her to Patna's Rajendra Nagar terminal in eleven hours. She intentionally didn't book a ticket so there would be no proof of her journey. When the TC came calling out for tickets, Ekantika made up a story of her mother's illness, told him she was a student and gave him some cash. After the TC received the cash, he didn't probe further.

During her train journey, she called Taksh and told him she had some tests coming up in Topsie so she wouldn't be able to meet or call him. Taksh was all right with it. He only wanted her to take care. Then she called her mother. Charulata picked up the phone this time.

'I'm sorry, ma,' Ekantika said.

'How could you hide so much from me?' Charulata's voice was still choked. As if she hadn't stopped crying since their last phone call.

'Ma, I know you would have freaked out if I told you I had a boyfriend and I was living-in. So I thought I would tell you when the time was right.'

'*Shonai, bodo ho gechish, na?*' Shonai, you've grown up now.

The call took an emotional turn until Ekantika told her that she had a few UPSC mock tests after which she would call and tell her everything. That everything, she knew, however, would still not have all the details. Like the fact that she was going to Patna for a kill.

To keep her alibi strong, Ekantika called up Guddu bhaiya, the local grocery storekeeper in her area and ordered bread, Maggi, eggs and a Thums Up. She Paytm-ed him the money but asked him to tell the delivery boy to leave the things outside her flat. She was out and would pick them up the moment she was back. In her Paytm, it was recorded she had paid Guddu bhaiya that night.

The only thing that remained now was, once she was in Patna, whom she should select as a target. All she knew was it had to be a random person but the age group had to be around Faizaan's. And he could not be physically very strong, else she wouldn't be able to overpower him.

Later that night, around 10.30 p.m., a young man boarded the train from Kanpur Central station. He had a reservation. But he was surprised to see a girl sitting on his seat.

'Excuse me, that's mine,' he said, sounding meek and polite.

Ekantika looked at him. He was lean. Looked physically weak. From his dress it was evident he belonged to a middle-class family. He looked around Faizaan's age as well.

'I'm sorry, my mother is sick. Didn't have the time for a ticket. So . . .' Ekantika apologized as she stood up. The young man's inner chivalry took over as he said, 'It's okay. I just need a little space to sit.'

'It's your booked seat. I should . . .'

'Not a problem. I'll manage,' the man said.

Ekantika shifted a bit. In her mind, she'd found her target. She only needed to confirm a few things. The young man sat beside her. After a few lame smiles, Ekantika said, 'I'm Rani Tyagi. You?'

'Myself Jaideep,' he sounded surprised that Ekantika had talked to him on her own. She kept the conversation going, cleverly squeezing out the information she needed to confirm him as her target. Jaideep, being the typical Indian male who rarely got any female attention in his life apart from his mother's, enjoyed the attention Ekantika was giving him. By midnight, Ekantika knew he was from a small village in Bihar but lived and worked in Patna for a courier company. He was in Kanpur for official work. Jaideep had also been to Delhi a few times. That was it. When Ekantika and Jaideep decided to sleep in a sitting position, she intentionally laid her head on his shoulder. It was to create the illusion of an emotional connect. After that, no man like Jaideep would say no to her requests which would be made the next morning.

In the morning, when Patna was a few stations away, she asked, 'I don't know where to go the whole day.'

'Why, what happened?' Jaideep asked. His inner knight-in-shining-armour had been activated from the time he felt her head on his shoulder.

'The bus to my village is in the afternoon,' she said with a helpless face. Jaideep immediately replied, 'Of course you can freshen up at my place if you don't have a problem.'

As suggested by Jaideep, Ekantika accompanied him to his place in Rukanpura after the train reached Patna. Her mother called while they were on their way. Ekantika told her she would call her later as she was studying. She replied to Taksh's messages normally, as if she was at home in Delhi, preparing for the tests.

The place was a mess. Though Jaideep didn't show it, he was overjoyed to have a girl in his home. He was quick to apologize, telling her that apart from his few male friends, she was the first girl to have stepped in there. She didn't mind it. She excused herself to go to the washroom to freshen up. She remained there for some time, not doing anything except keeping the water tap open. After ten minutes, she called out to Jaideep.

'Jaideep, could you please hand me my towel and fresh clothes? I forgot them in my bag. Now I'm all naked. Can't come out,' she said. The last mention was deliberate. She wanted some sexual tension creeping in. She'd read in a psychology book that when a man is charged up sexually, his brain stops working for other things and he drops his defences.

At first, Jaideep thought he hadn't heard her right. He was preparing tea in the kitchen. He filtered the tea into two cups and then went to the bedroom to pick up the towel and clothes from her bag.

With a slight shiver he knocked on the bathroom door. It opened. He put his hand forward with the towel first. He was expecting Ekantika, Rani for him, to take the towel but she pushed the door wide open. She was fully dressed. Before he could do anything, she leaped on to him with the cloth she had taken inside, which was now drenched with chloroform. The suddenness of the attack didn't allow Jaideep to fight back. He lost consciousness soon enough. She did the needful after that with the cello-tapes she'd kept ready.

Ekantika went to the kitchen, sipped her tea, flushed his tea in the sink, washed the cups and made sure there was no sign another person had been in that place. She also wiped her fingerprints from all the places she had touched. She punched Faizaan's number into Jaideep's phone and saved it. She made a call as well but ended it before it was picked up. She waited after that. When Jaideep came to his senses, she watched him die as she had watched Preeti die. After that, she ordered some breakfast on Zomato for her home in Delhi. Another ruse if anyone questioned her alibi.

Ekantika took the same train, followed the same method of bribing the TC with cash and a sob story, and was back at New Delhi railway station in thirteen hours.

As she picked up the eggs, bread, and breakfast from her doorstep, Ekantika's phone rang, flashing her mother's name.

'Where are you, Shonai? I'm standing outside your flat in Karol Bagh. And there's someone else staying here,' Charulata said.

5

The one good thing Preeti had done on her trip to Bihar, following one of the cello-tape killer's victims, was to brief the Patna police on the case and request them to contact her if they found anything related to it. Now they had a dead body killed with the modus operandi of the serial killer she had been chasing.

It was Inspector Gagan who received the call from the Patna police. One minute into the call and he knew he had to involve ACP Pradeep immediately.

He updated Pradeep about the murder of Jaideep Kumar. By the time he was done, the Patna police informed them that they hadn't found any diary in his belongings but in his phone contacts, there was a Faizaan Ahmad saved. As they matched the number, Pradeep realized it was the deceased Faizaan Ahmad's number. *It can't be a coincidence,* Pradeep thought and asked Gagan to collect as much information from the Patna police and share the report with him.

'Also, find out if Jaideep Kumar or his family had any connection with the cello-tape killing.'

Gagan went straight to work. Pradeep called up Ekantika immediately.

'Hello sir,' she said, while sitting in an auto rickshaw which was taking her to Karol Bagh.

'Does the name Jaideep Kumar ring any bells?' Ekantika smiled to herself cunningly and said, 'Not really; why sir?'

'I'll tell you later,' Pradeep said and ended the call. Ekantika sighed, feeling relieved. *Everything had gone smoothly*, she thought. Now UKC wouldn't question her audio statement or revisit it with questions, she was sure.

Ekantika reached her old apartment in Karol Bagh where Charulata had set her up before leaving for Baruipur two years back. A lot had happened since then. None of which Charulata had any hint of, Ekantika thought as she asked the auto rickshaw driver to stop by the building's main gate. She was about to pay him off when she saw her mother standing by the gate.

'Ek minute, bhaiya,' she said and climbed down from the auto rickshaw.

'What are you doing outside?' she asked.

'Don't ask me questions,' Charulata said.

'Let's go home first.' Ekantika almost pulled her, picking up one of her bags.

Charulata followed her. She looked pissed off with her daughter. Ekantika took the same auto rickshaw back to her place in Old Rajendra Nagar. They didn't talk in the auto rickshaw except for Ekantika asking her why didn't she tell her she was coming, to which Charulata gave her a piercing look-whose-talking glance.

Once home, Charulata asked, 'Now I want to know what's going on, Shonai. I get to know from a news channel that you are living-in with a guy? He is no more. And now when I come here, you aren't even living where I left you? Did you intend to hide everything from your mother?'

She sounded hurt. There was pain, ego, pride—everything concocted in a dangerous emotional mix in the way she spoke. Ekantika took a deep breath and told her of all that had happened in the last two years, confining her revelations to those things that she could no longer hide from her mother.

'You were staying with a boy?' Charulata sounded scandalized.

Ekantika rolled her eyes. She had anticipated her mother would lose her temper about the matter.

'I loved him, ma. I know I'm guilty of not telling you anything about him but . . .'

'What all haven't you told me, Shonai?'

In the next half an hour, Ekantika told her more. This time focusing on how Faizaan died, when she shifted here and why the female journalist, Kisha Bhargav, was at her place after the assistant SI's death.

Charulata hugged Ekantika tight and with an emotional voice and moist eyes said, 'You know how much I love you, Shonai. There's nobody for me but you. I understand you are a young girl now. And you won't share everything with me like you used to . . .'

Ekantika broke the embrace and looked into her mother's eyes. Her own eyes welled up with tears. She knew in her bones all that Charulata had undergone to make her reach where she was in life.

'Don't say that, ma. I would have told you. Maybe after some time. But I would have surely told you,' Ekantika said.

'I trust you,' Charulata smiled through her tears. Then she looked around. 'How is this place?'

Ekantika helped her inspect every nook and corner of the flat.

'You shifted here all by yourself?' Charulata couldn't hide her surprise.

'No, Taksh helped.'

The mention of Taksh's name brought a smile to Charulata's face. The kind that happens when one mentions spring amidst teeth-stuttering winter. And with that, Ekantika understood what Charulata had in mind when she gave her number to Shukla maashi.

'He is a nice guy, isn't he?' Charulata asked.

'Yes,' Ekantika said.

'Let's call him over for dinner. I also want to meet him. Does he live nearby?'

Ekantika nodded and messaged Taksh: *Hi, my mother is here. She wants you to come over for dinner. Possible?*

A minute later, Taksh's reply came: *Sure. Tonight?*

Yes. But let's meet outside before. Works?

Ekantika left for her classes at Topsie. She explained to Charulata thoroughly that she should not open the door if any journalist came. After Topsie, Ekantika met Taksh at a nearby cafe.

'So, what's this secret meeting before the dinner?' Taksh asked jocularly.

'All right, my mother came here without any prior notice.'

'Prior notice?' Taksh laughed at the manner in which she put it.

'And right now, I can't have her here. What I've understood from talking to her is that she wants us to hook up.'

'Us?'

'Sorry, not hook up. Get married, probably.'

'What?' Taksh realized this conversation already had a tumultuous graph within one minute.

'She didn't say it directly but . . . you know Indian parents. Their indirect allusion is direct enough.'

Taksh laughed some more.

'So, let's pretend we are in love and will soon be a couple.'

'So that she gets us married?' Taksh looked surprised.

'No! So she leaves for Baruipur soon. Once she knows her daughter is being protected by someone, she will relax. More so if that someone was chosen by her.'

Taksh gave her an awed look.

'What?' she shrugged.

'You think pretty meticulously.'

Ekantika smiled at him.

'Done deal. When I come to your place tonight, I will be totally in love with you.'

'Me too.'

They shared a laugh. Ekantika didn't exactly know when Taksh had become a buddy for her. He was someone with whom she could be herself without the fear of being judged. The best thing about Taksh, she felt, was that he never probed unless asked to. Much like Faizaan. He knew how to give someone just the kind of space which made them comfortable with him. And he was never scared of being friend-zoned. Probably, he too was looking for a friend in Ekantika to begin with. Or so she thought.

'By the way, I heard that the Patna police found Faizaan's friend dead. Probably killed by the cello-tape killer himself,' Taksh said. There was a buzz about it in his office.

'Yeah, I also heard so, but I don't know the details.'

'Such cases are a rarity,' Taksh said, adding a little sugar to his coffee like always.

'Why?'

'I've been part of some murder cases before. This is my first serial killing case. But I've always found something or the other in the crime scene. Not that it led to the killer always but something which proved useful in the case. But in this . . . nothing.'

'Is that a problem?'

'Not a problem. But unusual. Just goes to show how minute the planning has been.'

'Hmm.'

Ekantika left soon after they finished their coffee telling him that she would wait for him around 8 p.m. at her place.

Later that evening, ACP Pradeep and Inspector Gagan reached UKC's house. They had taken a prior appointment from him. Pradeep had updated him about the development in Patna over a phone call. By then, Gagan had also learnt that there was nothing in Jaideep's or his family's past connecting them with the serial killer.

'There was a phone contact named Faizaan whose number is the same as that of Faizaan Ahmad who was killed,' UKC spoke as the two police officers settled opposite him. He continued, 'Whereas Faizaan Ahmad's phone contact list didn't have any Jaideep Kumar's name.'

'Right sir,' Inspector Gagan said. Pradeep gave him a look. UKC didn't like people speaking up when they were not asked to. UKC didn't react though. He looked totally immersed in his own thoughts.

'However, if it was the other way around, it would have made more sense from Ekantika's statement. She'd said in her audio statement that Faizaan had sent messages to Jaideep but he didn't respond. It means Faizaan's phone must have had Jaideep's number. If Jaideep didn't respond and was out of touch with Faizaan then, ideally, we should have found Jaideep's number in Faizaan's phone. At least the old one, if this was a new number. That's because the one who goes out of touch, generally, is the one who deletes the other's number first. And yet Faizaan Ahmad's phone didn't have his number. Jaideep did. Interesting.'

The police officers frowned.

'But who knows, this could be an exception as well,' said UKC. Their frowns disappeared.

'May I, please?' Pradeep asked softly.

UKC nodded.

'There's some information we received while we were coming here.'

'When were you planning to tell me that?' UKC sounded his normal self; rude.

'Sorry. After the body was found, Jaideep's phone was given to the cyber cell. They told me that their initial investigation shows that Jaideep had tried to call Faizaan only around the time he died. Never before did Jaideep message or call Faizaan Ahmad's number from his phone.'

'This means two things: either Jaideep had changed his phone number. And never gave the number to Faizaan. This also answers my initial query as to why Jaideep would have his number while Faizaan's phone didn't. Or did Jaideep want to tell Faizaan something about the killer? Which means he didn't know Faizaan was already dead. Or . . .'

The officers sat forward in anticipation.

'The second scenario is, Jaideep was killed and Faizaan Ahmad's number was fed into his phone so we'd think he is indeed his friend.'

'Why would the killer do so?' Pradeep asked.

UKC looked at him in such a condescending manner that Pradeep felt he was going to abuse him. Instead UKC calmly asked, 'Did the Patna police get the diary which the killer had supposedly stolen from Ekantika's place?'

Pradeep shook his head in the negative.

'But if the killer had stolen the diary, then why would we find it at Jaideep's place?' Gagan asked.

'Ekantika had said that Faizaan had told her the diary belonged to his friend. We wanted to get to his friend because we thought the friend could possibly be the killer. And if this was true, then why would the killer kill himself?' It was UKC trying to see the same thing from different perspectives.

Sometimes one missed nailing a murderer, UKC believed, because one failed to understand his perspective.

Pradeep and Gagan looked at each other, clueless. An uncomfortable silence followed.

'My instinct says we aren't after one killer. We are after four killers.'

'Four?' Pradeep said and realized he could have been a little subtle in his pitch.

'One original cello-tape serial killer. And three copycat killers.'

UKC's face stretched to form a faint smile. The kind which appeared when a case started to become interesting in a complicated way.

6

'Thanks Taksh,' Ekantika said. They had come down from her flat after Taksh was treated to a sumptuous Bengali dinner.

'Thanks? Are you kidding me? I should thank you. It was such a . . .' He burped and added, 'Sorry. The food was too good.'

'Ma prepared it. I helped a little.'

'And that presentation with all the bowls around the main plate?'

'She was serving you assuming her *jamai* had come home.'

'Jamai?'

'That's Bengali for son-in-law,' she said with an amused smile.

'Ah, now I get it. But I must tell you, your mother is pretty hot.'

Ekantika's eyes widened as she looked at him.

'I mean she has maintained herself well.'

'I know what you mean. If I wasn't your friend then you would have termed her a MILF, right?'

Taksh stood there with a guilty face.

'It's funny how we as a society bracket women across ages. If a forty-five-plus-year-old woman maintains her physique, she is a MILF because we are used to a certain image of Indian women at that age. Just as if a young girl of my age parties, wears revealing clothes and goes out with men, she is a slut for the majority. Whereas if a forty-five-year-old uncle maintains his body, we don't have a term like DILF for him. Or do we?'

'I didn't mean it that way, but I know what you mean. Society is hopeless. And DILF is legit funny,' Taksh said, not realizing a fun jibe would take a serious turn.

'No. Society's rules are good. They maintain a certain overall sanity. Except that times have changed. The rules need to be updated and made gender neutral.' Ekantika paused and then continued in a contemplative tone, 'After my baba's death, do you know how my mother brought me up? She was a surrogate for wealthy infertile couples. She had to keep her physique intact. She always tells me that a mother can go to any distance to protect her offspring.'

Taksh was quiet. He didn't know what to say.

'I'm sorry,' Ekantika said, controlling her tears. 'All I want is that she remains happy always. And that's why I thanked you. You agreed to do what I asked. I'm sure she is convinced we are going to marry in time to come.'

Taksh managed a smile. So did she. His Uber arrived. He climbed in after giving Ekantika a tight hug.

Charulata, standing by the bedroom window of the flat, saw them both. She smiled looking at the two. She prayed in her heart, hoping the two would make it together in life.

Ekantika was correct when she'd told Taksh about her mother leaving early if she knew there was someone to take care of her. Charulata left two days later. From the time Ekantika had joined college in Baruipur, Charulata had started to teach young girls, whose parents couldn't sponsor their education. She wasn't giving them academic lessons. As she told Ekantika, she was training them in certain soft skills, which she knew they could use to get some kind of job somewhere. She had three girls to begin with and by the time Ekantika moved out for Delhi, the number had grown to fifteen. Now, Charulata had thirty girls in her class. She had to rush back to Baruipur for them.

Taksh was in Karol Bagh for some work. He'd asked Ekantika if they could catch up for some lunch. She agreed. He told her he would meet her by the Karol Bagh metro station. Ekantika had almost reached there when a voice called out her name. She turned to notice Kisha Bhargav, the journalist.

'Hi, how are you?' Kisha asked.

'I'm good. How are you?'

'Fine. I wanted to talk to you,' Kisha said pleadingly.

'That means it's not a coincidence we are seeing each other now?' Ekantika sounded stern. She didn't want to do anything on television any more.

'I'm sorry to stalk you like this but our last interview was a major success. The TRPs were crazy.'

'So?'

'I was wondering if we could do a one-to-one interview with you.'

'You know I told you . . .'

'Please hear me out. It's not about the case as such. Not about who the killer could be and all that.'

'Then?'

'We want to focus on the love story you had with Faizaan. It's an aspirational love story.'

'I don't think that's a good idea,' Ekantika said, looking around to see if Taksh was there so she could excuse herself from Kisha and move on.

'Why? India needs such a secular love story today. They will love it.'

'Listen, you don't have . . .' Ekantika stopped, averted her eyes and said, 'Hey Taksh.' Kisha turned to see whom she was referring to.

'Sorry, my friend is here,' Ekantika said. Kisha's jaw had fallen by then. Taksh stopped for a second, then came up to Ekantika.

'Hey,' he said, softly. Looking at Kisha, Ekantika realized something was wrong.

'You have my number. We will connect later,' Kisha said and scurried away.

Ekantika gave her a puzzled look, then turned to Taksh.

'What was she saying?' Taksh asked.

'You know her?' Ekantika asked. He was silent.

'Oh my God!' Ekantika exclaimed. 'That's your ex?'

Taksh nodded. As they took the metro and went to CP for lunch, Ekantika told Taksh how and why she'd met Kisha before. And that she was asking for an interview about her love story with Faizaan now.

It was only after they'd ordered in the Chinese restaurant they went to, that Taksh brought the subject up.

'I think you should say yes.'

Ekantika gave him a look and asked, 'Why?'

'It would help her career. Also, now that she knows you and has a feeling I'm your friend, if you say no, she would think I made you say no.'

'Damn, you still love her, isn't it?' Somehow, Ekantika found it appealing.

'If you love someone from a distance, you will love the person for the longest,' he said, finishing the water from his glass.

'Oh yes! How could I forget that? You'll forever love her like this? From a distance?'

'I will. Love, when in the bracket of a relationship, transforms with time. For better or worse. But the kind of love that is free of any brackets remains just the way it began. Same intensity. Same madness,' he said, beaming.

'All right, I'll call her and say yes to the interview,' Ekantika said. While Taksh was talking, she was calculating in her mind. It wasn't a bad idea. She would remain in the news. She would have public sympathy, which may come in handy any time if the police still showed some lag in the case.

After they were done with lunch, she left but instead of Old Rajendra Nagar, she went to Gurugram. To Anjuman Baghiya where Faizaan's grave was.

She had bought some flowers from CP itself. It was evening by the time she entered the cemetery and went to stand in front of Faizaan's grave. She put the flowers she'd bought on the grave. Then knelt down staring at it. There were numerous thoughts in her mind . . .

I'm sorry, Faizaan. I know that nothing I say or do will ever absolve me of this sin and crime, both, which I've committed. Pretty wilfully. I know I killed you. I had to. Otherwise my mind, my body, my soul wouldn't have rested in peace ever. But please do believe that what I never planned was falling in love with you so passionately, so desperately and so insanely. I love you and always will. Whether you forgive me or not, Ekantika will always be yours, Faizaan. Now that you have gone to your heavenly abode, I can tell you what I've never told anybody. My baba, my father, didn't die of pneumonia. He was the last victim of the cello-tape killer. And I won't rest in peace till he is caught. And punished.

'I love you,' Ekantika muttered under her breath, stood up and left the place.

Ekantika: 8–13 Years Old

Her father's photograph became a holy object for Ekantika. She kept it with her every time she stepped out of the house to go to the local market with Charulata or to her school. She had been shifted to a private school from Standard Two onwards. And here nobody teased her in any way. In fact, everyone loved her because she was an ace at studies and sports.

Though the report card or class test results were signed by Charulata, they were first shown to her baba. She treated the photograph as an entity which, in her mind, used to talk back to her giving her suggestions and advice whenever needed. A time came when she confided in her baba more than her ma. But she never received the answer to one question.

'When are you coming back, baba?'

With another surrogacy going successfully, Charulata shifted home. This house was better than the first. It was also a new locality. And when a single mother and her daughter stepped in, the male gaze didn't spare them. In particular, the eyes of Dhononjoy Adhikary.

He was a forty-four-year-old government bank employee who stayed with his ailing mother and an authoritative elder sister who was a spinster. He lived two houses away from Charulata's newly rented house. He noticed Ekantika for the first time from the window of his room, when she was going with Charulata to the vegetable market. He had immediately masturbated standing right there by the window. From then on, he never let go of any moment to watch her surreptitiously. From the local males, who gathered at Ghonsha's tea stall every evening to gossip, he learnt that Charulata's husband didn't stay with her. The information emboldened Dhononjoy.

He started visiting Charulata's place pretending to offer a helping hand. And every time Charulata invited him inside for a cup of tea, for etiquette's sake, he used to come out and spread the gossip amongst Ghonsha's tea stall members that she was trying to seduce him because of his bachelor status and settled government job.

In a month, he started telling the males that Charulata had slept with him when actually, whenever he went in, his eyes were seeking out Ekantika. Neither the mother nor the daughter, unaware of the gossip, minded his home visits because he started helping Ekantika with mathematics. But what he was actually looking forward to was some time alone with her. Finally, the opportunity presented itself one evening when Charulata asked him to wait while she went out to fetch some sugar from the nearby shop so she could prepare tea for him.

As Charulata went out, Dhononjoy who was teaching Ekantika, suddenly started rubbing his hand on her bare thighs above the hem of her frock. The touch didn't feel good and she jerked his hand off.

'What happened to you, uncle?' she asked. Dhononjoy smiled and said, 'This is a game.'

'What game?'

'The touch game. I will touch you somewhere. You will touch me on my body somewhere,' he said.

'I've played touch and run, but this is a new one,' she said.

'You'll enjoy it,' he said and touched her chest. There was a perverse satisfaction on his face.

'Uncle, who wins this game and how?'

'First, don't call me uncle when your mother is not around.'

'Then what should I call you?'

'Call me baba.' Dhononjoy said, this time putting his hand on her nape.

Ekantika did not recall what happened next. All she knew was her mother was shocked when she returned while Dhononjoy rushed out of the house with a blood-smeared shirt and a compass jabbed in his right eye.

Nobody can take my baba's place, Ekantika muttered under her breath, her body shuddering with anger.

Within a fortnight, Charulata had to vacate the house owing to the pressure from the neighbours. Dhononjoy, after losing the vision of his right eye forever, had made sure people hit the mother-daughter where it hurt the most. He told everyone the mother was a professional escort and she wanted her daughter to follow her profession. When Dhononjoy protested, the daughter took away his vision.

Charulata didn't fight the men. For she feared they would somehow scar Ekantika forever. She decided to remain pragmatic and shifted homes once again, going to live in another neighbourhood of Baruipur.

This time their neighbour was a warm lady and her young son. The husband worked in the Gulf. Ekantika called her Shukla maashi. They were there for a year, after which

Mrs Shukla and her son, Taksh, shifted to the Gulf with her husband.

Stepping into puberty, Ekantika wasn't the same gullible girl any more. Looking back, she now knew what Dhononjoy had been doing to her. She had grown up quickly with a high EQ and IQ. She understood more, talked less. She now knew where her mother disappeared to for nine months at a time, but didn't confront her about it. She knew Charulata was subjecting her body to all the pain, so she could study. And study she did. She was a topper all through. She won all the school Olympiads and extempores and shared it all with her baba.

Now that she had grown up, Ekantika knew she had her father's chin, nose and jawline. But she also knew by now she would never meet her father. A year ago, Charulata had told her that he was coming to meet her. He was in Bihar to meet a friend when he died of pneumonia. So close, yet so far. Ekantika went into self-subjected reticence. She even stopped talking to her father's photograph.

Apart from studies, the only thing she did was binge on crime shows on TV. This was something that she'd picked up from Charulata. One day, the crime show that she watched regularly showcased one of the country's unsolved serial killing cases. The cello-tape serial killer case. Ekantika was shocked out of her wits to see her father's picture as one of the victims of the killer. Her mother had lied to her. He hadn't died of pneumonia. He was coming to meet his daughter and this killer had intercepted his journey.

She felt her life had come to an end.

7

UKC hadn't slept well. And he was happy about it. He always maintained that one who slept well is a contented person. And UKC never wanted to be content while working on a case. The sleeplessness only proved to him that his mind was constantly thinking about the cello-tape serial killer case.

To be specific, he was thinking about the recent murders. Of Nagma, Faizaan, Saira, Preeti and Jaideep. Nagma was related to Faizaan who was related to Saira who was related to Preeti through her son's death and finally, Preeti was related to Jaideep again via Faizaan's death investigation. A link in the recent murders had been established pretty easily unlike the original serial murders in the 1990s in which no dots had been joined till date. This led him to consider that the concept of copycat murders was true in this case. Or had the original killer lost his randomness and was now killing to prove something? Sometimes patterns change in serial killing cases as well. But after twenty-one years? UKC couldn't accept it wholeheartedly.

As he did some research into the history of serial killings, by listening to audio books on the subject, he learnt that copycat murders took place because of the glorification of the original killer in the media. Becoming famous was part of the deal. And most of the people taking part in copycat murders had past criminal records as well as poor mental health. The media part in the cello-tape serial killing didn't hold much ground because the murders began in the years before cable TV news became popular in India.. News channels were few and most of the reporting was done by newspapers. That too whenever a killing happened. There wasn't much glorification of the killer as such.

UKC's gut told him there was some clue hidden within the killing of the last five victims, which had taken place within the span of a few months. It was as if the killer was in a hurry, knowing that the killings were being investigated actively. He asked Neema to call Pradeep and ask him to round up all of Nagma's close friends and take their statements about the kind of relationship Nagma and Faizaan had. Whether there was any third person involved. Whether Nagma had mentioned a certain Jaideep, her boyfriend's supposed friend, to them. In particular, he asked that the statements be video-recorded so he could watch them speak. Neema made a note to call Pradeep and then switched the television on to a news channel that was telecasting Ekantika's interview. The television in the house was switched on only when something case-related was being shown.

Ekantika was ensconced on a sofa while Kisha was opposite her. They were in the news channel's Noida studio. The backdrop had a blown-up picture of Ekantika and Faizaan together, projecting the perfect love story to the audience. The name of the programme was *Pyaar Koi Khel Nahi*

(Love Isn't a Game). Ekantika had told Charulata about it so she could also watch it without it coming as a surprise.

The show, as promised, focused on her love story with Faizaan. How they met, where they met, when did they decide to live together, did their parents know about them, any funny or romantic memories, how she found him dead. Ekantika made sure she didn't mention the Miss Mixo part in her interview. It was something really private and she didn't want to make it public. In between, as Ekantika talked, the channel showed photographs of them together to rouse the viewers' emotions well. The show ended in fifty minutes.

As Ekantika's mic was being taken off, she looked at Kisha. She had sensed an awkward energy working between them since she met Kisha after knowing she was Taksh's ex.

'Thanks for this, Ekantika,' Kisha said in a professional manner.

'Can we talk for some time?' Ekantika asked.

'Sure,' Kisha said, sensing this wasn't going to be something professional.

Kisha took Ekantika to the coffee vending machine first. Took two paper cups of black coffee and walked out to the smoking zone. She offered her a cigarette. Ekantika took it saying, 'Faizaan loved it.'

'I'm sure you miss it with Taksh. He doesn't smoke,' Kisha said curtly. By then, she had guessed why Ekantika wanted to talk to her.

'Just wanted to clarify; Taksh and I are friends. There's no romance brewing between us.'

Kisha blew out a puff of smoke and smirked.

'Even if there was something, why would you tell me? I hope Taksh told you we are done with each other.'

'Yes, he told me everything.'

'Everything? Great. He must have turned me into a nice little bitch who couldn't handle a relationship, isn't that so?'

Ekantika wanted to clarify when a colleague of Kisha peeped around the door, 'Kish, boss calling.'

'You have to excuse me. And it's perfectly fine if you guys are dating or not dating or whatever. I'm done with him.' She dropped her cigarette on the floor and stamped on it before going inside.

Ekantika continued to smoke. The smoke puffs reminded her of Faizaan. Then she remembered another man who was dead too. Her baba. She opened her bag and took out a hard copy of a photograph. She stared at it for some time till her cigarette burnt out. By that time, her eyes moistened. The tears only solidified her promise to her baba. A daughter will avenge her father's death. Come what may.

Taksh, who was in the area, decided to drop by Ekantika's home that night. He had messaged her before. It was only when she said she was okay with him coming over, that he dropped by.

The moment she opened the door for him, he knew she was drunk.

'I'm sorry. Drank with Faizaan after a long time. Come in,' she almost pulled Taksh inside and locked the door. Taksh noticed an untouched glass of alcohol on the centre table.

'Faizaan loves Miss Mixo, so . . .' she said, slumping on the sofa. Taksh sat opposite her.

'Sorry you have to make your own drink,' she said.

'Sure.'

Taksh knew where things were kept. He went to the kitchen, got himself a glass and made himself a drink with whisky, soda and some ice. He sat opposite her again.

'Cheers,' she said.

Taksh raised his glass and said, 'The interview went well?'

'Yeah. Kisha didn't mention you. But I have a feeling she thinks we are dating,' Ekantika said and laughed.

Taksh smirked with a nod and said, 'That makes two people who think we are dating. Kisha and your mother.'

He knew that was an obvious assumption Kisha would make. That was one perennial complaint of his against her. She never looked beyond the obvious. He sipped his whisky. And picked up a couple of chips from the bowl on the table.

It was then his eyes went on to a hard copy photograph on the table beside the bowl. It was a black and white close-up of a man. He picked it up and looked at it closely. One thing which caught his eye was that the man's nose and chin resembled Ekantika's.

'That's my father. Wasn't he handsome?' Ekantika said. She had finished her drink. She was grabbing the pillow which she had placed on her tummy with both hands.

'He was.'

'I never met him though. He died when ma was pregnant with me. This is the only connect of mine with him.'

Taksh didn't know what to say.

'Well, even I had a pretty disturbing relationship with my dad. So much so that it kept tormenting me till I was a young adult. Childhood is so fragile. Sometimes, we also don't know what scars we carry to our adulthood,' Taksh said in a trance-like voice. Then he looked at Ekantika and smiled. She had dozed off with her eyes closed and mouth open. Taksh went to her, made her lie down on the sofa. He went to the bedroom, brought out a blanket and covered her with it. He finished his drink. And then switching the lights off, he left. Ekantika was awake but she was drunk. She pretended to be asleep so she didn't blurt out any information which wasn't meant for Taksh. Sometime after Taksh had left, she actually slept.

It was a busy morning. Pradeep was going through all the files on his table. Though there were three or four more cases he was investigating, he preferred to read the file with Preeti's phone call records. As he studied it for some time, he realized there were too many calls between Preeti and Ekantika. He checked the dates. Most of them had happened after she had shifted to a new place from Preeti's. And also on the day Preeti was found dead. Not that this discovery led to anything concrete in his mind, but he did call up Neema to relay this information. During the call, Neema asked Pradeep to line up all of Nagma's friends and video record their statements as per UKC's insistence.

In the evening, Pradeep called Ekantika, asking her to video call a certain number at 7.30 p.m. sharp. The number belonged to Neema. Ekantika was alert. She did ask Pradeep what the video call was about, but he didn't tell her much. She thought of a lot of questions which UKC could ask her but she could never have anticipated the one he did ask her.

'Did you know Preeti at a personal level also?' he asked. Though it was a video call, Ekantika could see Neema while she heard UKC talk.

'Not that much,' she said.

'Then any special reason why there were so many calls between her number and yours? Especially on the day of her murder?'

Ekantika knew she didn't have much time to frame a foolproof lie. Nor could she confess the truth. She decided to go with a half-truth. It took UKC by surprise as well.

8

Ekantika sounded confident when she said that Preeti was trying to gain some sexual favours from her, by calling her incessantly and trying to convince her to come on a date She hadn't reported this to the police, Ekantika told UKC, because she didn't want to tarnish a dead person's name unless pushed for it.

The day when she'd emotionally broken down and Preeti had hugged her, pressing her a little too tightly, Ekantika had understood it wasn't just a woman to woman touch. It was more. Till then she had only seen Preeti eyeing her from time to time.

Ekantika also knew there was a camera inside the bathroom in Preeti's flat. That's why she was careful not to give any facial shot to the cam. She was playing with Preeti in the hope that she would be of some help if the need arose. She didn't know help would mean killing her altogether. To justify her claim, Ekantika asked UKC to look for her bathing video in Preeti's phone that the latter shot without her permission or knowledge.

After the video call with Ekantika ended, UKC told Neema to cross-check the video part with Pradeep, who asked the cyber cell to update him immediately. By the time they called him, Pradeep was having dinner with his family. His daughters were talking about some movie while his wife was informing him about some relative's gastro issues. Pradeep was not listening to a word of what she was saying. His mind was someplace else. Preeti had shot a nude video of Ekantika? The cyber cell told him they had found the video before, but there were a lot of other porn videos on her phone so they thought it was one of them as there was no face in the video. *Preeti was a lesbian?* Pradeep didn't know about the concept of a bisexual. Humans were either straight, gay or lesbian for him. And now when he thought back as to why she had been dry during their last few sexual escapades, he understood Ekantika must be telling the truth. It also made him consider the drought his sex life was experiencing now that Preeti was gone.

The woman with whom he was having sex in the room when Preeti came in was a prostitute whom he'd hired only to teach Preeti a lesson. He was sure she would apologize and they would revert to their old arrangement. Nothing of that sort happened and now the side-effect of not having the kind of fetish sex he wanted was making him irritable as a person.

It wasn't that he hated his wife. The constant need for a sexual thrill was what had made his wife look boring in comparison. And Pradeep wasn't the let-me-have-sex-for-money kind. He loved an emotional connect before he took a woman. He was a demisexual of sorts. But that needed time. With Preeti, he had invested that time. There was nobody in the vicinity after her. As Pradeep finished his dinner and went to wash his hands, his phone started ringing.

'Who is it?' he asked his wife.

'Unknown number,' she replied, still having her dinner. Pradeep came and took the call.

'Hello sir, this is Taksh Shukla from forensics.'

'Oh, hello Taksh, tell me.'

'Sorry to bother you at this hour but I had something to share.'

'No problem. Tell me.'

'This is about assistant SI Preeti Jangra's death.' Taksh had Pradeep's full attention now. By the time the call ended, Pradeep had a feeling it was a good development as far as the case was concerned.

Ekantika was in her class in Topsie when she received a screenshot of a chat from Taksh. She opened the message to realize it was a chat between Taksh and Kisha. As the teacher carried on with his lecture, Ekantika couldn't stop herself from going through the chat.

Kisha: *Hi.*

Taksh: *Hello. I thought you'd blocked me.*

Kisha: *I had. Unblocked just now.*

Taksh: *Thanks for the clarification. Felt good.*

Kisha: *You have many things to thank me for.*

Taksh: *Of course.*

Kisha: *What's up with this girl Ekantika?*

Taksh: *What?*

Kisha: *Are you guys dating?*

Taksh: *No.*

Kisha: *Good.*

After five minutes.

Taksh: *Hello? Blocked me again? Great!*

Ekantika smiled reading the last line. The fact that Kisha had made it a point to unblock Taksh and ask what she did, told Ekantika that what she'd felt talking to Kisha at the smoking zone was true. Kisha hadn't moved on. Else this chat wouldn't have happened. And perhaps the hatred which she had for Taksh was only a layer of dust over her love for him. Ekantika knew Taksh wouldn't reach out to Kisha. But she couldn't let this love story remain incomplete. She was already living one incomplete story. That had to remain incomplete because of her own demons. Her own mission.

Weird, isn't it? Did she tell you anything? Taksh messaged.

No. In class. TTYL. Ekantika responded.

After Topsie, she went to the Noida office of the news channel. The security told her Kisha was inside. Ekantika waited outside for some time; then realized it was a stupid idea. She messaged Kisha instead: *Meet me at Starbucks, DLF Mall at 3 p.m. Need to share something urgent.* It was a bait.

Kisha called her a couple of times, but she didn't pick up, nor did she respond to her messages. She had simply gone to Starbucks, taken a frappé for herself and studied there, sitting alone. Till around 3 p.m., when Kisha joined her.

'What happened? Where's your phone?'

'I forgot it at home.'

'But you messaged!'

'Yes, then moved out. Forgetting the phone at home,' Ekantika lied. By then, Kisha had settled opposite her.

'Coffee?' Ekantika asked.

'No. Too much coffee already today. So, what's the urgent thing you wanted to share? Any update on the case?'

'Taksh loves you,' Ekantika said, removing her books from the table and putting them inside her bag.

Kisha was visibly taken aback. Then she said, 'And he chose you as his mouthpiece? Can't he simply say this himself?' There was hurt in her voice. Ekantika didn't blame her.

'Taksh loves you but doesn't want to be in a relationship with you.'

Kisha looked at her for a few seconds and then laughed.

'Does that even make sense?'

'I know, right? Even I didn't understand it at first. But I wouldn't have cared to waste my time here with you if I didn't feel it in my guts that he genuinely loves you.'

Kisha gave her a thoughtful look.

'So what do you want me to do?'

'I don't want to trigger any action in you. I only wanted to tell you that he still loves you. If you think you should do something about it, it's up to you. I won't interfere henceforth. After all, it's between Taksh and you,' Ekantika said and picking up her bag, added the last bit which she knew would make the difference, 'But you seem like a mature girl to me who wouldn't take any rash decisions. Certainly not something about which you would repent later in life. Take care.' Ekantika flung her bag on her shoulder and moved off. Kisha remained still for some time. Then she unlocked her phone, and went to her WhatsApp, to her block list. There was only one number. A moment later she unblocked it. And typed a message.

UKC had a deep frown on his face. Pradeep was sitting at some distance from him on the couch, sipping tea. He had told him what Taksh had called for. Forensics had found out that the cello-tapes on Preeti's nose and mouth had only her fingerprints. Nobody else's. And that chloroform wasn't used in her case. It was the first time it happened that way. Never in the history of the cello-tape serial killings had there been any fingerprint on the tapes. Not even in the recent killings. It stood out as a strong odd point.

'Even if we consider that Preeti was probably trying to fight the killer and thus the fingerprints were on her tapes, it doesn't hold water because the obvious thing is to tie her hands first and then tape her. Nobody tapes before and then ties the hands. Unless one is unconscious. But then if she was unconscious, how could she fight the killer? Also, as forensics states, chloroform wasn't used in her case. So she wasn't unconscious for sure.' Pradeep made his thoughts clear. UKC heard him quietly and then went into his own pensive mode.

'This discovery takes me to an absurd line of thinking. It is as if Preeti was trying to kill herself,' UKC finally said.

'Exactly. There was no reason for her to kill herself. That too by copying the cello-tape killer,' Pradeep said, finishing the tea. He put the cup on the centre table.

'There have been only two aberrations till now in the recent killings,' UKC said. He wasn't looking at anything in particular.

'What are those?' Pradeep asked.

'One is this. Preeti's fingerprints on the tapes.'

Pradeep nodded.

'The other is Ekantika being alive. I don't think any of the killer's victims have been alive till date.'

'That's correct.'

'And in that flat, Preeti was there when Ekantika was attacked. While Preeti's dead body was reported by Ekantika.'

Pradeep frowned, trying to figure out the link he thought UKC was trying to create.

Were they up to something together? Pradeep wanted to ask but UKC spoke up before that.

'Unless . . .' UKC turned to look at Pradeep, and said, 'Nagma, Faizaan, Saira and Jaideep were all planned murders. Only Preeti's wasn't.'

Pradeep's pupils dilated a little with the realization. His gut told him they were getting closer to a truth which would be ugly.

9

Pradeep briefed the police commissioner with UKC's latest conclusion. It had become almost an everyday duty for him to update the commissioner on the case. Apart from the media pressure, the ruling party too was behind the commissioner's ass to get the cello-tape killer caught before the elections so they could claim their party man, Hari Prasad Mishra, was innocent. And regain public confidence in a big way. Their cyber PR machinery would do the rest. The commissioner further updated the home minister. The good thing was, as the minister noted, there were strides taken in the case, however small; at least it wasn't a cul-de-sac.

Taksh rushed up to Ekantika's second-floor apartment. He had finished work when he got a text from her asking if he could come over. She needed some urgent help. He called her but Ekantika didn't pick up.

When Ekantika opened the door, the first thing Taksh asked was, 'Everything fine?'

'Yeah, why?' Ekantika said in a casual tone. She went and sat on the floor.

Taksh closed the door and came in. He was about to sit on the sofa opposite when Ekantika gestured for him to sit on the one beside her. Taksh came over. She picked up a bottle of hair oil from the centre table and gave it to him.

'I called you for this,' she said jovially. 'I don't have any friends. Back then, Faizaan used to give me a *champi*. And now you are the only one whom I could think of,' she said.

'Crazy, you are,' he said, relaxing.

'Guess so.'

'Why, Kisha is also your friend, isn't that so?' Taksh said, opening the bottle and pouring some oil on her scalp. He started massaging her head.

'Gently please,' Ekantika said and then continued, 'Kisha called you?'

'Messaged me. She wants to meet. She didn't even ask if I was interested. She simply said she would wait for me at her place tomorrow after work.'

'At her place, huh? Nice.' Ekantika deliberately tried to sound naughty.

'Oh shut up! What was the need to tell her whatever you told her? I thought we were friends. And nothing would go beyond us.'

'We are friends. That's why I told her. Look at you. This isn't the age to philosophize so much about love and relationships. You love someone, you go and tell the person. If there's some issue, sort it out. Taking a step back is the easiest thing to do.'

'You can't be serious.'

'I am. I wish I could have Faizaan by my side always. You don't know how terribly I miss him. I don't think I'll ever be able to connect to a person at the level Faizaan and I connected.' Ekantika said. And wished Faizaan's life had not trespassed on her own mission in life.

'I know what you are saying but what am I supposed to talk about with Kisha? I can't apologize all the time. Especially when it's not my fault.'

'What was her fault?'

'It's not one single fault. Several small things also add up to a bigger problematic picture. And when it happens that way, we call it a compatibility issue.'

Neither talked for couple of minutes.

'You know, I finally have a counter to your theory,' Ekantika said. Her eyes were closed as she enjoyed Taksh massaging her scalp with his fingertips.

'Which is?'

'You say loving someone from a distance is better than being in a relationship. And you got to that realization because you don't want the person's flaws to outweigh your love for the person, correct?'

'Kind of.'

'It also means by going away you won't have to face her flaws.'

'Yeah.'

'But then is it love if you only know and are comfortable with one aspect of a person? That's mere admiration. The way we admire our favourite film stars, sportspersons, authors, etc. We don't know them as people. But we think we love them, whereas we only love their work or performance. That's also what we do from a distance. Who gets into a relationship with their favourite movie star or the like? Nobody!' Ekantika realized Taksh's fingers had stopped. It meant he was contemplating something.

'If someone you love has a flaw, and it disturbs you in any way, talk to the person. Communication is underrated. Tell her and make her aware of the thing that pisses you off. If she isn't able to rectify it, then either you accommodate or arrive at a decision that it's not working. Otherwise, a successful relationship is all about how amazingly you proof-read yourself for the other. Every day! Like Faizaan and I used to do with each other. If a person is adamant and isn't able to change that one thing which irks the other, then I guess it's time to move on even if the love persists. In that case, I'll agree with your theory. Else, it's just a defensive stance to love someone from a distance. Especially after knowing their flaws. You'll never know a person from a distance. And if you distance yourself after knowing the person, and are still in love, I think it's a kind of denial.'

Taksh's fingers started again on her scalp but were slow. As if he was thinking more than he was massaging her head.

'Have you ever told Kisha about the small faults you are talking about?' Ekantika asked.

'Sometimes. But never strongly. I only observed them.' It was a soft confession.

'I guessed it. After you felt it, you decided it's better to stay away. You simply went ahead and created situations so you could break off with her. And continue to love her from a distance? Sorry, I won't encourage anyone to do such a thing. And Kisha has only blocked you. If someone I loved did that with me, I would have screwed him over.'

Ekantika sounded conclusive. Taksh continued to give her a quiet champi. In his mind, he'd made a decision. He would go and meet Kisha. Once.

At UKC's house, Pradeep had brought with him the video recordings of all of Nagma's close friends. UKC had formulated the questions himself that Pradeep made Gagan ask. As the recordings were projected in his room, UKC kept looking at the youngsters featuring on them one by one.

Most of them were basic questions regarding Nagma, Faizaan and their relationship. And if there was anyone who was trying to threaten the relationship. Two questions—did Nagma ever complain of being stalked and what was Nagma and Faizaan's sexual life like—none of the friends could answer. Until one girl, Bhagyashree, who worked with Nagma in the same office, answered them. She was supposedly close to her.

'Did Nagma ever complain of being stalked?' It was Inspector Gagan's voice.

Bhagyashree thought for some time and then said, 'Twice she told me while coming to office that she thought there was someone behind her.'

'When was this?'

Bhagyashree thought again and said, 'I don't remember the date but it was a month or so before she went missing.'

'Did Faizaan and Nagma have any physical relationship?' It was Inspector Gagan's voice again.

'Of course. We shared those details often.'

'How was it?'

'She used to tell me how gentle and respectful Faizaan used to be towards her. Nothing rough or abusive. I remember this because my boyfriend used to be the opposite. And I imagined how nice it would be to have a guy who'd respect me when we were intimate.'

UKC asked Pradeep to pause. He did.

'Ekantika's recorded statement tells us something different about Faizaan. She clearly states that he used to be a beast sexually, giving her bite marks and all,' he said.

'That's correct.' Pradeep said recollecting the same. Then a pause later, he said, 'It's possible one person behaves differently with different people.' He knew how he was with his wife and what his avatar used to be with Preeti.

'It is possible,' UKC said thoughtfully. Then asked, 'Nagma goes missing. A week later, Ekantika comes into Faizaan's life. Then when Faizaan dies, Nagma's dead body is also found. Killed at the same time when she had gone missing.' *This girl Ekantika is featuring too many times,* UKC wondered, *both in Nagma's and Faizaan's case as well as Preeti's.*

Pradeep understood where UKC was going with that.

'But Ekantika told us that it was Faizaan who approached her. It's there in her audio statement.'

UKC nodded first and then with a smile said, 'Her audio statement is whatever happened . . . according to her.'

The last part did make Pradeep moisten his dry lips. *Does it mean . . . fuck,* Pradeep thought.

10

Taksh reached Kisha's place after work. It was the same place where he had spent a countless number of days and nights. There was a time when he used to have a spare key to the flat. When he gave up the key, he had given up on the rights for everything on her and *them*. Kisha opened the door. For a few seconds, neither said anything.

'Come in,' she said. Taksh went in. She locked the door. It had been a year and a half since they had broken up. Taksh noticed from the corner of his eye that nothing of the interior had changed. He went and sat in his favourite armchair in the hall. He saw there was already a coffee mug on the table.

'You want some?' Kisha asked. Taksh nodded. She came and sat on the furry mat adjacent to the armchair. That was her favourite place. He'd visited her with a clear thought: he would only react. After all, she'd messaged him to come over.

'You still love me?' she said.

Taksh neither nodded nor said anything.

'You can tell that to a girl whom you met recently, but you can't tell it to me whom you've known for five years?' Her voiced choked a bit. She was now looking straight at him.

'Kisha, things aren't as simple as you stated,' his eyes met hers.

'Then let's simplify it. It's not that I'm happy breaking off with you. Maybe because I never wanted to break off,' she said.

'Even I'm not happy but I realized somewhere my love for you was decreasing.'

'Why? I never cheated on you. It's only after our break-up that I fucked a random Tinder guy. That's all.'

'That's not cheating. And there are more things in a relationship than just cheating on the other.'

'Like?' Kisha now rose up on her knees with her hands on her hips. That was her fighting stance, Taksh knew well.

'Come on, let's not get into details,' Taksh said, sounding defensive. And realized probably that's where the problem lay, after Ekantika had shown him the mirror. He had never come clean with Kisha regarding what irked him about her. It was always 'Let's not get into details' while in his head he knew exactly what irked him. *Should I detail it out for her now?* Taksh wondered.

'No way I'm letting you get off. You have problems talking to me but you go on talking to other girls about me and how much you love me so they think you are one helluva lover and I'm the bitch who doesn't deserve true love.'

'What? I only told Ekantika. Nobody else.'

'That means you met a lot of girls after we broke up.' Kisha stood up now on her feet. Aggression came naturally to her.

'Yes, I met a lot of girls, so what? Why are you patronizing me?' Taksh too stood up.

'Now I get it. You wanted to fuck more girls which was difficult while being in a relationship, so all this break-up drama.'

'What?' Taksh couldn't believe the way Kisha was steering it.

'What, what? You men!' Kisha said, stamping her feet with anger.

'Shut up, okay. If I was one of those men, I would have fucked Ekantika also.'

'You want to?'

'Shut up, Kisha. She is a friend.'

'Don't try to shut me up,' Kisha said and came close to him.

'Look at me and say if you want to fuck her.'

Taksh looked at her and said, 'Fuck you.' His pitch was raised by then.

'No, no, you don't get to do that any more. Those Tinder guys are better than you at least. They say what they want. You go in a roundabout manner.'

'Ah, so how would I know all you want is a good fuck and not a good relationship,' he said in a derogatory tone. Kisha picked on it.

'You bloody swine,' she pushed him. Like old times. He fell on the armchair. She rode him, with her legs on either side, to slap him. Taksh put his hand on her waist to support himself on the wobbling chair. Her tee rose up exposing her waist. And that's where his hand rested. As their skin touched the other, it seemed someone had charged them with a sexual current. As she pulled his hair, they came a little too close because of the armchair's wobble. Their lips brushed. His hand went a little down on her butt. He grabbed it tight. She kissed him. He reciprocated. The next minute they were on the furry mat, half naked, with Kisha on top of him. Her forever favourite sex position.

She rode him while digging her nails into his exposed chest. That was the punishment for breaking up. The riding was the gift for coming back.

I'll never be able to complain about this sonofabitch's dick size. He always opens me up, she thought, riding him fast.

She came in the next few minutes. While Taksh flipped her and took her legs on his shoulders. He gave harder and deeper thrusts and then came in a rush.

As they lay half naked beside each other, there was pin-drop silence in the flat. Both didn't know what had just transpired. *Was it a nasty dream or had it happened for real?* Both wondered. It was Kisha who broke the silence.

'Now that it's out of the way, let's talk like two mature adults.'

'That's a good idea,' Taksh said, hating himself for not able to control his lust. For while Kisha had one Tinder guy, Taksh had gone sexless since the break-up. He didn't mention it. They dressed up and sat down relaxed. To only talk this time.

That night, Pradeep was fucking his wife after a long time. His horniness had reached its pinnacle. And he needed a hands-free release. But while fucking her, in the banal missionary position, he had his eyes closed. Images of Preeti, Ekantika's naked video, then Preeti again kept flashing in his mind, which did affect his hardness. Not so much that it popped out of his wife's vagina. He came soon and lay on his wife for a few seconds. His phone rang. Pradeep moved away from his wife and picked up the phone from the bedside table. His wife climbed off the bed and went to the attached bathroom covering herself up. She was happy to have her old husband back. Pradeep saw it was Inspector Gagan's call.

'Yeah, Gagan.'

'Sir, I just received a call from one of my friends in Bengaluru city police. They have found a young techie's dead body near MG Road metro station, Bengaluru, with his nose and mouth cello-taped and hands tied.'

Ekantika: 14–20 Years Old

For weeks, Ekantika couldn't accept the fact that her mother had lied to her about her baba. He wasn't in a faraway land. He was dead. Killed. Murdered. A life cut short. A relationship cut short. Had he lived, she would have made sure they had countless memories together. Her baba and her. She could also stand in the storm holding his hand and smiling like her little neighbour once did. What wrong had she committed to deserve a childhood without the physical presence of her baba? Ekantika never had an answer to this.

She didn't sleep at nights wondering how her mother could lie. Then it dawned upon her that, if she had been shocked to learn of her father, even her mother must have been shocked by her father's death. She still had her mother's shoulder to cry on but whom did her mother have? She would have done the same if she was in Charulata's place. She too would have protected her daughter from being scarred. That's what one does for family. To take the heat oneself to keep the other warm.

There were moments when she wanted to blurt out to her mother that she knew her father hadn't died because of pneumonia. But she couldn't. Ekantika was mature enough to gauge that somewhere the lie Charulata told her was not because she just wanted to keep the truth away. Ekantika understood she'd lied because Charulata herself must have not been able to accept the truth. And she didn't want her daughter to be as broken as her. If Ekantika told her that she knew what the truth was, she would have snatched that one straw of pride from her mother. The pride of securing her daughter against a life-altering scar. It was a life-changing realization for Ekantika. It was that moment when her obsession about meeting her baba took a dangerous turn.

Ekantika swore to herself that she would get the one who was responsible for not allowing their relationship to blossom, her family to remain normal and her mother to be broken within. The one who snatched her baba from her, the one who made her mother toil extra, taking in all the societal harassment and abuses, only to safeguard her daughter, had to be caught. The cello-tape serial killer. He had to be punished. And she would gift her mother the identity of the killer who had murdered her father.

Ekantika's obsession turned into a mission now. On one hand, she studied with a dogged focus; on the other, she started keeping a personal diary where she jotted down all the information out there in the media about the cello-tape serial killer.

Ekantika did it all. She used Google to locate articles from old newspapers. She watched crime shows on YouTube to create a profile of the killer based on his modus operandi, selection of random victims and his possible temperament. She stalked the victims' family members on Facebook for leads. And by the time she was eighteen years of age, she was an encyclopedia on the cello-tape serial killer. But she didn't know his identity and she didn't know why he did what he did.

By the time she was in the second year of college in Baruipur, Ekantika had started researching on how she could shift to Delhi. Not only was Delhi where most of the cello-tape killings had happened but, living in Baruipur she had understood, a big incident in a small place is a small thing in India. A small thing, aptly marketed in a big city, has the potential to become a pan-India concern. And Ekantika wanted to do something which would shake the capital in a way that all of India would demand the reopening of the cello-tape killer case. She'd seen and understood the power of the common people in putting pressure on the legal system in both the Jessica Lal murder case and also the Nirbhaya gang-rape case. It was time people did the same for the cello-tape serial killer case as well. All she had to do was bring it back in their conscious mind.

Ekantika had aspirations of becoming an IAS officer. She had seen too many aberrations in the system to feel motivated to play a role in cleaning a few dirty spots in it if not all. Delhi was an obvious choice. She located one of the most-sought-after coaching centres there and soon after her graduation, shifted to Delhi.

While she continued preparing for UPSC, she knew she hadn't come to Delhi only to study. She had to locate a target and flag off a series of events that would bring the cello-tape killer back into the limelight. And once the original killer saw his killings were being copied, he would do something to prove he was the only one there was. The fire of revenge was burning too intensely within her for someone to convince her how much a shot in the dark it was.

Being in Delhi, Ekantika started to zero in to a possible target. Around the place she lived, in Topsie or even at random places when she met guys through Tinder and Bumble. But none fit her bill. She wanted to be in a relationship with the guy first and then kill him so she remained within the investigation all the time. Otherwise it would be a task for an individual to stay abreast with the proceedings of the case. Why would the police tell you anything if you were unrelated to the case?

Two weeks after Ekantika's admission in Topsie, she noticed a guy. He was a student at Topsie but was clearly her senior. There was something about him that she couldn't keep him out of her mind. A little digging told her that his name was Faizaan Ahmad.

11

Ekantika got to know about the young techie's murder by the supposed cello-tape killer from a news app on her phone. A capsule had appeared in the form of a notification vibrating on her phone. It was 8 a.m. and she was studying. One look at the notification, and Ekantika ran to switch the television on.

She saw Kisha presenting the news from the studio in Noida. She was talking to a correspondent in Bengaluru. As the reporter spoke energetically, Ekantika learnt that the murder had happened around 1 a.m. in the night. The techie, Sravan Reddy, was riding to his office on his bike. The bike and the body, lying on the road, were found by a police patrolling van. Sravan Reddy had his limbs tied and his nose and mouth were cello-taped. Initial reports suggested it was done by the cello-tape serial killer. The reporter tried to run after a few Bengaluru city policemen to squeeze out some more information but they didn't say anything.

Ekantika had a big smile on her face. The last time she was this happy was when she realized that Faizaan's diary was stolen. For Faizaan's diary wasn't his. It was hers. And when it disappeared from Preeti's flat, Ekantika was sure the original killer's eyes were on Nagma's and Faizaan's deaths. She had done what she had set out to do. She had pulled the trigger.

Ekantika's phone suddenly rang. It was Pradeep.

'Hello sir,' she sounded as if she was unaware of what had happened.

'Ekantika, meet me at GK-1, UKC's house in an hour.'

Before she could say or ask anything, Pradeep ended the call. She sensed he was in a hurry himself.

A little more than an hour later, Pradeep and Ekantika were in front of UKC's house. Every time Ekantika stepped into that house, a haunting silence welcomed her. There was a foreboding energy all around that disturbed her. It was simply too quiet. Silence could be intimidating, she learnt from being there.

'How was your sexual relationship with Faizaan?' UKC asked. Ekantika noted this time there was less warmth in his voice.

'I've mentioned it in my audio statement,' she said, throwing a furtive glance at Pradeep.

UKC repeated his query as if he hadn't heard what Ekantika had said. And didn't care. She understood there was no escape without answering the question again.

'It was pretty active.'

'What was his nature when he was intimate with you?' UKC sounded sharp.

'Wild. Rough. Adamant.'

'But Nagma's friend told us he was gentle with her all the time. Any reason why he'd turned rough with you?'

It could be a trick question, Ekantika thought, for she didn't know whether Nagma's friend would have told them that. And with that question it was clear to her that UKC was testing her against her own statement. Yet again. *Is he suspecting me?*

'Now that you ask me, I remember Faizaan did tell me once how unsatisfied he remained with Nagma. But I never asked him the details. Maybe Nagma didn't like it rough. Not all women are the same,' Ekantika said with renewed confidence.

True, not all women are the same, Pradeep thought, comparing Preeti to his own wife.

'You didn't mention it in your recording, did you?' UKC asked.

This was coming, Ekantika knew, and she was ready with the answer, 'No. Perhaps I missed it. I was asked by Pradeep sir to only record everything between Faizaan and me. Not between Nagma and Faizaan.' Ekantika was slightly curt with the last part.

There was nothing that UKC could ask her then that would prove that she was lying. When two out of three concerned people were dead, then one couldn't help but give the benefit of doubt to the third one. Unless some solid evidence proving the third's lie emerged.

'May I know where you were on Tuesday, 18th, last month?' UKC asked.

Damn, there is something which is making him doubt me, Ekantika thought and said aloud, 'I was here in Delhi only. Haven't travelled for a long time.'

'Are you sure?' UKC's eyes pierced Ekantika like arrows.

Pradeep couldn't hide his obvious surprise with this line of interrogation from UKC. The date he mentioned was when Jaideep was found dead. *Is he thinking Ekantika went to Patna and killed that guy? Come on,* he thought.

'One second.' Ekantika took out her phone and opened her calendar to the previous month.

'Yes, I'm sure I was here. In fact, wait,' She tapped her phone a few times and then turned it towards UKC.

'You can ask Guddu bhaiya,' Ekantika said. She was flashing her Paytm payment record on her phone.

'Who is Guddu bhaiya?' UKC asked, while Neema checked the date and time of the record. There was a slight nod from her towards UKC.

'The grocery store wale bhaiya in my area. I'd ordered eggs, bread and some more stuff from there that night.'

UKC glanced at Pradeep. The latter made a note of cross-checking the details.

There was nothing more for UKC to ask her at that moment. But as Ekantika and Pradeep left, UKC did wonder how quickly she recalled she'd ordered eggs and bread on a particular date even though they were items one bought every alternate day or so.

'I need a head wash,' he told Neema.

Later that evening, Taksh took Ekantika to Kisha's flat. Taksh and Kisha had arranged for a small party. It was their collective way of thanking Ekantika for getting them back together.

As Ekantika settled down in the cosy flat, she looked around with appreciative eyes.

'The interior is so relaxing.'

'Yeah, we both did it,' Taksh said.

'Once upon a time,' Kisha said with a hint of sarcasm. Taksh gave her a funny look and turned towards Ekantika, 'What will you have? Wine, vodka or whisky?'

'What are you guys having?' She was still looking around. There were some photographs of Kisha pinned on the wall.

'Some wine, maybe,' Taksh said, turning to Kisha. Ekantika nodded and gave her consent. Then realizing most of those framed photos were of Kisha in yoga poses in various places, she asked, 'Wow, you're a yoga guru?'

'That would be pushing it. I love yoga. I've been into it for a decade now,' Kisha said, glancing at Ekantika who was admiring the photos.

'Anyway, what music do you like?' Kisha asked, holding up her phone.

'Not much into music,' Ekantika said, getting back on the mat.

'Cool, so I'll put my favourites on then,' Kisha said and tapped her phone. Enrique's voice came alive from all four corners of the hall. Kisha lowered the volume to a soothing level and then joined Ekantika on the furry mat.

Taksh first brought the small table laden with drinks and snacks close to the mat. Then went in to bring a bean bag from the bedroom. Placing it beside the mat, he ensconced himself on it.

'To homecoming!' They clinked their glasses. The mood was disturbed with a phone call. It was Taksh's.

'What *yaar*!' Kisha lamented.

'Work call, sorry guys. Joining in a bit,' he said and took the call, moving into the bedroom. Kisha and Ekantika were alone in the hall. Both sipped their drinks.

'I'm sorry I may sound crazy but I have to ask you this,' Kisha said. She knew she needed a drink to speak her mind on this. And she didn't want Taksh to hear it.

'Sure,' Ekantika said biting into a succulent chicken lollipop.

'Have you ever had angry sex?' Kisha asked.

'I heard about angry birds. What's angry sex?' Ekantika looked genuinely innocent about it.

'I mean, you and your guy are both angry at each other. Like pissed off kind of mad and then with that emotion you fuck each other?'

'No!' Ekantika was quick to respond.

'Didn't know that too could be so intense.' Kisha sounded as if in her mind she was reliving their angry-sex episode.

'Damn, I thought you guys talked it out like adults. I didn't know you two fucked it out like teens,' Ekantika quipped, swirling her wine a little.

'I know, right? But the talks also happened. I think the angry-sex part released such pleasure hormones that it took care of all the negativity we had stored up against each other for a year now.'

'I knew there was a male ego playing a part when Taksh told me about being-in-love and not being-in-a-relationship.

But when I met you, I knew you guys weren't done yet. You look at a couple and just know who's done and who's not.'

Kisha took a few seconds and a sip later said, 'I didn't know it was that obvious. It's funny, in the last year and a half since we broke up, I swore so many times not to think about him. I even hooked up with a Tinder guy.' Kisha stopped, seeing Ekantika smile. She shrugged.

'Sexorcism!' Ekantika said and smiled. A word which Faizaan had once told her.

'But I guess it's difficult to move on when your mind is done with the relationship but your heart isn't.'

'The worst thing is when your heart and mind both are still into the relationship and yet you know some day you have to move on,' Ekantika said, looking up at the ceiling. Kisha sensed what she was hinting at.

'You still love Faizaan, right? Taksh told me.'

'Love is an understatement. He gave me more than what I deserved. While I gave him what he never deserved.'

'The first few months, the first year is difficult.'

Ekantika nodded, 'I'm not moving on from Faizaan for sure. Not now. Not ever.' Emotions clogged her throat. She gulped the wine.

'May I ask you something?' Kisha said. Ekantika nodded.

'Didn't you feel attracted to Taksh? Like even if it meant a rebound kind of thing?'

Ekantika averted her eyes from the ceiling to her with a faint smile.

'I mean he is a nice guy,' Kisha continued, 'I know girls generally fall for bad guys but they always leave us in a mess.

Not Taksh. Even after we broke up, more than feeling like a wreck, I missed the comfort he used to be in my life. In fact, I was the one who blocked him. He didn't do anything other than step back.'

'To be honest, I was tempted initially. More so because Taksh is similar to Faizaan in some ways. Even he was a nice guy. And I totally relate to the comfort that you are talking about. It's like guys like Faizaan and Taksh become your shock-absorbers.'

'Absolutely.'

'But then I understood my attraction towards Taksh was because I was getting attracted to the similarities he had with Faizaan. I'm too mature to commit the mistake of seeking someone within another person.'

Kisha absorbed it all quietly. Then Ekantika spoke.

'You know Wabi Sabi?'

Kisha nodded, saying, 'I've heard about it. Some Japanese belief?'

'To find beauty in imperfections,' Ekantika said, remembering her conversation with Faizaan.

'We rarely do that. We rarely remain happy, thus,' Ekantika said softly.

Their attention was drawn by Taksh who rushed into the room.

'So, what did I miss?' Taksh asked, sitting down excitedly holding his wine glass.

'That you are one lucky son of a dog,' Ekantika said, giggling away. Kisha joined her giggles.

'Huh?' Taksh didn't know how to react.

'Nothing, just girl talk,' Kisha said.

As the three continued to drink and chit-chat, UKC had skipped dinner. He was too immersed in the case, going through the materials with Neema's help, as carefully as he could. It was for the umpteenth time that he had read the case history of the original killer. Twenty-six kills and then no more. *Why?* Did he recover from whatever motivation or psychotic behaviour was leading him to commit the murders? Did he become bored with killing people if it was a game for him? Or did he simply die after the twenty-sixth victim? And nobody ever knew who he really was.

Another odd thing about the case, which Preeti had pointed out in her report to Pradeep, was that most of the twenty-sixth victim's direct family was dead. Unlike the families of other victims. While the wife and son were untraceable. There weren't any age profiles in the report. It seemed like a dead end. And dead ends irked UKC the most.

Pradeep's wife, after that one night when he showed interest in her sexually, according to her, was on a high. Since then, she made it a point every day to prepare his favourite dishes. That night, the excitement with which her husband sat at the dining table appreciating the appetizing fragrance of the food, she knew another sexual night was awaiting her. Discovering your sex life in your mid-thirties with your husband once again, was orgasmic in its own way.

The moment Pradeep had one morsel of the food, his phone flashed a call from the commissioner. He quickly finished the food he was chewing and took the call.

'Yes, sir.'

'Any update?' the commissioner asked.

'Not yet.'

'Hmm, next time you have a talk with UKC, tell him there's a time issue now as the home minister is thinking of handing over this case to the CBI. Especially after the Bengaluru killing. The media and the public on social media have gone mad. The home minister had to inform his social media cell to counter the organically trending hashtags against the government with fake ones.'

'I get it, sir.' Pradeep said. The call ended. Pradeep joined his wife and daughters at the dining table with a pensive look.

'You two will sleep in the same room tonight,' his wife said. The kids started making faces. The two older daughters liked to sleep alone in their respective rooms while the younger one still wanted to squeeze in between her parents. As his wife tried explaining to them why one of them should take the youngest one with them to bed, Pradeep suddenly spoke up.

'Let her sleep with us,' he said. The kids were happy. His wife's face fell.

The party went on till 3 a.m. at Kisha's place. Finally, Ekantika realized she had to go home. Kisha asked her to sleep over. Old Rajendra Nagar was too far from the Ghaziabad border where Kisha lived. Ekantika was about to say no when Taksh too said the same. More adamantly. Kisha went inside to bring some of her night dresses for Ekantika.

'I forgot to ask, how is aunty's health? Ma said she wasn't doing too well,' Taksh said.

Though Ekantika was a little tipsy, she registered what Taksh said.

'But I had a talk with ma this morning itself. She was all right,' she said and immediately picked her phone up and called Charulata knowing well that it was late in the night. Her instinct told her something could be wrong with her.

The call connected and an automated voice said the number was unreachable. Ekantika stared at the phone as if she had seen a ghost. Not because the number was unreachable. But because the automated female voice was speaking in Kannada instead of the usual Bengali.

12

There was a new visitor at UKC's house along with Pradeep. It was Faizaan's younger brother, Mohsin Ahmad. He was called in at UKC's behest. UKC had an inkling that Ekantika was lying about a few things. He didn't know why she was doing this. What made him curious was how Ekantika had a proof for everything. People who don't have an alibi for everything are as much a suspect as people who have an alibi for everything. The only person alive, apart from Ekantika, who was connected to Faizaan in some way, was his younger brother.

Though Pradeep had been asked to convey to UKC that he had to speed up else the case might go to the CBI, he had confidence in UKC. For his own self-interest, he did not share the news with UKC. Pradeep knew that once the case went to the CBI, his own role in handling the entire case would subside. There would be no professional brownie points considering how big this had become. All Pradeep told UKC after coming in was that Guddu bhaiya had confirmed Ekantika had ordered the goods from him a night before Jaideep's murder. A delivery boy had gone to drop the things off at her place.

'Did your mother ever have an abortion before you two were born?' UKC asked Mohsin.

'Not that I'm aware of.'

'Hmm.' UKC wanted to check the part about Faizaan talking to his imaginary sister that was mentioned in Ekantika's statement. Saira Ahmad was no longer alive while Hari Prasad Mishra, who had fathered both Faizaan and Mohsin, wouldn't sit for a Q&A, UKC knew. He understood it was difficult to know whether Ekantika was lying or if Faizaan indeed talked to his imaginary sister.

'Give him the audio statement,' UKC told Pradeep. He did as asked.

Pradeep sat quietly watching Mohsin listen to Ekantika's statement on a headset. The first time he heard it, he said he didn't find anything contradictory about his brother. He was asked to hear it one more time.

Mohsin suddenly pressed the stop button of the recorder somewhere in the middle of the statement.

'What happened? It's not over yet,' Pradeep said.

'It just struck me . . .' Mohsin said. UKC gave him an eager look. Mohsin looked uncomfortable as he glanced at UKC, then at Pradeep as if he wasn't sure if he should blurt out what he had in mind.

'Whatever it is, just say it,' Pradeep said.

'Actually, Faizaan bhaiya couldn't have been that great,' Mohsin seemed to think before he spoke, 'with Ekantika.'

'As in?' Pradeep urged him on.

'Bhaiya had ED,' Mohsin blurted.

'ED?' Pradeep had a confused look on his face as he turned towards UKC.

'Erectile Dysfunction,' UKC said aloud. *Ekantika had mentioned Faizaan's bad performance once in the statement,* UKC wondered, *but that was a lie to ward off the female attention he was getting at Topsie Coaching Centre.*

'I know this for sure,' Mohsin continued, 'because he was undergoing treatment and I'd accidentally found the doctor's prescription. Even mummy didn't know about this. It was our secret.'

I don't think even Ekantika knows about it, UKC thought.

'Do you remember the doctor's name?' UKC asked Mohsin. The latter took his time but could only recollect the clinic's name that he'd seen on the prescription.

'That would do,' UKC said and turned to Pradeep. 'Please check with the clinic as to which doctor was seeing Faizaan.' There was a rare sense of excitement on UKC's face.

'Does that mean . . .' Pradeep was cut short by UKC's boisterous laughter. Even Neema stood still. She could count on her fingers how many times she'd seen UKC laughing like that.

Ekantika woke up with a hangover at Kisha's place. Her phone was ringing with an unsaved number. She thought it was some sales call and she cut it. Ekantika remembered calling her mother; her phone was unavailable as she heard the automated voice say so in Kannada. She didn't know where to call to check on her mother. She simply sent a message to her asking her to call back the moment she read it. As she waited for a response, the alcohol made sure she dozed off.

The same unsaved number called again. Irritated, she picked it up.

'Hello, who's this?'

'Shonai?'

'Ma? What happened? Whose number is this?' Ekantika was concerned.

'This is my new number, Shonai. My phone was stolen a day ago,' Charulata said, sounding hassled. As she continued to speak, Ekantika's mind was elsewhere. *Phone stolen . . . the automated voice in Kannada . . . the kill in Bengaluru . . . he is screwing her up now.*

'Ma, did you lodge an FIR with the police?' Ekantika said with her pitch raised.

'Not yet. Should I?'

'Yes ma. Just go and lodge an FIR right now. Let me call you back,' she ended the call and immediately dialled Pradeep.

'Hello sir, I think the cello-tape killer stole my mother's phone before committing the murder in Bengaluru.' *He is trying to get back at me for digging him up after these many years,* Ekantika thought.

'Hmm, I'll look into it,' Pradeep said calmly. He was in his police car heading towards his office in Gurugram. Mohsin was sitting in the front. Pradeep was supposed to take his official statement regarding Faizaan's ED. Pradeep scrolled through his last dialled list and tapped on a name: UKC-Neema.

'Hello.' Neema picked up the landline on the third ring.

'ACP Pradeep here. Just wanted to inform UKC that Ekantika called up and said she thinks her mother's phone was stolen by the cello-tape killer before committing the Bengaluru murder.'

'One moment.' Neema covered the receiver with her palm and updated UKC.

'UKC says it would be great if the stolen phone could be tracked,' Neema said.

'Sure. And we still need to track Ekantika's phone on the night before Jaideep's murder and during that day as well, right?' Pradeep was confirming. He was told to do that before leaving UKC's house with Mohsin.

'Hold on,' Neema said and a second later added, 'Yes. That we have to do.'

'All right, thanks.' Pradeep ended the call.

Once in office, Pradeep asked Inspector Gagan to talk to his counterpart in the Bengaluru city police and begin a search for Charulata's phone. If Ekantika was to be believed, it would take the case somewhere closer to the killer if the phone was found.

After tracking the phone's last network to a town named Guntakal in the Anantpur district of Andhra Pradesh, a rigorous search was initiated involving the Andhra Pradesh police as well. Finally, the phone was found in a semi-damaged condition beside a lamp post facing a railway track. Pradeep was informed by Gagan. He called Neema. And updated UKC. He even WhatsApped a picture of the damaged phone to Neema.

UKC had a look at it once Neema put the landline down.

'The fact that the phone was found in Andhra Pradesh, near a railway track makes it obvious the phone was thrown from a running train,' he said to himself. 'And that too when it just entered Andhra Pradesh. Else the automated voice

Ekantika told Pradeep about would have been in Telugu, not Kannada. It also means the killer had moved out of Karnataka. Or maybe he is in Karnataka but threw the phone in a different state as a ruse.'

Neema nodded like an obedient student.

'The question is, why would the killer steal Ekantika's mother's phone specifically before his thirty-first kill? And never before?' UKC was lost in thought.

Kisha was feeling a little tired and worked up. She had not taken a work break since her break-up with Taksh. That was intentional though. Work was a saviour, helping her divert her thoughts and emotions from her own life to other's lives. Crime journalism had its own challenges. There were never good things awaiting you. Even the 'good' stories from a journalist's point of view were gruesome stories of the levels of decadence a human being could go to. Not that Taksh's work was any different.

If Kisha's work led her to gut-churning stories, Taksh's took him to bowel-bulging visuals of dead bodies. Last night itself they'd decided to take mutual work breaks and perhaps travel a bit. They zeroed in on a Leh-Ladakh road trip. A good twelve days break with proper social media detoxing and making up for the lost togetherness that had happened in the last one and a half years. Starting fresh with Taksh, she suddenly felt she was reliving the first phase of their relationship where every message, every call from him used to make her blush.

Come home tonight. Kisha messaged Taksh in between work.

Anything special? Taksh replied after some time.

Yes. I'm on the menu. Limited time offer.

Rushing!

Not in your pants, boy.

No, no, inside you.

The naughtiness in the message made Kisha smile like a fool sitting in her boardroom. She felt blessed after a long time. After their heart-to-heart talk, both decided to give one hundred per cent to their relationship. Neither would point out to the other what the other didn't do. Instead, they would focus on what they could do to keep the relationship as fresh as it was on Day One.

Kisha's plan was simple. She would leave office early. Go home, freshen up, prepare dinner for both of them and then have some orgasmic love-making all night. Kisha didn't say this to Taksh. She simply left office around 5.30 p.m. Taksh was supposed to reach her place by 9 p.m. As Kisha drove her car out of the office parking, she didn't know she was being followed by . . . the killer.

Ekantika stretched out after studying straight for four hours. She was feeling drained. There was no update on the cello-tape killer case. She stood up and went to the kitchen to prepare some tea for herself. That's when the doorbell rang. She went and opened the door. There was Inspector Gagan and two constables; one male and one female by the door.

'You need to come to the police station with us,' Gagan said.

'What happened?' Ekantika asked. Never before had she been fetched from her home. It was always Pradeep calling her to meet up or being picked up. *Have they discovered something against her?* Ekantika thought and felt a knot in her stomach.

'Some questioning needs to be done,' Gagan said.

'Let me call Pradeep sir.'

'You'll be wasting your time. He ordered us to take you there.'

Ekantika thought for a moment and said, 'Okay. Let me change.'

Kisha was putting up at Shipra Suncity in Ghaziabad. As she went inside the main gate, the killer asked the cab driver to stop a little ahead so he wouldn't know where exactly he'd dropped the passenger. Then, as a family was entering the complex, the killer too started walking alongside them and entered without attracting the security guard's attention.

Kisha parked on the ground floor at her designated place and went up to her flat. She headed straight for a shower. Once done, she was on WhatsApp messaging Taksh while preparing dinner, when she heard the doorbell. She left her phone in the kitchen and went to open the door. The moment she did, she was attacked.

Ekantika was sitting in front of Pradeep in a room. A video camera was set up ready to record her while Pradeep had video-called Neema from his own phone so that UKC could ask Ekantika the questions.

'Ekantika, you mentioned in your audio statement that Faizaan used to be rough with you in bed. Is that correct?'

Ekantika nodded.

'Please answer clearly yes or no,' Pradeep said.

'Yes,' Ekantika said. Though she was doing her best to maintain her poise, she had an ominous feeling inside about all this.

'How long did he last in bed?' UKC's voice reverberated loud and clear in the room.

'I don't remember the exact time but forty-five to fifty minutes approximately.'

'Every time you guys had sex, it was the same?'

'Yes,' Ekantika said. A glance at a surprised Pradeep told her she must have committed a mistake by saying so.

By the time Kisha came to her senses, she realized she was lying on her furry mat. A little fidget told her that her hands and legs were tied while her nose and mouth were taped. She opened her eyes. As her vision became normal, she saw the killer squatting down beside her, looking arrow-straight at her. The killer was wearing a mask and had on latex gloves. She knew pleading or making a noise wasn't an option. Feeling breathless, she started moving, fidgeting impatiently . . . till her body went quiet.

'You're lying, Miss Pakrashi,' UKC said. 'It's high time you tell us why.'

'What? Why would I lie?' Ekantika threw a questioning look at Pradeep, at Gagan and then at UKC on the video call.

'Faizaan Ahmad had erectile dysfunction.'

'That's not possible.' Ekantika knew it had to be a trick statement. To corner her perhaps. She had a don't-kid-me look on her face while in her heart she knew she had lied about their physical intimacy in her statement.

'Gagan, please show her the reports,' Pradeep said.

Gagan gave her a few sheets of paper. They had the name of the clinic in bold letters at the top. Ekantika looked at them incredulously.

'The last time Faizaan went to the doctor was when he was still in a relationship with you,' UKC said.

There was pin-drop silence in the room. Ekantika could feel the hair on her nape rise. She was thinking hard to come up with something which would negate this.

'We can be conclusive about this that Ekantika didn't know about Faizaan's ED condition. Maybe he never mentioned it to her because of the nature of the condition. It's also obvious now that they had never been intimate. Nagma telling her friend about Faizaan's gentle prowess was certainly hogwash. Which girlfriend would want to tell her friend that her boyfriend had ED? Stigma is a funny thing. Especially when she loved him genuinely,' UKC almost said it like an announcement.

Ekantika sat frozen. And yet she could feel a shiver down her spine.

'There's something else as well. Inspector Gagan, could you please give her the phone call sheet?' UKC said.

Inspector Gagan was quick on his feet. He was carrying those sheets with him. He gave them to Ekantika. The phone call sheet clearly stated her phone number was constantly catching a phone tower in Patna on the day of Jaideep's murder.

'Why would someone order eggs and bread from Guddu bhaiya when she was in a train travelling to Patna?' UKC asked.

With that, Ekantika knew it was checkmate for her. She should have left the phone at her place and taken another phone perhaps. But it was too late now.

'I'm asking you, Miss Pakrashi,' UKC said.

Ekantika remained silent. There was a connection problem from UKC's side. His face froze on the screen. A few seconds later, he was online again.

'ACP Pradeep, please get an arrest warrant for Ekantika Pakrashi made for misleading the Haryana police intentionally in the murder of Faizaan Ahmad. And for killing the innocent Jaideep Kumar. The rest, I'm sure, she would confess like the good girl I feel she is,' UKC said. Neema ended the video call.

By then, Kisha's body had gone still. The killer stealthily left the flat, certain that Kisha was dead.

13

The police were preparing the charge sheet against Ekantika. As per the district magistrate's order, she would be arrested and kept in custody in the district jail, Gurugram, for fourteen days after which she would be produced in front of the court. That night, though, she was kept in the lock-up.

Ekantika had confessed to her crimes. The killing of Nagma, Faizaan and Jaideep. It didn't come out immediately though. Ekantika sat in silence for a good three hours. Her mind was blank. She had planned everything meticulously for years. And yet it was busted. Not that she hadn't anticipated this situation. But all she prayed was if she ever got caught, the original killer was also caught as well. That hadn't happened. Yet.

Three hours later, after she analysed the situation in her mind and realized there was nothing she could do to delay her arrest, she called for a female constable and told her that she wanted to confess. The constable informed Gagan and Pradeep about it. Ekantika was given a pen and a paper and was asked to write down her statement. With eyes filled with tears, she wrote down all of it. This time, she told the truth unlike what she'd recorded in the audio statement to the police after Faizaan's death.

'My mother, Charulata Pakrashi, is unaware of my intent or agenda. She still thinks I came to Delhi to prepare for the UPSC. Which I did, but it wasn't the only thing. Once my mother left for Baruipur after settling me here, I started looking for my target. I wanted someone whom I could get into a relationship with, then kill him being the copycat of the cello-tape killer and project it to the police that there was a personal loss involved. My intention behind it was simple: I wanted the cello-tape serial killer's file to be reopened and the original killer finally caught.

'I first saw Faizaan in Topsie. He didn't notice me. But there was something in his eyes that didn't let me forget him. I started stalking him. And understood he was a loner, didn't live with his family and didn't have many friends. He was the perfect catch for me. But the only bone of contention was Nagma. His girlfriend. I thought it wouldn't be a bad idea if Nagma was killed first and then Faizaan. But I couldn't let Nagma's body be found, otherwise Faizaan wouldn't have got close to me quick enough. He had to believe Nagma disappeared suddenly. That would have made him emotionally vulnerable. And I was right. Though her parents filed a missing person FIR, she wasn't found because I'd kept her dead body with me. I'd Googled and read several articles on how to preserve a dead body without raising any suspicion. I was also inspired by the Debjani De corpse case that had happened in Kolkata. Even when Faizaan came to my place, Nagma's dead body was very much there. He didn't know it, of course. Even when I shifted with him, to his pad first and then to Gurugram, he didn't know I was still holding on to the rented flat at Karol Bagh. I was paying the rent without his knowledge.

'Most of what I mentioned in my audio statement to the police before were mostly lies. Faizaan never was a beast in bed. In fact, we had never had sex. Perhaps that's why I never knew he had ED. He didn't show any inclination for physical intimacy towards me and I now know why. While

Faizaan for me was a step in my mission, I also didn't push him towards making our relationship physical. Except that I too didn't know when that step of my mission became my genuine love. His behaviour, his thoughts, his attitude towards women and me, his constant care and concern for me somewhere made me fall for him. Somewhere he fitted into the image I had of my father. Maybe that's why I fell for him. That doesn't make me innocent but I thought of mentioning this. The audio statement had one thing right for sure: that I loved Faizaan Ahmad. He never clipped my nose. I deliberately said all those things to create a certain image of Faizaan in front of the police. So they would suspect that he may have had some links to the killer. In my opinion, only then would they have been all the more interested in reopening the serial killer case. And relooking at everything.

'That night when we came back after watching a movie, he asked me to go up to answer nature's call. But I didn't. By then, I had rehearsed the scenario too many times for it to go wrong at any point. I took the elevator up, which had a camera and then took the stairs to go down. The back stairs and the floor lobby didn't have any cameras. When he was inside the car parking it, I knocked on the door. He opened it. I asked him to smell my handkerchief for there was some weird smell on it. He did. I used all my energy to press the handkerchief on his face. He did fight back but it was nothing that I couldn't handle. I used the same modus operandi as the cello-tape serial killer. I should mention here that the diary which I said belonged to Faizaan actually belongs to me. Though it's not with me. The real killer had stolen it from Preeti's flat when I was living with her. I told all those lies in my statement so the police would believe Faizaan had some connection with the killer and the case would remain open longer as I didn't know whether the original killer would strike or not, come out in the open or not, contact the police or me or not. But he did. Saira Ahmad wasn't killed by me. I only killed Nagma, and put her body inside the pipe in a

deserted construction site and dumped it with earth two nights before I killed Faizaan. I was as happy when Saira Ahmad was killed as I was when my diary was stolen, for it only meant the original killer was still out there. And had taken notice of my copycat attempts.

'In fact, the attack on me when Preeti was with me at the Gurugram flat was only a self-attack. I did that more for the real killer to take notice than the police. I knew the news would fly and the killer, if alive, would know there was indeed his copycat around and that wasn't me. For I too was attacked. I hadn't used chloroform because I knew I would survive and nobody would test me. There were no fingerprints on the tapes I used on myself as I wore gloves to put them on. I did so before killing Nagma, Faizaan and Jaideep.

'Jaideep was collateral, really. To begin with, I'd mentioned about the fictitious friend in the audio statement to make the police suspicious if they picked up on him. I knew they would go on a wild goose chase, thereby helping the case to stay open longer. At that time, I didn't know about UKC or the fact that the real killer would steal the diary. When I met UKC, I knew he had doubts about the friend. I didn't want UKC to catch my lie about the friend and the diary. I knew if one lie was cracked, everything else would open up. So, to prove to everyone how truthful I was with my audio statement, I made sure the police believed there indeed was a friend.

'Coming to Preeti, it wasn't planned by me. Preeti wanted to take revenge against the Gurugram police for reasons she knew best. She told me that the police weren't taking the case seriously and an attack on a police officer would keep the case afloat. It was only meant to be an attack. But it was only at the last minute I thought perhaps killing a police officer would really churn the system up. And give the case a sensational twist. Preeti had tied and taped herself. The plan was that I had to release her at the last moment. But, I didn't.

'There's nothing more I know. Whatever I've written above is the truth which I've written with all my conscious mind and self without being under any kind of pressure from the police or any individual. Or any other influence. I don't care what happens to me but I really want to see the original cello-tape killer caught and die with me if that's where I'm heading after these four kills.'

Ekantika signed the sheet. And put the date underneath her signature. Her hands were still shaking. She wondered what Charulata would go through when she learnt of all this. She had been a terrible daughter for a mother who gave her everything to cushion her life. A daughter who had not been able to unmask her father's killer, which had basically triggered the disintegration of her family. As the female constable came to collect the signed statement sheet, she saw Ekantika howling as if someone dear had died in front of her.

If there was one person who was the most confused, it was Taksh Shukla. With the recent developments, he didn't know whether to meet Ekantika or be with Kisha. The latter was admitted to a hospital diagnosed only with trauma. She was fine otherwise. He was glad he had reached her in time. The killer didn't know that Kisha was a yoga practitioner. She was an expert at holding her breath, which helped her save her own life. After the killer left, Kisha told Taksh after she was admitted to the hospital, she had managed to sit up holding her breath. She started hitting the tape on her mouth with all her might with a stiff tongue. After some time, luckily, one side of the tape opened up slightly. She managed to open that side up and breathe some air from her mouth. She remained in that position till Taksh came, expecting a dinner as planned.

She narrated the same to Pradeep when he came to visit her in the hospital. By then, the doctor had told Taksh everything was normal with Kisha and she could go home in some time. Her parents had also come down from Agra.

Later that night, Charulata reached the Gurugram police station. She introduced herself to Inspector Gagan and pleaded to be allowed to talk to her daughter. Gagan consulted Pradeep. When Charulata was taken to the lock-up, her knees weakened seeing her daughter.

'Ma?' Ekantika was surprised. And then she couldn't stop her tears.

'I saw all this in the news, Shonai. I had to take the flight from Kolkata. There has been a big mistake, isn't that so?' Charulata said with ragged breaths. She was sure her daughter was innocent. It was one of those things that a big bad city does to a girl from a small town.

Ekantika didn't say anything but kept weeping.

'I've let baba down. His soul won't forgive me. I have let you down as well, ma. Please do forgive me.'

'Don't worry Shonai, I will take out all my savings. I've some jewellery too. I'll sell it. And will connect with the best criminal lawyer. You will be out in no time,' Charulata said, caressing her daughter's head through the iron bars.

'I've already confessed, ma. Nothing will help any more.'

'Don't talk like that. As long as I'm alive, nobody can touch you.'

'I just had to tell you, ma, that I love you a lot. There's something I never told you. I know you'd told me baba died of pneumonia, but I found out quite early that he was the last victim of the cello-tape serial killer.'

Charulata swallowed a lump. She didn't know how to react. It was too much of a shock all at once. The lies she had told her daughter so she could grow up with a healthy mind now seemed pointless. Everything seemed pointless. For the next five to ten minutes, neither said anything. Their tears were their language. Their helplessness the theme of their silence. A female constable came and informed Charulata that she had to leave. The time was up.

'Take care, ma. And be alert. The cello-tape killer may attack you as well. He killed Saira and the techie in Bengaluru.'

'I don't think there's anything left in me that can be killed,' Charulata said and walked out of the police station like a zombie.

Neema helped UKC sip his Scotch. With every sip, his thoughts were getting intense. In particular, he was wondering what could have been the killer's motivation in attempting an attack on Kisha. That too after the Bengaluru techie's murder. Now, he knew the intention behind Nagma, Faizaan, Preeti and Jaideep's murders. But about Saira, the techie and Kisha, he was still in the dark. Who was the second copycat? Or was it indeed the original cello-tape serial killer? The possibility of it excited UKC.

While he was musing over important questions about the case, Kisha's interview from the hospital was being telecast live on the news channel where she worked. As Kisha narrated her ordeal with the killer to her colleague, mentioning that she couldn't see the face because the killer wore a mask, the killer watched her on television. After the brief interview, the news presenter also said that the man behind cracking the case was UKC. They went on to share with the viewers a brief bio of UKC. After a minute, the presenter went on to another news headline. By then, the killer's mind was already made up, as to who the next victim would be.

As UKC took the final sip of his Scotch, Neema held up her phone in one hand which had the photograph of Ekantika's confession statement. He next checked her profile as written by one of the police officials in Hindi. What caught his attention was a person's name. Ekantika's father's name. He had read the same name somewhere recently. And it was a Eureka moment for him. Ekantika's father's name was the same as that of the last victim of the original cello-tape serial killer: Sahabzaade Samsher Khan.

14

If Arfa Khan and Shaheen Khan are Sahabzaade's wife and son, as per Preeti's report to Pradeep, then who is Ekantika? UKC wondered. *Or should I ask, who is Shaheen Khan? Or is it that Sahabzaade had two kids? Or . . . two wives?* With those thoughts, UKC retired to bed with Neema's help. She switched off the lights and went to her room, closed the door and went to sleep.

Around 4 a.m., the killer managed to climb over UKC's house compound wall and get inside the premises. There was no security outside. The killer looked around. The house was slightly lit by a few street lamps. There was absolute silence all around. The killer quietly went behind the house, climbed the wall using the kitchen window, shifted to the drainage pipe and then reached the terrace two floors above. There were clothes hanging on a rope. All male. And on another rope were some female clothes. The killer forwent the plan of getting in using the terrace door. It would alert the people inside.

The killer climbed down to the ground and went around the house to the kitchen. Though the window had iron grills, it was open. The utensils stand, pinned to the wall, was visible. The killer picked up a tiny stone and threw it at the stand. There was some noise. Half a minute later, the lights of the kitchen came on. Neema came in and looked around. She didn't spot the stone on the floor. Sensing everything was all right, she switched the lights off. *One lady*, the killer made a note.

The killer then went around the house and did the same with the three bedrooms. And every time it was Neema who switched the lights on, looked around and finding nothing, switched the lights off. The killer realized there was nobody in the house except in the third bedroom from where a male voice was heard. The target: UKC. This much the killer knew from the news, that UKC was wheelchair-bound. There would be no need to tie his limbs.

The killer waited for half an hour so Neema could go back to sleep again. Then went to the front door and pressed the doorbell, knowing that Neema would be the one to open the door. The delay was because the killer wanted Neema to be sleepy when she opened the door. The lights of the hall were switched on. The next moment, Neema opened the door. Before she knew it, she was hit. She collapsed on the floor. The killer made sure Neema was unconscious.

'Who is it, Neema?' It was UKC. The killer remained silent and closed the main door. And tiptoed to the bedroom where UKC was. The killer entered the room as UKC asked again from the bed, 'Who is it, Neema?' The silhouette of a body covered with a blanket on the bed could be seen in the dark.

The killer took out a roll of cello-tape, scissors and then, in the dark, went to the bed. The blanket was flung aside. The killer saw UKC under it. But he had a big smile on his face.

The killer frowned as a gun was cocked in the silence. The killer turned around to see in the faint light, ACP Pradeep Ahlawat holding his service revolver rock steady with a finger on the trigger.

'Both Saira Ahmad's and the young techie's murder in Bengaluru were a distraction, isn't that so?' UKC said, still lying on the bed. Neema entered the room holding her head. She switched the lights on.

It was midnight when UKC had cracked the case in his mind. And if he was correct, he knew he would be attacked. Sooner than later. He woke up Neema by pressing the calling bell in his room. He made her call Pradeep and explain that if he wanted to catch the killer red-handed, he had to station himself at UKC's home for the next forty-eight hours. UKC was sure, for he had estimated the emotional desperation of the killer to kill him.

'Killing me was an act of revenge because I was instrumental in catching Ekantika's lies. And it would have also opened the case because if the killer was still outside, then Ekantika still had an iota of a chance to fight for her freedom,' UKC said in his typical emotionless tone.

Pradeep leaned forward and ripped the mask off Charulata Pakrashi's face.

'Charulata Pakrashi or Arfa Khan? The biological mother of Ekantika Pakrashi or Shaheen Khan? What should we call you?' UKC asked. This time his voice was soaked in sarcasm. Charulata gave him an intense, hate-filled look. If Ekantika was there at the moment, she wouldn't have recognized her mother.

'My daughter is innocent,' she said.

'I wish, Mrs Pakrashi. I so wish,' UKC said. ACP Pradeep and his team arrested Charulata.

The moment the media got a sniff of who the real killer was, it was a TRP feast for them. Everyone was busy giving exclusive news. Charulata Pakrashi, alias Arfa Khan, the mother of Ekantika Pakrashi, had been taken into immediate custody. Kisha couldn't believe it. Even Taksh was speechless when he was told about it.

It was during her custodial interrogation that Arfa Khan spewed out the truth, which she had cocooned inside her for twenty-one years now. She sat in front of Inspector Gagan. As she narrated her story, a female constable wrote it all down in Hindi on a sheet of paper.

'Start from the beginning,' the constable said. Though Arfa was looking at the floor below, everything flashed in front of her as if it had happened recently.

'I was first impregnated by my lover,' Arfa began, 'in my village in Bihar. When my family came to know about it, they thought it was best I was married off before my belly started showing. My lover had run away by then. Sahabzaade Samsher Khan's family was the seventh one who was considered for a match. The family said yes. And my destiny was intertwined with Sahabzaade's who, I was told, was in Bombay at the time.

'I was happy since I was told they had accepted me with my out-of-wedlock child. But after marriage, when my in-laws got to know about it, they created a huge ruckus. Sahabzaade came down and took a stand by my side. I felt proud of him. But after I had delivered the child, he killed her. I knew it in my guts he had poisoned the infant. I thought it was because it was a girl child. He never admitted it though. We hardly talked. He was mostly away; on work. And once when he came, much later, he impregnated me.

'I lived in constant fear for all of my pregnancy. What if it was a girl child and he killed it again? I wanted to meet him. Talk to him. Convince him that even if it was a girl child, we should let her live. Maybe we could have a boy later. I was emotionally damaged with what had happened before. I kept waiting for him but he didn't come. I only heard from him when he used to do a trunk call to a nearby grocery shop that had the only phone in the entire village. By the time I reached my fifth month, he was in Lucknow. I noted the hotel's name where he worked when I last talked to him. And then without telling anyone, I left for Lucknow one night.

'I somehow reached Clarks Avadh hotel and asked for him. The guard said he had left the job but knew where he lived. He took me there. Sahabzaade was shocked to see me. Though I must say he was courteous enough to welcome me and allow me to live with him without any questions. At that time, he was jobless. We were living on his meagre savings. I tried to talk to him about why I was there. But I never got a chance. He was a recluse. Never talked to me. Or to anyone actually. He used to go out daily, I don't know where. And one day when he was out, I happened to clean the house. I found a bag of his where I found a few photographs. Faces of dead people with tapes on their noses and mouths. I recognized a couple of them as I'd seen them on television once when I had gone to the grocery shop to take his trunk call. They had been murdered or so I remembered, but I didn't know what those photographs were doing in his bag. Then I found a pair of scissors and two rolls of cello-tape. My heart skipped a beat but I let it be.

'When he came home that night, I talked to him about my pregnancy. He told me he would kill the infant if it was a girl. He believed we hadn't yet made a society where girls could fit in. The calm with which he said this scared me. Then when I asked him about the photographs, he said he had killed them. And he went to sleep. But I couldn't. For the first time I realized I'd married a serial killer. The cello-tape killer was my husband, Sahabzaade Samsher Khan.

'A week went by. I too stopped talking. And then one night I decided I couldn't let my child die if it was a girl. It would kill me. I went mad at the thought. After a week of being in utter emotional distress, an idea struck me: if I killed him the same way as he had confessed he had killed others, my baby would have a life. And I wouldn't be caught.

'That night while Sahabzaade was asleep, I taped his nose and mouth and tied his hands. I watched him die helplessly. And then called the police. They took my statement and let me leave. I understood, as a few journalists had come around then, that my plan was successful. They thought Sahabzaade was killed by the cello-tape serial killer. I left for our village by train that night itself.

'I gave birth at my mother's place and with her help was able to spread the news that it was a boy. So nobody had any problem. But in reality it was a girl. I named her Shaheen. Nobody from Sahabzaade's house cared much about me.

They had labelled me a bad woman from the day I told them about my pre-wedding pregnancy. And when they learnt about his death, they washed their hands off me and my family.

'A week later, with Shaheen in my arms, I went to the nearest railway station from our village and caught the first train that was about to leave. I was afraid the police would reach me some day. In the train I met this burqa-clad Muslim woman, Alvina, who got talking with me and somehow understood I was on the run. She asked me if I knew where I was going. And that it didn't matter where I went, I could be found easily. I had no answer. She proposed to arrange a meeting for me with an agent. She too was going to him. It was then I realized the train was going to Kolkata.

'Once we reached there, we caught another train and both of us went to meet the agent in Baruipur.

'He gave us a new identity. From Arfa Khan, I became Charulata Pakrashi. I told myself if I was faithful to my Allah in my own way, in my deeds, how does a name change matter? The agent gave me my fake voting ID card as well. Shaheen became Ekantika, which was easier since she was only one week old. A birth certificate was given to me that said that she was born in a government hospital in Baruipur. Alvina went her way while I decided to stay put in Baruipur, taking up a cleaner's job at a clinic. A couple of years later, I was given my first job as a surrogate there itself. I couldn't believe the amount of money I was paid for my womb. Looking at little Shaheen, I didn't think twice about it. In a way, I too was selling my body to raise my child. But somewhere it was helping a couple be happy. I accepted perhaps that was what Allah wanted of me.

'Almost twenty-one years went by. I thought the past would never catch up. Shaheen, now Ekantika, had grown up as well. But one thing didn't change in these two decades. My protectiveness about her. When I settled Ekantika in Karol Bagh, she thought I went back to Baruipur. I didn't. I stayed on in Delhi. Only, she didn't know.

'I had my eye on her. Mainly because I wanted her to be safe. I don't know how to explain this. I'd stayed with only one thought in my mind in the last twenty-one years. *My Ekantika should be all right.* And suddenly when she had to be away from me, how was I supposed to embrace it easily? I thought I would return after I saw her settling down on her own, but when I saw her with Faizaan, the motherly instinct in me was sharper than before.'

'Didn't you see Ekantika following Nagma?' the constable asked.

Arfa shook her head and continued, 'I didn't. I don't know when she did all that. I wasn't spying on her anyway. I was in Delhi just to be close to her. A sight of her once a day, even in secret, used to relieve me. With Faizaan on the scene, I soon realized they loved each other from the way they roamed about and the way he frequented her place. I was okay with it. Finally, I told myself, it was time to let go. My daughter too would get married and have kids and have her own happy life. I couldn't have my eye on her all the time. I had booked my tickets to Baruipur after two years of living clandestinely in Delhi. But before I could board the train, the news came in about Faizaan's death.

'People were talking about the cello-tape serial killer. I was instantly alert. I wanted to approach Ekantika, but the day I went to her place in Gurugram, I saw officer Preeti entering the flat. Hence, I stayed away.

'Whatever I knew was from the news channels. I saw Ekantika being called for interrogation to the police station. I didn't want the police to have anything to do with her. Then I was confused when it came out in the media that even Ekantika was attacked. I thought a copycat was doing the murders. I was scared. To distract the police as well as the other possible copycat killer, I went to Preeti's flat and looked for anything suspicious. I'd made her inhale chloroform in her sleep after I entered the flat.'

'Why did you go to the flat like that? Stealthily?' the constable asked.

'There had to be something which belonged to Faizaan or Ekantika in there. Why else would the copycat killer attack Ekantika? That's when I found the diary and stole it. It's still with me. It had all the details of the killer.'

'That was, by the way, Ekantika staging an attack on herself,' the constable clarified.

Arfa pretended she didn't hear it. She continued, 'I knew it was Ekantika's handwriting in the diary which further confused me. But when I saw her going to the ruling party office with officer Pradeep, I wondered if she was a suspect. Or was to be made a scapegoat. I wanted to distract everyone. From the police to the copycat killer. Hence, I chose to kill Saira Ahmad, Faizaan's mother, so the police would think it was the personal vengeance of the copycat killer towards the Ahmad family. And let go of Ekantika. But after I killed Saira, I checked her phone and found out she was having a relationship with a minister. I leaked the chats to the media to give it a political twist so my daughter would be spared.'

There was silence. The constable was a tad behind finishing writing whatever Arfa had narrated. Once she caught up, she looked up at Arfa and said, 'What about the techie's murder?'

'Again a distraction. By then, I had an inkling Ekantika was somehow involved. Especially when I saw her going to New Delhi station and then coming back after a day. I didn't know where she had gone, but later understood it was Patna. Killing the techie was my penultimate attempt at distracting the police and letting them know that they were wasting their time with Ekantika, whereas the killer was in Bengaluru. Unfortunately, Ekantika brought up the Kannada issue up with them without my knowledge, even though I had thrown my phone off the train after I received her message around 3.30 in the morning. I knew she must have had some doubt, else she wouldn't have messaged at that time. I reached Delhi later that day.'

'And the attack on Kisha Bhargav?'

'That was my final, desperate attempt at distracting the police away from my daughter. I didn't know she had been arrested by then. I failed. I failed to protect my daughter.' The last bit trailed off.

Once done with her narration, Arfa Khan was quiet. She felt weak from within. Something which she never felt even after delivering so many lives from her womb for several couples.

'Take her signature and file the paper,' Inspector Gagan told the female constable. As the latter approached Arfa with a pen and paper, she took it and asked, 'I have one request. If I sign this statement, will my daughter's crimes be forgiven? Can I take the punishment for her crimes as well?'

Inspector Gagan could only sympathize with her. *Promises had no place in law*, he thought.

'Let's see what the court decides,' he said. He waited till Arfa signed the statement in Hindi and then walked away following the constable.

Outside, he could hear Arfa's sobs. And in that he could feel a mother's pain.

Epilogue

Nineteen Months Later

The Honorable High Court of Delhi made three major decisions in the cello-tape serial killer case. One was, it allowed Ekantika Pakrashi/Shaheen Khan and Charulata Pakrashi/Arfa Khan to remain in the same jail. Second, it allowed Ekantika to study for her UPSC exams. The police had brought her all her books and study materials and allowed her to appear for the exam. She was escorted to the examination centre for her prelims. When she passed, the same procedure was followed for her mains as well. She passed the mains for the first time. But by the time her interview dates came out, the court's third order had taken precedence. That Ekantika Pakrashi/Shaheen Khan and her mother Charulata Pakrashi/Arfa Khan should be hanged till death on multiple counts of murder as they had done so in their full conscious mind and sparing them would be a grave danger for society at large. They were to be the first women to be hanged in India. There was a media and social media uproar both for and against the order, but neither meant much to the mother and daughter. The date of their hanging was one week before Ekantika's UPSC interview was scheduled.

The mother and daughter spent that night together in one cell. They'd requested for some hair oil which her mother applied on Shaheen. They chit-chatted about old memories together. The hard times, when Arfa had to surrogate her womb to raise Shaheen. The times when little Shaheen was almost sexually abused by Dhononjoy. Shaheen knew everyone in her locality had labelled her mother a whore which she never could fight. The time when she had to leave for Delhi. And the time when she got to know her father was the original cello-tape serial killer while her mother was the killer of her father. She had gone quiet for a good two months after learning this. And now they were together in one cell. The irony of her life was that the killer of her father, who had turned her life into one mad obsession, was the person for whom she wanted to catch the killer. Shaheen didn't have anything to say to anyone. Not even any complaint against life. She stopped further dissecting the emotional complexity of the whole scenario. One thing, though, kept coming back to her. Why did her father kill? Nobody—be it UKC, or her mother or even she herself—could exactly decipher why Sahabzaade used to kill people. With him, this fact was also buried forever.

In the last one year, their conscious minds had accepted their fate. There was no more trying to fight it or showing any kind of resentment towards it or anybody. Both had forgone all kinds of grudges against everyone who had hurt or humiliated them knowingly or otherwise. Shaheen still carried her father's picture with her. And she still loved him the way she always did even after knowing who he really was. The cello-tape serial killer. Someone who had killed twenty-five people. Somewhere within the daughter that she was, Shaheen believed, even though her father was a serial killer, he would still have been a generous father if he was alive. And if he would have seen her. *Once.*

The date and time of their hanging arrived. The time as determined by the court was 4.45 a.m. Both took their last bath that morning and wore their jail uniform. The jailer had asked them the night before if they wanted to eat anything or if they had any last wish.

'I want my mother to have Miss Mixo with me,' Shaheen had requested. She was provided with all the ingredients to prepare one glass of Miss Mixo. Since Arfa didn't want to consume alcohol, Shaheen substituted the alcohol part with a syrup. As a female constable came to usher them to the hanging room, both sipped it together. While Arfa's mind remained blank throughout, Shaheen was talking to Faizaan in her mind as they both moved out of their cell to the hanging room.

I know I lied to you a lot, Faizaan. But I'm coming to you soon. Maybe I'm coming to you because I never lied about my love for you. Just that I loved my father more than you. Let's meet beyond this life, and we will sit with ease so I can whisper to you all my truths. Hope you'll listen.

As the mother and daughter entered the hanging room, the magistrate, the jailer and the *jallad* (hangman) were already there. Even the ropes were ready. Two nooses hung in front of Arfa and Shaheen. They hugged each other for one last time. There were no more tears. Both smiled at the other.

As the jailer looked at his watch, he held a white handkerchief in his raised hand. The jallad's focus was on it. Exactly at 4.45 a.m., the handkerchief dropped, the levers were pulled and the two bodies were suspended in the air. Arfa's body went still before Shaheen's.

The cello-tape serial killing case had finally come to an end. It was time for a father, mother and daughter to reunite—if there was something beyond life, beyond the body and beyond this which we call reality.

Acknowledgements

I wanted to write a crime thriller for a long time. It was only last year when I finally found an exciting plot that not only allowed me to pen one but also do it in my own signature style, which I've developed over the years and to the liking of my dear readers.

Heartfelt thanks and gratitude to:

Milee Ashwarya—for always being the guiding star in my storytelling universe. Can't thank you enough for everything. Here's to many more stories together. Cheers!

Vijesh Kumar—for coming up with the best solutions always. Thanks for supporting my books the way you do.

Pinaki da—for all our 'bong' talks and your valuable inputs. Always cherish our meet-ups.

Saloni and Ralph—for the smooth copy-edits.

Shams Tahir Khan—though I don't know you personally but have been an avid viewer of 'Crime Tak'. It kept the itch of writing a crime thriller alive in me.

My readers—for showing love and appreciation for more than a decade now. You guys are my strength.

Friends and family—for being there whenever I need you all.

Ranisa—for being my 'education'. Every day's a lesson. Every night's a realization.

R—for making a *home* with me with walls of our tears and a ceiling of our smiles.